I0547648

The Remedies Of Pachili

A Novel by Michael Craig

Publisher Data

Logical Soul LLC
6050 Peachtree Parkway, Ste 240-340L
Norcross, Georgia 30092 USA
publisher@logicalsoul.com

Copyright © 1995-2013 by Michael Craig.

All rights reserved. No part of this book may be reproduced, stored in a retrieval system or transmitted in any form or by any means electronic, mechanical, photocopying, recording, or otherwise without express written permission of the author.

ISBN-13: 978-0-9800674-9-1

Editor: Lexie Ross
Cover Photo and content layout: Michael Craig
Cover design: Gaurav Sikka.

Disclaimer: The characters in this novel are fictitious.   Any resemblance to any person either alive or dead is coincidental.

To Soma

SECTION I: THE FIRST REMEDY

Chapter One

The image of his face ebbed and flowed before me as if it were a fading hologram. Sparkles shone on either side of the tensile strands: beams of color and light that thrust themselves into empty space. I quickly slipped into another state - somewhere between Arizona and the far side of Pluto.

I suppose I asked for it. No one actually takes this journey to the subconscious who does not "ask for it." And yet, being here, I could honestly say I didn't want it: the *real* cure for my persistent headaches. Or whatever it was I *thought* I wanted . . .

"Shift! ... Shift!!"

A familiar voice pierced my consciousness. I remained indifferent: trapped in an astral wonderland where stillness is punctuated with bursts of sight, sound and feelings, a chaotic security that begged me to stay. There was something very familiar about it - comfortable. But it was not the world I was used to, the world of logical thought and predictable events.

"Wake up, you stupid pig!" cried the voice again. A thumb rudely jammed me, somewhere between my nose and upper lip. I snapped out of it . . . wide awake for the moment.

"Can you not listen?" raved the orange man as I gathered my senses. I recognized him: Pachili, the German-Buddhist monk I had come to visit. "You slipped around the Zone like some drunken slob. You lost awareness. Now we must wait . . . next time. No access now."

Lost awareness? Access? Zone? For the moment I was lost. Giddy. Confused and groggy. I started drifting again. I felt him shake my body again . . . it didn't matter. He yelled something else. To hell with it. All he did was give me drugs, that's all. Any medical quack could do that!

My body again drifted in this space . . . Not hearing. Not seeing. Not caring. Just drifting. I wanted to throw up, but couldn't. There was ringing of high-pitched bells in the distance. Or was it just my ears? I couldn't tell. Dizzy.

I started to daydream . . .

****

The day we met he was sitting on a putrid-green retaining wall outside the clinic, talking with two interns. I had just begun my second month as a visiting doctor at Dr. Alfred Jayawardene's clinic - a student of acupuncture and alternative medicine. It was a typical August day in Colombo, Sri Lanka: rainy, hot and muggy.

The man appeared to be in his mid-fifties. Average in height, he was closely-shaved. In fact, his head stuck out through the top of his neatly-wrapped orange robe like a garish orange-and-white carnival ice cream cone. I overheard he was a homeopathic doctor from the mountains.

"How much are your textbooks, Sir?" asked one of the interns. He mumbled something, so I moved closer to hear. The two men, apparently displeased with the offer, shook their heads and walked away, leaving us alone. I smiled at the monk and turned nonchalantly to follow the others. Something made me stop.

I glanced back. Two of the largest, blackest eyes I had ever seen bore a hole right through me! I turned around and started to say something, but couldn't. Like a midnight deer caught in headlights, I was fascinated . . . and afraid. He said nothing, silently commanding my attention. Was I being hypnotized? I'd heard about those mind-control cult leaders running around . . .

I shook my head, logically dismissed the whole thing as just my imagination, forced a smile, then I walked towards him. No matter how I tried to relax, however, I couldn't. He appeared harmless enough - even familiar - like a long forgotten friend. I offered my hand, but he didn't respond. He just looked at me.

"I'm Dr. Cannon from America," I said, feeling mighty awkward with the silence. "Do you have any information on . . ."

"On headaches?" he interrupted, raising one eyebrow like Mr. Spock on some old Star Trek episode. His eyes sparkled as he smiled for the first time. "As a matter of fact I do, doctor."

How did he . . . ? I dropped my head and held my breath, amazed at the apparent ease at which he read my thoughts. I felt suddenly naked. Vulnerable. No one else appeared to notice.

"How did you . . . ?"

"Explanations are boring," answered the man crisply in a German-British accent. "You are average height and weight. About thirty-five years old. Reddish-blond hair. Your father was very strict, but fickle. Your mother controlled the family. You are near-sighted and wear glasses. You want me to go on?"

"No, " I interrupted, reeling from information overload, "What's all that got to do with my headaches?" The monk continued his piercing gaze for a moment then softened into a more benign demeanor.

"One must start from the beginning," he said simply. "Your whole history - your being - must unfold before any so-called 'cure' can be given."

I was both amused and amazed. All doctors should be so thorough . . .

****

I noticed my bench was very hard . . . Suddenly, I was back in my body, aware I was witnessing my recent past . . . like a translucent painting, a lucid dream, a crystalline image excised from the dregs of my body and thrown to the wind. I just watched the characters as their peculiar and seemingly insignificant drama unfolded. I wanted to pinch myself. Was I witnessing another reality? Or a Deja-Vu? Some experience flowing from my memory?

In all my years as a chiropractor, I'd never experienced any dreams like this one. I could vaguely relate it to some LSD trip I took when I was a 19-year-old hippie, but no drug ever prepared me for *this!*

Shifting uncomfortably, I tried to open my eyes, but couldn't! I drifted again.

****

7

"But how can you cure *my* headaches?" I inquired.

Pachili's answer came softly, as if by telepathy . . . a whisper in the wind. I was arrogant, and utterly desperate. I wanted answers, but had fallen for too many con artist stories. Too many promises from those who claimed to have the truth, but didn't.

"Other doctors have told me this too," I stammered, trying to sound confident, "I'm a doctor too, you know! The results you get with others doesn't guarantee you'll get results with *me.*"

Pachili didn't argue. He just listened. No longer the inquisitor, he seemed rather pleasant. Amiable. Mature. I noted the change . . . a sudden attraction to him. Perhaps it was the memory of my deceased father. Perhaps he could do what he claimed. No matter. I wasn't going to let down my guard. I'd been burned too often.

"My condition hasn't responded much to any mode of treatment - medical or alternative," I explained. "I often wonder if I'm *ever* going to get well!" I added, feeling rather pitiful.

Pachili just sat quietly for a few moments. He scratched his nearly shaved head with a right hand, I noticed, was missing a little finger. I started to ask, but didn't.

"You may be right," he acquiesced. "There is much work to be done. It will take preparation and much time. True healing is a catharsis. Such pain comes from very deep within you . . . are you willing to do what it takes?"

I was scared. Doctors don't ask questions like that except from a dying patient. Was my condition terminal? I thought not. Other than the headaches, I felt perfectly fine. But why would he use such terms? I felt a lump rise into my throat. He appeared to know what he was talking about. But *do what it takes. . ?!* What was the risk? Did I dare trust another con man? I hesitated too long . . .

"Perhaps not," uttered the soft-spoken mystery man with a sigh as he rose to his feet. "In this case, I can only offer my best wishes." He held out his hand to say good-bye.

"Wait!" I squealed, knowing he would leave if I didn't respond. I was used to bargaining with the natives. I forgot: he was no native. He was German. A simple *yes* or *no* is all he wanted.

"You don't understand," I argued weakly, looking for reassurance. "Many doctors have tried and failed. Its not that I don't believe you . . . I've spent years seeing chiropractors, nutritionists, general practitioners, neurologists, ENT specialists, and even the best neuro-surgeons. They can't decide whether I have migraines, cluster headaches, cranial faults, or some hidden tumor! After years of this, I'm no better off!"

Pachili again took his seat, listening matter-of-factly to my whining like a father to his teenage son's confession. I felt uncomfortable baring my soul, but also desperate.

"Mr. Pachili, I know you probably can't appreciate what I'm saying, but it's important to me. . ." I implored.

"I will listen," he said patiently, managing a weak smile.

"You see, my practice suffered. I've been miserable. CAT scans, MRI's . . . scads of blood work . . . special diets, medicines and remedies. They were all a waste of time and money.

"I even swallowed my pride and tried psychics and acupuncture. *Hell,* I've even put my license on the line - came here to Sri Lanka to *study* acupuncture. Even *that* hasn't cured these damn headaches . . . *I've had 'em for seven long years,* do you hear? Sometimes three or four times a month, and I'm sick of them! Sometimes I just feel suicidal."

Pachili just sat quietly, looking at me, staring off into the distance. He twirled a piece of straw between white teeth exhibiting barely a trace of plaque. I waited vainly for some sign of pity. A minute passed. It never came.

"O.K. . ." I capitulated, suddenly willing to let go of my ego and my money, "What do I have to do, dammit?" The silence was relentless. He continued to just sit, picking his teeth with that stupid straw, periodically squinting into the hot morning sun. I was enraged, and almost walked away from this conceited jerk. The memory of my pain, however, wouldn't let me. "One more time" I muttered silently to myself. "One more *freaking* time . . ."

I knew he could read me. His eyes and demeanor portrayed a soul much older than his years, someone I could follow. But my mind screamed at me. I wanted to trust him, but couldn't. A sickening mixture of fear, anger and desire came over me as I caught his silent glance. I suddenly realized these feelings contributed to my headaches . . . one was coming on as I spoke.

I needed this guy. He had something I wanted, and he knew it. I knew it. He could help me, but I had to let go of all the mind games. They didn't work with him. Or me. Slowly, the fear and anger melted into grudging acceptance, even as the headache receded. I shuffled my feet and didn't know what to do with my hands.

"Wh-what do want me to do?" I repeated, trying to understand this person like a hungry laboratory rat gazing at a wired food bowl.

"Nothing much," he said, finally breaking the silence with a smile. "Come to see me in the mountains. Take a homeopathic remedy that I give you, wait a while - a few weeks or a month - then come back. I must see the results and give another remedy. There are three remedies in all . . ."

I sighed with relief. Three? Was that all? I almost laughed when I realized this was how many of my patients must feel before *I* gave *them* treatments. Now the joke was on me!

Chapter Two

Suddenly, I lost all concern for everything. My thoughts drifted into the vortex of swirling light and sound; a mixture of orange and green color danced into my awareness. I shook my head and forced open my eyes. The ground beneath my feet, blurry at first, quickly came into focus, like solving a visual puzzle. I sat up and looked around. The 3-D effect was startling. I had no idea where I was, or - for that matter - *who* I was. Strangely, I didn't care!

I found myself sitting on a porch bench, staring at a spider's web and an empty floor. I had been in some near-mindless state for hours. Different realities merged as I shook my head, trying to recall where I was and why. Sunday, September 27, 1987. No clinic today. Why was I here? What was I doing? My wife Cheryl was in America, 13,000 miles away, wisely tending our business while I was off chasing moonbeams. Was I a lunatic, or what??

I began to slide around on the bench. My back ached against the hard wood of Pachili's *avasa,* or small cabin near the monastery. The monk himself sat across from me on a small log. He appeared entranced by a clump of trees gently undulating in the late afternoon breeze. In spite of the stiffness from sitting, I was remarkably relaxed, as if awakened from a long-needed sleep.

I remembered his angry attempt to revive me. Funny. I spend the whole day pouring out my guts to this guy. He then gives me some strange "remedy," makes me pass out, then jams a thumb into my upper lip and yells at me! What kind of masochistic trip was I on? I glared at him, waiting and watching for some sign of displeasure. None came. Pachili remained silent, gazing at the treetops. He looked more like a sailor checking the wind for the next chance to hoist the jib than someone angry at me. I missed something.

"Did I do something wrong?" I finally asked after summoning the courage. He didn't speak, instead gazing trance-like into the leafy canopy. Sensing he was deliberately ignoring me, my stomach tightened. The nerve of this character! What did I do? It made no sense at all to me. I was about to try for his attention again when he looked, smiling in my direction.

"Oh, good. You are back," he said as if I had just returned from the restroom. My anger subsided, replaced by curiosity. "That was the first remedy. It may take some time before you are ready for the next."

He walked over to my bench, handed me a small package and walked away. No expression. No instruction. I opened the wrapped paper. It looked like powdered sugar, probably treated with the same "remedy" he gave me earlier . . . the stuff that made me pass out!

For a moment I was dumbfounded.

Why did he give me this with no explanation? It was the same last time: when I tried to inquire, he just waved off my concerns, saying my knowledge was too meager for any sort of meaningful discussion.

If so, then why doesn't he at least tell me what to do with it?! Does he expect me to take it? To wait for him? Did I dare trust him after what had just happened? Was my life in the hands of someone trying to poison me? Anything could happen in this isolated spot of the globe, and who would know? In my stay at Kalibuwila Hospital, I had seen many quacks come and go. This Pachili had all the trappings of one, but I couldn't be sure. He was different than the others.

I folded the package and thrust it angrily into my pocket as I lay down on the bench, confused, waiting for his return; I had so many questions . . .

I waited, fidgeting restlessly. It was getting late and my host had not returned. I checked my watch for the hundredth time, knowing I had to catch my driver who would be arriving for me soon. He had asked me to meet him at the main road and I

12

was out of time. I wanted to ask him about the remedy, but couldn't wait any longer.

I rose from my wooden perch and slowly navigated the narrow path toward the monastery. The day was beautiful: a late afternoon sun shone brightly through the hazy greenness of a tropical countryside recovering from a monsoon rain.

Reaching the main building ten minutes later, I encountered one of the orange-robed Sinhalese (i.e., native Sri Lankan) monks, apparently on his way to dinner. He was fairly young, although it was hard to tell from his bald head. I had seen him talking with my host earlier that day.

"Pachili?" I inquired. He replied by pointing in a northerly direction, then waved and shook his head as if to say it would be a waste of time pursuing him. Apparently, the older monk disappeared for days, weeks, and even months at a time with no word as to where he was going.

"You Cannon?" asked the Sinhalese monk.

"Yes . . . Ov." I nodded. The young man handed me a note written in my host's scribbling hand. Before I could decipher it, I heard Thomas' voice.

"Dr. Cannon! Come, quickly," waved my Sinhalese driver hurriedly as he approached the edge of the courtyard. Reluctantly, I folded the note into my pocket and briskly followed him towards the road. I still had many nagging questions.

13

Chapter Three

Thomas, my driver, spoke urgently as I climbed into the middle of his express van:

"We must leave here before darkness, Dr. Matt."

"Why?" I asked, curious as to his sudden punctuality. He didn't answer, obviously avoiding me, intent on getting his old rust-bucket-tape-and-wire van out of the monastery and onto the south-bound highway before the sunlight faded. I dropped my curiosity for the moment and grabbed the overhead safety handles.

"You from UK?" squeaked the soft, high-pitched male voice that poured over the seat from behind me. I swung around and gazed at the elderly couple sitting behind me. His hands rested neatly in his lap. Hers clasped lovingly around bag of canned goods. They both appeared to be in their mid-seventies. Thomas apparently picked them up on this return trip to Colombo.

"No, I'm from America," I responded politely.

"Aaah . . . U.S.A!" replied the man, flashing me a wide grin. "And what brings you to Ceylon?" Only the older folks still called the island 'Ceylon.' They had a type of courteous gentility and spoke flawless English: traits I had not witnessed among the younger natives - those further removed from the days of British rule and English ways.

"I'm a doctor," I said, managing a smile.

"Medical doctor or Homeopathic?" Their faces lit up.

"Chiropractor," I said, almost apologetically.

"What is . . . chiropractor?" asked the old woman, puzzled. I sighed. Should have just let them have their fantasies. Instead, I had to open my big mouth. All I wanted was to be left alone.

Now feeling obligated, I babbled on about my profession and my trip here to study acupuncture, homeopathy, and various alternative medicines. While the old couple knew nothing about chiropractic and acupuncture, they appeared to have a laymen's understanding of western medicine, homeopathy, and local ayurvedic medicine. Wanting to keep things simple, I stuck with homeopathy. I explained I just came from a treatment session for my persistent headaches, but still had doubts.

"About what?" quizzed the old man.

"These remedies," I mused, "are thinly-diluted doses of poisonous substances, right?"

"This is so," smiled my companion.

"If these were normal doses," I reasoned, "wouldn't they cause the very symptoms they are otherwise supposed to cure?"

"I have heard such," agreed my fellow passenger, "but aren't western vaccines made that way?" His wife nodded in concert.

"That's not so strange," I conceded. "My only beef with homeopathy is the dosage: it's so tiny it doesn't make any sense!"

"Oh?" said the old woman, chiming in.

"Well," I pontificated, "According to this theory then, the more you dilute the remedy, the more potent it is. If that's true, then the most potent remedies are made having only *a few molecules* of the original substance in it!" The old couple looked at each other and shrugged their shoulders. My concern was obviously not theirs.

"Allow us to introduce ourselves . . ." squeaked the smiling little man, changing the subject. He told me his name, but I soon forgot it. I was sensing another headache coming on. Damn these things! The so-called remedy wasn't helping me much now! But I also figured it didn't hurt me. I mean, how much damage could a few *molecules* do?

After introductions, the old man droned on about his life, marriage of 52 years, children, grandchildren, great-grandchildren, and more. I briefly answered his questions about my children (none), my political persuasion (independent), and my religion (none), then slumped in my seat. I pretended to fall asleep while he droned on about the Sinhalese government, world bank, and the trouble with Tamils until he ran out of words. Even his wife fell asleep.

Then darkening silence: a welcome reprieve. It was certainly much better than the crowded, noisy ride earlier that morning. I never enjoyed public transport in this country: dozens of people stuffed into spaces meant only for a few. Heat. Sweat. Odors. It took a lot of getting used to.

I positioned myself as best I could in the hard leather seat. If I were to survive the numerous potholes that plagued the back roads of this small island, I would need some security . . . only regretted not having a seat belt for the long drive. I folded my extra shirt between my head, the seat, and the window and assumed the most comfortable position I could.

Eyes half-opened and half-closed, I watched the scene out my window to the east. The growing shadow of our van stretched out over the rice paddies and patches of forest. It was hauntingly beautiful beneath the early evening sky. I turned to catch the sunset on my right and barely missed it. The red ball quickly dipped beneath the mountains, ending another remarkable day.

I leaned against the window and relaxed. Then it started .

.

****

"Who is he?" I asked the old-timer at Kalibuwila Hospital. He merely shrugged and mumbled a few words. Apparently no one I asked really knew. All they could tell me for sure was that his father was a homeopathic doctor in Germany, and that Pachili lost his parents at an early age. Dr. Jayawardene, the head of our hospital, had met him in India in 1967, and invited him to come work at the hospital. The monk did for a while, but then mysteriously disappeared for years.

I heard other stories: he had traveled around the world, lived with Tibetan monks, North African tribesmen, and was once a disciple of some ancient master in India. Curiously, some even feared the sight of him, saying he was a *maha yaka,* or great devil . . . a walking ghost. When I mentioned these stories, he just laughed, neither affirming nor denying the accusations. He insisted these rumors - and other facts about his past - were unimportant.

He also spoke of strange things like the "Zone," a state of unlimited awareness, and the idea that my headaches arose from fears and beliefs attached to another plane of existence. Having heard new age explanations before, I humored him. I didn't care about philosophy; I just wanted to get well.

And those eyes . . . ! Quackery or not, I decided to try it. I figured I had nothing to lose but my headaches. A German walking ghost? Not likely. It was simple, really: he was a great actor. Perhaps an adequate doctor. *I* was the fool in *this* play, driven by headache pain. Harboring a secret death wish. Jumping in every pool of sharks I came across! What did it matter anyway? I would just take his remedies, feel better for awhile, then move on to the next quack. Same old story.

At least it gave me hope.

Chapter Four

Like water through a broken dam, memories flashed through the punctuated darkness before me. I opened my eyes, not sure whether I was witnessing the darkened scenes outside my window, or just dreaming.

Paula! Chiropractic college. Studied all the time. Never had time to feel anything; to be with her . . . to connect. May, 1984. The premature loss of our only child pushed her over the edge . . . My wife killed herself.

Her face! Blood was everywhere . . . I noticed I wasn't breathing. Just staring . . .

The loss of my family was a deep shock. It took years to get over it, if I ever did. I felt like an orphaned child myself: very aware, but also very afraid. Afraid of the unknown. Afraid of being so vulnerable. Then the colds and sinus problems started. I ate and drank too much. Dated women, then dropped them for no reason. Then the headaches started. I was angry at God, afraid of being alone or dying, and ashamed of who I'd become. . .

Thomas stopped the van at a small store and got out. I sat there, half-asleep, transfixed by the softly-glowing light bulb in the window of this small rustic house. The texture of my senses was alive. Full. The moving shadows within caressed my imagination. The thought occurred to me: I was the only one witnessing this scene. Here. Now. This place. In all its sensual beauty. Thousands of miles from home. Yet, somebody actually lived here. Their home. I wondered if they were happy . . .

Then drifted off again.

****

Arrival at Colombo Airport was quite a culture shock. So many strange things. Oxcarts and water buffalo crowding the main highway. The rampant exhaust from the cars and trucks. The ubiquitous scent of curry. I was scared . . . haunted by deep-rooted feelings of inadequacy. Everything was so different.

I had this feeling every time my parents moved. Dad was always losing jobs and moving us around. I hated it. Everything was strange. I didn't want to be there. I cried for days each time. No place was safe . . . nothing.

I always worked hard. I never understood. Debts piled up. Then these persistent migraines. Why? All I had was this noble commitment to better myself and the world. True healing. Leroy Cravett, M.D. aborted a patient's asthma attack within minutes with a needle . . . no more asthma. Miracle cure. That was my calling: to be a doctor; do these things. Dreaming was easy. Getting there wasn't. Somebody suggested Chiropractic College. I took out loans and went.

Then my only boy died. Then Paula. My whole world collapsed . . .

****

The door of the van slammed as Thomas once again cranked the engine and started down the highway. I shifted in my seat, trying to find a better place to rest my head. The headache was still there, but noticed the pain receding considerably as thoughts surfaced.

Finally, I lay down on the seat, giving in to the dream-thoughts. They continued, like a deep cleansing process . . .

****

Cheryl and I were good friends. My anchor. She was loyal. Safe. Two years later we married. She took care of the details in my life and my clinic. I could venture out a little . . . try new things. Meet new people.

I taught myself acupuncture and had great success with patients, but had to stop. Some showdown with the Georgia Chiropractic Ethics Board. They said acupuncture was illegal. Told me to stop or I would lose my license. Ethics? What a joke! Muzzling me was just an offering to the medical boys so they would leave us alone come time to pass chiropractic legislation . . .

I tried to get into pure chiropractic again, but all joy of discovery had disappeared. Depression set in. My headaches became more frequent . . . demons eating away the gray matter in my skull until, after hours of crying for mercy, I was allowed to sleep. Even the ergot medication that helped before didn't work this time. I vowed to find the answer behind the pain. Cheryl encouraged me to go away for a while. Get rid of the cobwebs. Leave the victim behind.

That's when I met Carl and learned about his group going to Sri Lanka to study ancient and modern remedies . . .

Chapter Five

Bam. Bam. Bam. I felt my leg. Damp. Wounded. Blood pouring everywhere. Strange. I felt little pain . . .

****

Bam. Bam. Bam. A different sound emerged: a knocking sound . . .

"Hey Doc! Wanna join us for breakfast?" I sat up, still caught somewhere in the twilight state.

"Thanks, Betty," I garbled. My voice was gravely and barely able to speak. "I'll join you later!"

Still groggy, I lay back down, buried my head in the pillow.

Betty Blakely's raucous southern voice this early? I glanced at the clock. 7:00 a.m. Monday, September 28. Not so early. I had really been out of it! I forgot about the group; I'd promised to go with them to the clinic. Betty was one of my six traveling companions. I usually admired her directness, but this early in the morning she was just irritating.

Strange. As I lay there, half-conscious, the sound of crows shattered the quiet dawn with their ghostly cries - cries that were almost human. Was it a dream . . . or something else? Paula's death came back to me like an open wound crying to be closed. Was this Pachili's so-called Zone: a strange, suspended mood of twilight where one dream seemed to link dusk with dawn? Surely I was hypnotized!

I drifted again.

****

Bam. Bam-bam. Bam. "Come on! Wake up, you lazy thang . . . We're leaving."

The Zone had seduced me again. I fell in; lost my sense of time, space, and identity. Betty's voice rattled around in my brain. I wanted to cry out but heard fading footsteps. Gone. I stumbled out of bed, watching my dream-thoughts evaporate. For some reason I felt sad. Lost. Unable to recall anything. I rubbed my eyes, prying them open.

Then I remembered. Thomas delivered me to the front entrance of my hotel last night, about midnight. I had agreed to meet my six travel companions - Carl's Group we called it - for breakfast. This was to be our last week together. Three months of clinic work was over and the others would be going back on October 13th. I paid extra to stay two extra months. I didn't know why; felt I needed to for some reason.

The face in the bathroom mirror was distorted: an old man with a beard! I shook my head in disbelief and looked again. As my hair, eyes, nose, and lips fell into place, a momentary chill crept over me. Something happened to my awareness. I also noticed I had several pimples and an oozing sore on my left elbow and leg.

But the group was waiting; I had no time to dwell on these bizarre occurrences I quickly shaved and washed my face, threw on my shorts, clinic shirt, and sandals, grabbed my pith helmet, and headed for the lobby. I had already missed breakfast.

After an excruciatingly slow elevator ride, I emerged just in time to see Betty and Dr. Anne Tiroli through the glass entrance, heading up the street. I ran to catch them, flipping a rupee to the beggar camped at the door.

"Hey . . . Wait up!" I yelled, running up behind the pair. In my haste I barely missed one of the ubiquitous puddles of Ceylon rainwater. "Where are the rest?"

"Well," said Anne coolly without looking at me, "Carl, as you know, is already there . . . and Delaney, Shay, and Ali already finished breakfast and decided to go ahead of us." I looked at my watch and saw it was already eight o'clock. I didn't respond. The ensuing conversation was lighter, more superficial.

"I'm sure glad Carl talked us into buying these pith helmets and cotton clinic shirts," said Betty as the equatorial sun beat down on us with an intensity few westerners have known. Carl had warned us about the constant threat of sunburns and heat strokes. While we ignored him on some other issues, we definitely listened to this advice.

The hospital trip of less than two miles felt like thirty. Our way was a veritable obstacle course of mud puddles, traffic, and crowded buses. Some days - if we were lucky - we found a taxi waiting outside the hotel. No such luck today; somebody had beat us to the punch.

After negotiating the mudholes of RamaKrishna Road, we approached The Road: a living, smoke breathing, crawling, noisy, massive, awe-inspiring tar-and-rock traffic serpent that ran through Colombo. Here all traces of the ocean disappeared, replaced by pure madness. Galle Road is no ordinary thoroughfare; it is a western commuter's nightmare. There are no stop lights. No cross walks . . . nothing to regulate the relentless churning of metal, rubber, smoke and flesh that obliterated all signs of nature.

But even Galle Road was not merciless. The first time I faced it, I was utterly at a loss. How do I take a breath, much less cross the thing? Yet, miraculously, I did it. I remember gulping as much air and smog as I dared, then following Carl and the others as they just . . . started walking! The cars and trucks slowed down, swerved, passed on either side. All of them appeared to me as having lost their minds, but no one hit us.

This time was no different. Adrenaline pumping, we lunged through the mass of moving machinery. No matter how many times I did this, I always felt like a scared rabbit running from the talons of a diving falcon . . . a weird sensation arising in the pit of my stomach, into my throat . . . a strange mix of power and harmony. It was a feeling that, even in the midst of total chaos, there was universal order. A feeling that western attempts at man-made order were, at best, a poor cousin to the orderliness of chaos. A feeling they somehow knew this in Ceylon.

Once through, we hurled ourselves onto the soft underbelly of the building on the other side. I rested briefly, then dutifully followed the others - beeline fashion - towards the next haven: the direct bus to the hospital. After two blocks we were there. I collapsed onto the hot, noisy pavement, and stared blankly into the chaos. Meditation on madness.

"Move in. Move!" yelled the young driver, interrupting my stupor. We obeyed, offering three rupees. He raked them greedily out of my hand, then stuffed me - along with about fifteen or twenty others - into the bowels of his small van. I found myself hunched over the heads a couple of Sari-garbed women, staring into the face of an old man with a big nose and a missing eye. The smell of sweat, betel leaf, and curry filled my nostrils.

Their void expressions told me the natives considered this torture as normal. How, I wondered, did Asians cope with so little personal space? I shuddered to think I could ever get used to this! After a jostling, sweaty, five minute expedition, we wormed our way out of the van, feeling like rats squirming off a sinking ship.

I wiped a large bead of sweat from my forehead and squinted into the haze of the morning sun. There, through the rusty gates, lay the monument of our destination. Kalibuwila Hospital. The place had an air of colonial mustiness. It was, in fact, a relic of the days when the British government held control of the island. When I first saw the ancient bureaucratic behemoth, I looked for Gunga Din to appear from around the corner.

The three of us marched toward the rear of the hospital towards the section set aside for acupuncture and alternative medicine. Turning the corner of the old building, we headed towards a clump of giant-leaf foliage. Beyond that lay the center for acupuncture and complementary - or alternative - medicine. I could already hear the booming voice of our teacher.

Chapter Six

He was big, boisterous, and fun. Like Bottom in Shakespeare's *A Midsummer Night's Dream,* Alfred R. Jayawardene, M.D. was a master performer. A jovial clown. At times, I even detected traces of divine wisdom in him . . . a diamond in the midst of a quivering jelly roll. A laughing Buddha.

Sporting a thick mustache, barrel chest, booming voice, and a penchant for the local whiskey, Dr. Jayawardene gave life to every story and joke he told. He turned otherwise dry talks about disease into a circus.

His world was a magnet for all kinds of people: doctors and laypeople, foreigners and natives, the rich, the poor, the sick, and the ones who simply came to hear the day's gossip. All kinds of disciplines - both orthodox and fringe - medical doctors to "magneto-therapists" - were represented here. Kalibuwila Hospital was a place they could practice - or receive - alternative medicine in an atmosphere unrestricted by legal or cultural taboos.

While most Sinhalese natives were meek, courteous, and traditional, Dr. Alfred was loud, boisterous, and irreverent. Where most hospitals were sterile, lifeless, and rigid, Alfred's wing had a dirt floor, patio, tropical plants, and hummed with informality.

While his many diplomas were practically worthless, the intense clinical experience was invaluable. In one month I saw cases I would never have seen even in a western hospital: polio, scurvy, elephantiasis, and other diseases so rare I had only read about them as some medical footnote. I soon accepted the rare and bizarre as a normal occurrence.

The most amazing thing to me, however, was his clinical success. Patients got better despite Dr. Alfred's shoot-from-the-hip way of prescribing and giving treatments. At first glance, he appeared almost careless - willing to sacrifice quality care for showmanship. Conditioned as I was to western detail, I first became unnerved when witnessing things like unlabeled remedies, bizarre treatments, and poor records. Still, his people got well.

"It doesn't matter how you treat the patients," he once preached, "the man gets well anyway. Eighty to 85 percent of his illness is self-limiting. The main rule is: do thy patient no harm!"

Sound advice. Something more medical professionals should heed, I mused. Acupuncture and homeopathy - and chiropractic - were fairly harmless therapies. All things considered, the law of averages was on our side.

What bothered me was the other 15-20 per cent. . . What about the ones who *didn't* recover? I asked him about it once during a lecture. He paused, cracked a few jokes, then confessed, "Things happen. That is their *Tao* . . . karma; some lesson for them. They learn . . . come back healthy next life. Be happy."

I couldn't. There had to be, I figured, more to it than that.

****

"Bring all the people and come!" bellowed the big man as he waved at us to join the festivities. Dr. Alfred never liked to be ignored - either in lectures or while treating patients - and used every occasion to create a party atmosphere. This time he chose an old rice farmer with a bad tooth.

"The tooth is rotten and must be removed," declared the big man, fluttering his arms and hands like a side-show hawker. The old farmer sat stoically, opening his mouth at the prompting of the physician. His tooth stood out in the gaping orifice . . . a final precious offering.

"That's the way it is in Sri Lanka. Too much whiskey. Too much curry. Some bad Betel leaf (a locally grown narcotic very common in the country). Too much . . ." He started to elaborate, but caught himself, smiled, then let out a roaring laughter that sent waves through the small crowd of twenty doctors. We figured it had something to do with sex, another of his favorite topics.

"Escussa me, doctor," interjected a woman from Spain, attempting to bring the group back to the purpose of the clinic. "Can dees mon be cured wis acupuncture?"

"In Spain? Or Sri Lanka?" quipped Alfred with the ease and crispness of a stand-up comedian. Ripples of laughter broke out from the crowd. The Spaniard looked puzzled, but managed an embarrassed smile.

"Not the tooth," responded Alfred on a more serious note. "The tooth, no. It is too much gone. But the pain, Oh, yes. We simply look to reduce the pain and make extraction as easy as possible. Now you come . . ."

With that, Dr. Alfred took the patient's hand and began to walk toward the main building. Two dozen doctors followed him like ducklings behind Mother Goose. I had seen this show before, but was curious to see how the new audience responded, so I tagged along. Betty came too, but Dr. Anne opted to stay and treat one of her regular charges.

We finally arrived at a small room on the second floor. It was dark and dingy, but adequate. Someone had arranged the room to accommodate a dentist chair and some rudimentary drilling tools, polish brushes, metal probes and other items.

"Come, come. Bring all the people. Here. You will see. Come over here . . ." Alfred gathered the group, then sat the patient in the chair and administered needles into the webs of the patient's hands, between the thumb and forefinger.

"You see, here, we put the needles into *Hoku* and apply the electrical impulses at 20 to 30 cycles per second." Dr. Alfred placed electrical clips onto the needles and began to turn up the volume on a small battery-powered stimulator box. He also stimulated the man's cheekbones bilaterally for several seconds. This ritual - like many of his others - was designed to build suspense. Although he evoked the scientist, Dr. Alfred was also aware of his role as magician.

"Now we wait a while for the sedative effect to take place," announced the entertainer. We waited.

Meanwhile, Dr. Alfred rambled on about the "bloody problems" as well as the advantages - of this mode of treatment.

The patient sat there, eyes growing wider, no doubt in mortal fear of this crazy person. I silently chuckled as tension filled the air. Knowing that Alfred's intent just made the whole scene ridiculous.

He began to tell us about the one dental treatment failure he had a few years back. Then, without breaking the tempo of his story, he reached over to the man's cheeks and massaged them again. The anxious patient reacted by tensing at first, then began to relax with the gentle massage.

That was Alfred's cue. He quickly grabbed some pliers from a table and yanked the last remaining tooth from the old man's gaping mouth. Blood spilled everywhere as patient and doctors alike recoiled with horror. A quick application of cotton balls to the gums and soothing words of comfort from Dr. Alfred brought breath back to those who had lost it.

"There you have it. Another success!" proclaimed the big man. He quickly redirected the group's attentions toward the door. As the small, bewildered crowd filed out, I glanced at the now-toothless fellow whose initial look of shock and anguish was replaced by the confused look of someone who was victim to a practical joke. He seemed lost without his tooth, yet somehow surprised that the operation ended so quickly . . . and with less pain than he anticipated.

This was classic Jayawardene. The big man had a natural talent - an ability to conjure up horrific images in peoples' minds, then just as quickly shatter the illusion. Despite what he may have lacked in technical details, Dr. Alfred more than made up for it as the consummate entertainer.

As I left the dental room, I felt a little strange. I soon found myself outside the building, leaning against a wall, vaguely aware that life was going on around me, carried away by some daydream. Betty had been talking to me about something - I wasn't sure what. Now, she looked at me with an expression of silent concern. I acknowledged her presence and confessed I had not been listening.

"Are you all right?" she asked urgently.

"I think so . . . I'm fine," I said, not quite convinced myself. "Just a few pimples and a sore . . .Why do you ask?" I queried, hoping I didn't do anything stupid during my recent blackout.

"Well . . ." Betty paused for a moment, looking deeper into my eyes as if struggling to find the right words to tell me. I started getting worried.

"What? What happened, Betty?!" I pressed, unable to recall anything but some daydreams.

"There's really nothin' to say about it, Matthew. It's just . . ."

"Go on."

"I don't know. I just felt that . . . for some reason, *you were not here* or somethin'. . ." I must have looked shocked. "You seemed a little out of it as we left the room. Then you stopped here, your eyes rolled up to the top of your head, and . . . *you just seemed to float away!* - not your body or anything - but *something* left . . . like you died standing up!!"

I was taken aback by her comments, but not totally surprised. It had happened before. Last night. This morning. *Something* happened. But what?

"A minute later," she continued, "you just unfroze yourself and . . . But you seem to be all right now. How do you feel, Hon? You want me to go get . . . "

"Don't bother," I shot back. "Really, I'm fine. Maybe just a little spaced out, but fine," I lied. I really felt confused, scared, and out of control . . . like my sanity was slipping away.

"Well, you let me know if you need some help or anythin', O.K.? I've got work to do, but I'll be keepin' an eye on you, y'hear?" With that, Betty twirled around and headed toward the acupuncture building to get her supplies for the morning. Still feeling bewildered, I paused, then followed her back to the clinic.

I was scared. Betty's words stayed with me all morning. As I went about my business I felt slightly groggy, but otherwise anxious. Why did I fade out so often? I tried to forget it.

Chapter Seven

"Whatever happened to Pabram Hussein? Yuan Po?" I asked Sam, my interpreter, making light conversation during a short break from patients. We were both sitting at the edge of the clinic in the place I staked out for my daily routine. Hussein and Po had crossed my mind throughout the morning. No particular reason.

"Returned to Pakistan. And China. You don't remember?" asked Sam with a look of concern on his face. The young man apparently noticed I was pale and not all there. He suggested I lie down for a while.

"I'm O.K., Sam," I said, still feeling drowsy but a bit stronger. I drank some coconut juice. "When did they leave?" I asked, my mind suddenly blank. I began to notice the heat - something I usually ignored. I also tried to ignore a noticeable buzzing in my ears, and accumulating sweat on my palms.

"In August . . . and September, doctor." answered the young man. Suddenly, I felt a little silly, almost senile. Memories started coming back in a torrent. Was I losing my mind?

"I remember now!" I said, smiling at Sam. "Hussein from Pakistan. Almost forgot about him. Introduced himself to me when I first arrived." Sam smiled faintly, betraying a look of courteous boredom - the way I used to react to my grandmother when she talked about "the olden days."

How could I forget Hussein and Yuan Po? Con men. Quacks. I fell for them both. Eager to learn about all the modalities - particularly acupuncture and homeopathy - I was naive to the point I suspended all common sense.

Hussein claimed to be a master homeopath. The Pakistani made a point to instruct me and others how to correct some of the so-called mistakes made in Dr. Alfred's clinic. He disappeared after milking a wealthy Canadian woman for over a thousand dollars to treat her mentally-ill son. I later found out he was really an electrical engineer, and had extorted money from her and several others during the course of his stay in Colombo.

Yuan Po, the so-called master acupuncturist from Hong Kong, was adept at explaining the five-element theory of acupuncture as if he invented it. He even appeared to heal some incurable cases. I discovered later he was a master at bait-and-switch. All the people he "healed" were hired strangers: not seen before - or since - their miraculous "recoveries." He worked his audience as cleverly as any tent show evangelist I ever saw in south Georgia.

Dr. Alfred eventually called Yuan's bluff . . . gave him a real case: a small baby with advanced hydrocephalitis, a rare fatal condition otherwise known as water on the brain. I remember looking at the infant's enormous, swollen head and big, innocent eyes. I was struck dumb as I studied the tiny form lying helpless on the mat before me. The child looked strong. Present. Alive, even as his body was sick and greatly deformed. My emotions ran the gamut: from respect and happiness for the child's obvious strength, to sadness and despair of his critical condition.

Dr. Yuan put on a great show, but failed. The baby died in two days. Yuan left Sri Lanka and never came back.

The child's death affected me deeply. For days I felt empty; sad. My belief in so-called miracle cures and master healers had waned. My lively innocence was gone - replaced by a keen awareness of life and death.

Dr. Jayawardene, meanwhile, went about his business as if nothing had happened. He had obviously seen his share of quacks and con men. In fact, the man himself was the biggest con man I knew . . . the only difference being he made no attempt to hide it! I actually admired him for this.

Chapter Eight

I collapsed on the floor. Someone approached. A woman's face. Betty.

"You need to rest!" she admonished. A group of men came and carried me over to one of the benches. Betty stuck some rescue remedy under my tongue. Everything swirled around me like the view from the middle of a Ferris wheel. My ears were on fire! Images of distorted faces appeared out of the corner of my eye. I felt life dripping out of the soles of my feet!

I was pretty sure it wasn't the rescue remedy, an alternative cure for fainting. Something else had taken hold of me. For some inexplicable reason, I felt death had come to pay me a visit. My worst fears surfaced. I squeezed Betty's hand and made an attempt to sit up when I heard the commotion outside the door.

"Bring all the people. Come here . . . a sick doctor," boomed the voice I knew so well. My heart jumped into my throat as the big man entered the room. "Not good, this fainting thing, but it happens. Heat stroke. Anxiety attack. Something. Obvious constipation. Sh . . t out of luck!" The crowd laughed nervously.

"Too much curry. Too much sleep in the morning. No sex. Too serious. Not enough whiskey . . ." More laughter rippled through the swelling audience. "We treat Neiguan."

Needles! I recoiled from the thought. Although ashamed to admit it . . . I *hated* needles! And knives. I had learned to cope with blood, dissection, even death. I could even use them on others. But *me?* No way. I was the consummate coward. Fear of pointed objects even prompted me to become a chiropractor instead of a medical doctor. There's even some kind of long name for this fear - I forgot exactly - but I had it . . . bad.

35

I don't even know why I came here. Some need for self torture, I suppose.

But Neiguan?? I had treated this point on the inside forearm for heart and lung problems. It didn't make any sense for fainting, but then again, was I in any position to decide? I felt helpless; vulnerable. Now I understood the patients, particularly the old farmer in the dentist chair! A crowd gathered - including a bevy of my so-called friends - to watch the show. I looked up and saw Dr. Anne chuckling in the back of the room. She had always wanted to see me as Alfred's guinea pig!

"Pulsatilla! Bring the Pulsatilla . . . and needles!" bellowed the big man to a nurse as she hurried toward the back room for some homeopathic bottles. Needles! The word hung in my throat like a swallowed chicken bone. My brain churned desperately as Alfred proceeded to give a ten-minute lecture on bowel movements and anxiety, describing my stool consistency in great detail. I just lay there, hoping to melt into the bench, alternating between laughing and tears.

Fear and embarrassment welled up in me and begged my mind - without success - to let go. I struggled like a moth in a bag for some escape. There was none. Realizing my predicament, I relaxed and welcomed this chance to overcome the raging demon within. The nurse appeared at the door with Alfred's remedies. More lecturing and laughter ensued, but I didn't listen. I closed my eyes and held my breath.

Then, without warning, I felt a deep, dull sting into my left forearm. Neiguan . . . needle . . . I needed no prompting. The Zone became my haven. No memory. No consciousness . . .

****

I floated in a dream-like state for an eternity. Strong emotions whirled about me as I felt a tugging on my heart and a vision of a sharp knife or machete cutting my leg, then pointed at my throat . . .

I froze, not sure whether this was real or a dream. I couldn't be sure anymore. Danger. I was about to die!

"Namaste," I said aloud.

36

"Namaste." Several times I repeated the word, each time softer and softer, until it echoed in my whole body. I surrendered to the fear and uncertainty of the moment. Thoughts, feelings, and time disappeared. For the last time I entered the Zone. Death was here. It made no difference . . .

****

"Namaste. Namaste . . ."

I came back from somewhere - I'm not sure where - finding myself taking the last needle out of a Tamil patient, suddenly realizing I had been gone a long time. She returned the "Namaste" with clasped hands and a humble bow, then walked away.

"More needles, Sir?" asked one of the local helpers, approaching me with a fresh tray.

"No, thank you . . . *Esthuti.*" I said politely, "I'm not quite through with the ones I have." I was on automatic, about to switch and do spinal adjustments on the next few patients.

I suddenly remembered: it was Tuesday! A whole day since I passed out from Alfred's treatment. The time had been flat. Other than a vague feeling of danger, I had no feeling or memory. Betty, and even Alfred became concerned at my reaction, although Dr. Jayawardene predictably hailed it as "another success!" Or so I was told.

I just smiled when I awoke, a different person. I heard of alcoholics going through blackout phases, but wasn't so sure this was the same thing . . . wasn't so sure of *anything* anymore. For some reason, life just seemed to cruise by without me.

While I felt happiness over the last 24 hours or so, it mostly faded into a *flatness* I found hard to describe. Nothing hurt. The fear of needles, the delusions. . . everything left me. But nothing seemed alive either. I just moved through the motions. Lunch. Rest. Dinner. Sleep. Wake. Walk. Clinic.

Everything appeared the same, but very flat. It's as if I had vacated my own conscious mind.

Chapter Nine

"Breathe in, then blow it out," I suggested to an older woman who lay face down on my adjusting table. I was trying to get her to relax, at the same time making a valiant effort to stay sharp. These last several days were rough. I had fallen into a dull haze as a result of Alfred's treatment. Slowly, however, my efforts at self-revival were paying off. I did conscious breathing, exercised, and actively engaged in conversations with others.

My patient turned her head and babbled something in French. My memory of French hovered somewhere between third and fourth grade.

"Un petit moment," I said while looking around for a French person - someone in a Legionnaire's outfit, toting a bonnet and parasol, or sporting one of those funny little artist hats. I didn't see any. Young Sam the interpreter (who spoke no French) shrugged his shoulders when I looked at him, as if to say "This one is your problem, white man."

"Excusem-moi." I patted the woman's back and pulled away from my table long enough to yell something into the milling crowd.

"Does anyone here speak French? Parlay voo Fransais et Inglish?! See voo play?!" I felt silly; being all I could muster at the moment was fractured French. But it worked.

"Oi, Oi!" I heard. Seconds later an attractive auburn brunette appeared wearing a safari outfit and multi-colored silk scarf. My eyes went first to her legs: long, smooth, sensuous . . . melting into a pair of multi-colored sandals; then her eyes: large, clear, and full of joy and life. I had seen her earlier and wondered who she was. Hopefully I would find out.

"Do you also speak English?" I held my breath waiting for her answer.

"Oh, yes, quite well actually. I'm from London," she said with perfect royalty. I released my breath with a sigh and a big smile.

"Are you with this woman?" I asked, rather curious as to the French connection.

"No, but actually we've met recently. By the way, my name is Ruth. Ruth Graham."

She extended her hand. I felt she was waiting for me to escort her to the coronation. I held her soft hand, not quite sure whether I should kiss it or shake it. I prudently chose the latter, slightly bowing my head and returning the introduction, along with a brief summary of my dilemma.

She told me the woman's name was Celeste and briefly explained to her - in French - what I was trying to do.

"Would you please tell this lady I would like for her to breathe in . . . then breathe out . . . then relax?" It worked. Ruth communicated the request perfectly, and I was able to get a release in the woman's mid-thoracic spine.

Ruth Graham's presence brought order and clarity. My head felt clearer; more awake. I was able to give attention to things easier. She was fabulous. Her speech, whether in French or English, was musical. Her manner flawless She walked and talked with an air of dignity that made me strangely uncomfortable. I didn't want to be so attracted to her, but I was . . . immediately. I tried to hide my admiration by putting on my formal clinic face. I finished the job with Celeste and helped her off the table. She smiled, thanked me in French, and spoke a few words to Ruth.

"She says she feels much better, thank you," said Ms. Graham. "Is there anything else?"

I wanted to say something bold, but didn't. There will be another chance, I thought. Another time.

"No, thank you . . . Ruth . . ." My voice must have betrayed me. She looked at me and smiled. The royalty melted away and I beheld a charming, almost sensuous beauty before me.

"Well, I'll be around sometimes if you need me," she said with a hint of flirtation. With that, she took Celeste by the hand and escorted her towards the crowd.

I squelched the impulse to pursue them.

This is ridiculous, I muttered to myself. I didn't know this person. I may never see her again. What was I feeling? Did I miss sex so much I had to fall for every female who spoke to me? What was I supposed to learn from all this? That Cheryl should have come with me? Why didn't I go home with the others? I felt like a love-struck teenager . . . my first date all over again. Miserable. Forget it. Let it go.

As it turned out, I didn't see Ruth again the rest of the day. Or the next day. Or all of that week. Although I looked for her, she never came back. I was both relieved . . . and sad. The emotional stress of our encounter was almost more than I could bear. I felt the onerous, yet delicious pull of temptation. I also felt an emptiness since the brief encounter . . . a strange longing for someone I didn't know, but couldn't live without.

Strange. Days after getting that so-called remedy from Pachili, I felt as if I'd lost control of my feelings, my memory, and, to a large degree, my senses.   At night, my dreams were translucent and vividly bizarre. Sometimes funny, sometimes horrific, the characters would suddenly change on me: take on ugly and onerous qualities. Once I was chased by a large python-like being. Once by a swarm of bugs. Another dream found me floating in rivers of multi-colored ooze. Sometimes blood. Often I had dreams of a bearded old man meditating in some marble ashram.

Dreams also filled my daylight hours - dreams so real I could reach out and touch them. Vivid, 3-dimensional daydreams. Reality, emotion, fantasy and memory came together in a kaleidoscope of richness that transcended anything I had ever experienced before. I often found myself staring at some flower or bush, awed by the splendor and intricacy of the petals or leaves. Once, I sat with a large ant, telepathically receiving information from him about the taste of tree bark! Sometimes, I talked with the bearded man. Like my dreams, each experience took on a logic of its own, a logic that faded when I woke up or came to my senses.

My practical memory, however, got worse. I forgot names more often. People remarked I seemed distant. Cold. Despite Alfred's treatment, the prevalent heat, and constant sunshine, my face continued to show a pallor that aroused particular concern in Betty. The headaches also continued, and my sinuses drained more often. Pimples on my face and body came and went, but the oozing sore on my left leg and elbow persisted.

Some of the older homeopathic doctors I met said my body was cleansing itself of toxins too quickly. They offered to slow it down with an another remedy, but I declined. I didn't know what Pachili had given me and I feared other remedies might make matters worse.

I still held onto Pachili's remedy, the one he gave me with no instructions. Should I take it? Was it the antidote to the previous one? Or was it poison? Would it help me, or make me worse? How could I call him? He had no phone. He may not even be there . . .

Indecision made me helpless to act. I simply kept the mysterious packet on my dresser at the hotel. Each day I picked it up like some sort of delicate religious icon, trying to decide what to do with it. Every time, I just put it back and walked away.

Fearing insanity, I resolved to pour myself into my work and take notes of any health progress in my diary. I decided I might have to see Pachili again after all . . . to resolve this unbearable state of affairs.

But when?

Chapter Ten

My travel partners returned to America as scheduled on October 13th. Despite nagging concerns, I resolved to see Pachili once again. Had he returned to the monastery? I didn't know, but it was worth a trip to find out. I left Colombo the morning of November 5.

The weathered Toyota I borrowed from my local friend Vimal Rasanaya was running well. I had kept it longer than expected - for trips to Galle and Kandy - but asked if I could use it another day or two and he agreed . . . provided I take care of it.

"What do you think I'm going to do?" I laughed over the phone, "drive it over a cliff?"

"You can never know . . ." warned Vimal in his rapid-fire Asian-English dialect, "many strange things happening in the mountains. Simply deliver to me the auto excellently, fill with petrol, and partake of little or no trouble that you see."

"You mean, take care of myself and the car?"

"This is what I say."

I cheerfully promised my friend I would return the auto in prime condition.

"Make a mind that you do, you idiot" snarled my friend playfully, "or I shall be forced to give you a *thunderrring rrrap* upon your head!" Vimal enjoyed hurling insults at me - a sort of male-bonding ritual I had forgotten since my college days.

I felt good about the trip, but detected in Vimal's playfulness a subtle sense of urgency. He had several cars, and rarely used this one. I offered several times to pay him, but he declined, insisting I use it free of charge. I promised to protect his property - and stay alert to any and all dangers.

He also cautioned me about traveling through the country during a civil war. I reminded him that the war was still mostly in the north and northeast, and repeated my promise to be careful. I had a strange sense of foreboding, however . . . something about a dream I had weeks earlier. I shook it off.

The day was still clear when I left my hotel, shortly before noon on Thursday, the full moon holiday of Poya Day. It had been raining sporadically earlier in the week, but the monsoon was coming to an end. Because 1987 was such a strange year for Ceylon weather, however, I could never be certain.

I stopped by to tell Alfred and the others I would be gone for a while to treat a friend in Galle, the old Dutch city-fort on the southern coast. I even called my distant friend Ifthikar, leaving the message I might drop by. Both were deliberate lies. I *was* heading south, but didn't want any problems with Alfred if I happened to end up in Balangoda.

The big doctor appeared to have a problem with Pachili. He had made several references to "those quacks" who live in the mountains, but never explained why we should avoid them. He could have only been talking about the Buddhist homeopath. There was no other mountain "quack." I also wasn't sure whether or not Alfred thought Pachili was *really* a quack . . . or wanted us to avoid him for some other reason.

Perhaps the big man was jealous . . . saw the monk as a threat to his authority. Maybe there was some unwritten law we couldn't have more than one *guru* at a time. Whatever the reason, it didn't matter. I knew what I wanted, and I'll be damned if Dr. Jayawardene - or anyone else for that matter - was going to stop me!

I headed straight for Galle Road. Like a gazelle chased by leopards, I felt the adrenaline rush as my car hugged the right sidewalk for a few blocks until merging with other noisy, sputtering vehicles. The Toyota purred effortlessly through the chaos, along the twisted highway, potholes, oncoming vehicles, and straw wagons. As always, Vimal's car never gave me any trouble . . . unless I count that one flat tire.

Leaving the explosive bustle of Colombo behind, I embarked on my first solo trip outside the city. I barreled along the now-serene-but-narrowing highway towards Panadura to the

44

south. My plan was to hit the small village, then head east. If all went well, I would spend the night at Ratnapura, the gem capital of Sri Lanka, then drive to Balangoda the next day.

The chaos of Galle Road soon imploded into silence, lush vegetation, and greenery. The sights and smells of the countryside poured into my open car window, a marked contrast to the smoke and fumes I left behind. The sickening blanket of smog had lifted to reveal a more pleasant side of the island. The aroma of palm and coconut swirled around me, along with that of various shrubs and flowers, hot peppers, the distant ocean, and other distinct yet pleasant fragrances I could not identify. An occasional oxcart, accompanied by children, dogs, chickens, and goats, provided more local color . . . fodder for my hungry senses.

I stopped only once between Colombo and Panadura. Passing through a stretch of lagoon and wilderness, I had to pull over and wait for a rare, five-foot monitor lizard to cross the road. Lugging its bulk slowly but deliberately along the road, the reptile reminded me of an overgrown Gila monster I once met in New Mexico as a child. I pulled out my camera, framed, and shot only once before the beast scurried to privacy into a nearby ditch.

"No doubt he's either looking for Mrs. Monster," I laughed to myself, envisioning his quest for some female monitor lizard . . . or equally delicious Ceylon bugs!

Continuing down the road, I felt alive. The Zone- at least for the time being - had vanished. I tuned into some Beatle songs playing on a Colombo radio station as the sadness of the last few days melted into a feeling of freedom. I stuck my head out the window, feeling the rush of wind and sun on my face. For the first time in months, I wanted to sing.

"What the hell," I said, looking around and seeing thick woods, deserted lagoons, and empty fields. I took a deep breath, opened my mouth and let 'er rip . . . singing loud and gloriously for miles:

"We-all-live-in-a-Yel-low-Sub-ma-rine . . ."

Signs of Panadura soon appeared, however, reminding me to concentrate so as not miss my turn-off. Feeling hungry, I decided this would be a good place to stop off for a bite of lunch. I pulled over to a small food shop and bought a coconut - or *thambili* to the locals - and a bag of chewy something-or-others to go with my homemade sandwich. I then proceeded to look for a place near the ocean to hang out in my car, breathe, freely, and enjoy my meal.

There was no decent place to be found. I drove south for miles, looking for a connecting road to the beach. None appeared. Other than a few patches of blue sky and sea, I could see nothing but clusters of thatched-roof houses, coconut groves, and thick forest between me and the Indian Ocean.

Determined not to let such a small thing disrupt my lunch, I pulled into a shady clearing on the side of the road. Sensing the rising heat of the afternoon, I downed the coconut first, hoping to cool off a bit. The juice disappeared quickly. As I unwrapped the cheese sandwich in my lap, I suddenly thought it would be better to park a little further away from the road. I threw the cellophane back around the sandwich, grabbed the steering wheel . . .

Then stopped. Deja-vu hit me like a ton of bricks.

The edge of the machete sharply raised my chin. I froze, unable to turn my head to see who - or what - was stalking me. The callused Tamil hand reached into the car and grabbed my sandwich, the bag of chewies, my camera, and a 100-rupee note sitting at my side. Time moved painfully . . . slowly; I flashed on both Vimal's warning and my dream. This was no dream; it was happening! Or was it?!

I shuddered quietly, my mind falling mercifully blank. I had no idea what to expect, but things did not look good. I said a silent prayer for those who would miss me.

Then, as if prompted by a script, I closed my eyes and spoke aloud the only Tamil word I remembered:

"Namaste," I said, repeating it again . . .

"Namaste."

46

Several times I repeated the word, each time softer and softer, until it echoed in my whole body. I surrendered to the fear of the moment.

"Namaste."

The sharp edge fell away from my chin. Would I be thrown out of the car and hacked to pieces? I followed the script laid out for me:

"Namaste" echoed into my throat, into my lungs, and into my gut.

"Namaste . . ."

Thoughts, feelings, and time disappeared. I entered the Zone once again. Now I was dying. Again . . .

****

"Wake up, you stupid dog! You are wasting my time!!" spoke Pachili harshly, tearing at my ego like eagle claws ripping the heart out of its prey. I gasped for breath. Was I dreaming again? Dead? I peered through a long tunnel, watching myself squirm before the onslaught of the master. Without effort, I dropped in.

"I'll have nothing more to do with you," he ripped coldly.

The brush-off shocked me. The lump in my throat swelled as the sudden agony in my solar plexus rose towards my head. The pain quickly mixed with such rage I wanted to run the car off the road, killing us both. Tears welled up inside me. My heart pounded. My head ached. I clutched the steering wheel, bracing for an act of violence . . .

I managed to pull of the road, then sat stunned, still clutching the steering wheel. I waited. There was only silence. I closed my eyes, witnessing a flood of emotion washing over me. The steering wheel became my only anchor in this swirling sea of uncertainty.

I couldn't let it go. Try as I might, the rage swelled within me like molten fire. I wanted to kill the bastard! I wanted to shred him from limb to limb! I wanted to . . .

****

More tunnels. More light. I shifted abruptly, not sure where I was, or why. I gripped the edge of the bed beneath me. Old stuff. Past. Although I knew this, I felt helplessly drawn in. Didn't want to give him the satisfaction of seeing me angry. I didn't want to let him know I hated him for beating me. What could I do? The belt came down . . . my exposed legs and buttocks withered in the onslaught, more from the anger than the pain itself. There was no escape!

Suddenly, I had a flash of insight: I was not this child anymore! I turned to my father . . . turned to him and looked him in the eyes . . . eyes burning with an intensity I had known for ages   "No more!" I said. He continued beating my body, but strangely enough, all the pain stopped.   I said again, "No more." He stopped.

"Namaste . . ."

****

Stillness prevailed. Slowly, I returned to my body consciousness, eyes closed. I put out feelers to my surroundings. All parts were present for now. My hands still gripped the steering wheel as I heard death stalking me, outside the car window . . .

"Mahatmaya. Rupees. Karunakara. Rupees . . ."

A small voice pierced my brain, the voice of a small child.

"Rupees, Mister? School-pen?" Another small voice joined in. They were sending children now to kill me!

There was a tap on my shoulder. Anxiously, I flashed my eyes open to see the hands of two little boys reaching into the car. I looked around the car . . . There was no Tamil Tiger in sight! Still mindless with fear, I reached into my pocket, produced two 5-rupee coins for the boys. Flipping out the coins, I cranked the ignition, forced the car in reverse, and shot out of my dubious retreat. A trail of burnt rubber became the only reminder of my visit.

Heart was beating wildly, I raced for miles. After driving for about ten minutes in the sun and wind, I began to calm down a little. I wanted to head back to Colombo and the safety of Hotel Brighton. As I got closer to Panadura and the turnoff, however, I reassessed my situation. I knew I had just survived a Tamil attack. All he took was my lunch, 100 rupees, and a camera. He left the car intact . . . and me still alive!

By some miracle, I had been spared. Perhaps it was the repetition of "Namaste," a Hindu word of reverence. Perhaps it was the approach of the Sinhalese villagers. Perhaps he was only hungry. But where did Pachili come from? Was this some dream of future events? Perhaps I was in the dream *now*. Perhaps . . .

Who knows. I quickly didn't care. At the moment, I was just glad to be among the living. Even my irritating sinuses had cleared up! Now, more than ever, I wanted to get to Balangoda. My whole life was turning upside down, and I needed to know what was happening to me.

The sign to Ratnapura appeared. Looking to put some distance between me and *that Tamil,* I cornered the curve, throttled the engine, and aimed my speeding chariot towards the interior . . . and into the unknown.

Chapter Eleven

Aside from my recent brush with death, this second excursion to Balangoda was better than the first. I had my own wheels. I didn't have to put up with the horribly cramped Sri Lankan public bus system, which actually consisted of a few beat up Japanese vans stuffed with human bodies. Also, the weather was good despite predictable mid-afternoon heat.

An hour later, I was singing again. The further I got from Panadura, the less threatening the machete incident became. Distance brought comfort. I felt safe now. I just needed to be more alert, more wary of stopping in isolated spots. Vimal was right. I had been careless.

Ratnapura lay ahead. I stopped the car next to a large rice paddy to check the map. I could hear the *Kalu Ganga,* or river, in the distance to my right and knew that the city was straight ahead. Probably less than ten kilometers by my estimation.

I cranked up the Toyota and headed due east, taking great care to avoid the increased number of potholes in the partially paved road. After being stopped twice - once for a herd of water buffalo crossing, and again for a pile of sticks that had fallen from an oxcart - I finally made it into the outskirts of town.

Unlike American cities, where fast-food joints create a ubiquitous monotony everywhere, the towns in Sri Lanka have their own flavor and character. This was certainly true of Ratnapura, Sri Lanka's "Gem City." The title is significant, considering the country itself ranks among the top five gem-bearing nations of the world, along with Burma, Thailand, Brazil, and South Africa.

Approaching the city, I could see gem pits dotting the rice paddies on either side of the road. A whiff of fresh, cool air caught my lungs as it came rolling down from the mountains. I felt alert; robust. The incident at Panadura woke up nerve endings I never knew I had! It was sheer joy just to feel the life force cascading throughout my body and mind. Since I'd just come back from the brink of death, every moment was a bonus.

I looked at my watch. It was three o'clock. I had options: stay in Ratnapura and spend the afternoon gem hunting, or press on to Balangoda. Feeling less anxious, I decided to stop for the night. The gnawing in my stomach had grown stronger . . . reminded me of my stolen lunch. I also felt the pinch of the 100-rupees, even if it *was* less than three dollars. I didn't know whether to curse the Tamil for robbing me, or thank him for letting me live.

I dug my hands in my pockets and came out with 500 rupees. Feeling lucky, I chose to forgive and forget. Besides, I didn't want to pass up an opportunity to look at cat's-eyes, rubies, moonstones, chrysoberyls, and sapphires.

Forty rupees paid for a curried rice dish and a fresh *thambili,* or coconut. Ten more paid off the immediate beggars. Finding a cool spot behind one of the stores, I sat in the grass and chased each bite of curry with a swallow of coconut juice.

Sri Lanka has probably the hottest (i.e., spiciest) food in the world. I learned this the hard way when a Pakistani friend and I order "medium hot" Byriani at a small cafe in Colombo. The ensuing pain was so severe, we guzzled water, soft drinks and yogurt until we were sick. My respect for Sinhalese curry is now similar to my respect for Sinhalese cobras: Look, but don't touch!

I finished my rice with a sense of accomplishment. Although it burned, I considered my ability to communicate *no spice* to members of the outback the equivalent of a non-violent coup. I capped off the curry meal with more *thambili* juice, then set out to re-discover Ratnapura before charting my course east.

Leaving the side alley, I headed down the dusty street of the main business district. Cheap, bright, hand-painted murals were everywhere. Beneath them sprawled equally garish goods and clothing. All were for sale: red, yellow, white, and blue; polyester and cotton; saris, dhotis, sarongs, and western-styled shorts and blouses. Curry smell sifted through the air, punctuated by the occasional odor of incense.

I began walking toward the nearest gem store . . .

"You from UK, Mister?"

A young boy stepped in front of me. He smiled, obviously bent on pawning some of his junk.

"Nah. U.S.A." I responded, wondering how much it was going to cost me to pay him off.

"I speak good English, Sir. My father is local magistrate."

I smiled and nodded, still wondering what he wanted. No response. He wasn't playing the game right.

"Well, young man, thank you for your smile," I quipped, and began to walk away. Much to my growing irritation, he followed. What was he selling? Why didn't he just come out with it like all the others?

Halfway to my destination, I noticed the boy still tailing me. Why was he stalking me? I quickened my pace to the gem store, figuring I could duck inside and escape. I stopped, feeling a burning in my heart I couldn't explain. Almost as a reflex, I pivoted to face the young man. He was standing in the middle of the road, looking at me in desperation. For a few moments, I struggled with my feelings of compassion for the kid, mixed with fear of getting stuck with an emotionally dependent child. I couldn't make myself go inside.

Resigned, I dropped both the compassion and the fear, determined to make the best of whatever he wanted. I returned, then kneeled down to face the boy at eye level.

"What is your name, little man?"

"Paratha, Sir." The boy's smile returned. I gave him a few rupees and made another attempt to walk away. He ran after me and stuck the rupees in my pocket. "No, thank you, Sir . . ."

I paused, astonished. I had not witnessed *this* before.

"Well, Paratha, what do you want? Money?" I asked, still resigned that he was setting me up for something bigger.

"No Sir."

"Nothing?" I quizzed suspiciously.

"Message, Sir. They wait for you before dark . . ."

"Who?"

"The *Vittas,* Sir," said the young man as he pointed at the sky. "That way!"

I looked towards the eastern sky and could barely make out a couple of blackbirds. It was eerie, but something in the lad's voice gave me goose bumps.

"Pachili!" I blurted out, then ran toward the car. Whether or not the young man's message meant anything, I didn't know. All I could feel was the sudden urgency to get back on the road.

"This has been the strangest day of my life," I muttered under my breath as I sought the familiar confines of my little Toyota. I was tired, a little irritated, and had no more desire to sight-see. I just wanted to keep moving.

A few miles down the road, I had a distinct feeling I had witnessed something extraordinary. How did that boy know I was going east? "They" waited for me? Who? How did he know I could be there before dark?

I couldn't shake the feeling that the boy was telling me something important and I just wasn't getting it. Talking to birds? Is that normal in Ratnapura? I laughed nervously, feeling like the straight man in a much-too-subtle comedy sketch.

Chapter Twelve

Balangoda is small. If it weren't for the large Buddhist altar, or Dagoba, near the road and a few shops, I might have missed it. I turned off the main road, onto the winding, dusty path leading to Pachili's monastery. Everything took on an orange hue as the sun settled close to the western horizon. I was arriving just before dark.

Unlike the onset of dusk in countries further north, darkness here came with little warning. Sure enough, within minutes of arriving at the monastery, the sun plunged beneath the western horizon as hints of the full moon greeted me from the east. The monks were just now adjourning from their evening meal. One recognized me and signaled towards Pachili's *avasa,* indicating he was at home. I took a deep breath, relieved I didn't miss him.

Bumbling along the trail in the sudden darkness, I made my way beneath a few low-hanging tree bows toward the small wooden cabin a short distance away. As I approached the tiny unlit abode, a sense of eerie anticipation hung in the still air. The full moon cleared the horizon and rose sufficiently to give me a clear view of the trail and the porch. I knocked on the rustic door, but sensed no movement inside.

"Pachili?" I said, then listened for an answer. None. Walking around to the back of the small frame house, I saw a robed figure sitting on a wooden bench about fifty feet away. His eyes were closed, facing a tiny herb garden. Not wanting to disturb him, I leaned against the wall of the small house in a soft pile of leaf mulch, closed my eyes and began to meditate.

A long time passed - I'm not even sure how long - before I heard Pachili's voice pierce the evening stillness:

"I've been expecting you," he said mysteriously. My mind froze as I experienced another moment of deja-vu. It was as if I suddenly knew the reason I was there . . . an inner feeling that gave no clue to my conscious mind. I felt a sense of awe in this place - as if I were truly sitting at the feet of a holy person about to impart some significant piece of wisdom to me.

"Are you hungry?" he asked.

"A little . . ." I responded, somewhat amused at my tendency to manufacture cosmic significance where there was none. "I had a small rice dish for lunch."

"Come. I've got some herb soup."

Pachili then led me toward the cabin. I followed his shadowy figure through the rustic wooden door. "Have a seat on the wooden bench over there," he said, making some motion with his hand. Although I could barely see, I managed to locate the bench with my shin, grab it and sit down. I heard Pachili fiddling with a lantern on the wall. Within seconds we were wrapped in the warm glow of his small kerosene lantern.

"I don't usually light the lantern," he said, finding a spot on his mattress on the other side of the room, "but today I have some honored guests." He paused, then arose suddenly before I could ask him who the others were.

"The soup!" He walked slowly and silently to the end of the room, took a large bowl and poured some liquid from a thermos container. He served me what looked like a bowl of vegetable broth. "Here. Take this. It will erase the journey for you."

I hesitated, then tasted the soup. It was lukewarm, mild, and very pleasing. There was a taste of some familiar herbs: sage, some oregano, and some other herb mixture I didn't recognize.

"Have you eaten already?" I asked, not wanting to be impolite.

"Oh, yes. You enjoy your meal and we talk when you finish."

I proceeded to down the bowl as Pachili sat regally cross-legged on his small mattress. The cabin had a good vibe. As I the warm broth filled my stomach, I began to relax and feel more at home.

I had not been inside Pachili's cabin before, only outside. It was a very simple unfinished frame house. He furnished it with a couple of wooden benches and chairs, a small table, a woven linen rug, and a single mattress with a few pillows and blankets for sleeping and meditation. Some bowls, plates, utensils, the thermos bottle, a pot, pan, and a small kerosene burner were in the makeshift kitchen: a table in the corner next to a little window.

There were herb jars in the corner and freshly picked herbs on the table. Incense permeated the air, along with a faint trace of burnt sage. A shelf in another corner contained a few books and bottles of remedies. There was no need for heating or cooling. The cabin itself sat under a cluster of trees for shade, and was, as I recall from my last visit, very comfortable even during the hottest part of the day.

Suddenly I felt uncomfortable. I looked up and noticed Pachili staring at me. His eyes seemed wider than I remembered, almost hypnotic. I wanted to say something, yet found my mouth unable to move. As he continued to glare at me, I felt dizzy and wanted to look away.

Chapter Thirteen

"So how do you feel about facing death?"

The question pierced the air like a knife and hit me between the eyes. The bolt of energy shot down to my feet and back up to my solar plexus. I glared back at Pachili, half expecting some sort of cruel joke to follow. He remained fixed on me with unflinching eyes.

I sputtered into my soup, mind racing to the incident at Panadura. What did *he* have to do with it? Did he set it up? Impossible, I thought. He couldn't know about that, or even that I was coming. And yet, he asked the most direct question. I decided to find out what he knew.

"Wh-what do you mean?" I stammered unconvincingly. I must have sounded really dumb. Pachili broke the gaze, laughed, then rephrased the question:

"You had a taste of the Zone," he added, shrugging his shoulders. "Death. So, how did it feel?"

I didn't know what to say. All I could do was stare into what remained of my herb soup. I wasn't hungry anymore. Was he *there?* If so, how could he have gotten here before me . . !? There is no telephone in the monastery. How . . .

"The Zone contains all the gaps in space and time," spoke the Buddhist, "You can enter there, but fear, anger, and unconsciousness will not let you stay present. Wake up! Be present!" The older man barked his commands with the precision of a drill sergeant. I had no idea what he was talking about. Yet somehow, part of me knew *exactly* what he was talking about! I had to respond. My feelings shifted . . .

"Are you willing to be *here?*" he asked, "To bring consciousness back into the body . . . full consciousness?"

Pachili pressed me to respond with some kind of answer to this powerful question, as if asking for the salt and pepper. For minutes all I could do was stare at my soup. I felt an ancient stirring in my heart and solar plexus, a fire dampened by decades of conditioning, but not destroyed. Feeling lost, I closed my eyes and responded to his voice, trusting my intuition. I didn't know what to think or feel.

"Yes," I said weakly, tears straining to come out.

"Fine," guided the voice. "Now trust. Go to the door of your mind and let in someone you trust . . . an older woman."

The image of my beloved grandmother burst forth inside.

"Mimi!" I cried out with joy. I ran up to my grandmother as she approached the doorway of our ranch-style home. She was delivering one of her special southern pound cakes. What was the occasion? I felt suddenly lost; afraid to open my eyes. Reality and fantasy became blurred: intense fear coupled with a strange overwhelming sense of bliss.

I jumped up and down as I opened the door and clamored for my loving Mimi who then joyfully took me into her open arms. I cried. The reunion with my grandmother was electric. I felt my body jerking in a seesaw motion as I rocked in her arms, crying and laughing, laughing and crying. Finally, I felt the wave of deep emotion wash over me. Mimi was here and wasn't going to leave. I was safe. Loved. Pachili's voice rolled in like a small wave on the beach:

"Now bring awareness of your adult into the picture," rang the voice clearly. Suddenly, I was separate from them - Mimi - and me as a small child. I pierced the thought veil with my adult mind and asked my grandmother if that was O.K. if I joined them. She said yes.

"Now go to them," said the voice. I did as told, not really understanding what was happening to me, making every effort to flow with it. The vision was so strong, so real, I found little difficulty in following directions.

I found myself holding hands with Mimi and my little child as if they were really in the room. Other things happened - I'm not sure what - then I saw myself lifted out of the room - into old memories, places, and times I thought I had long forgotten . . . times when I felt unloved, unprotected, and unacknowledged.

At each incident along the way, I was gently told to correct the situation, rewrite the script, then move on to the next.

After some time - not sure how long - I became mentally and emotionally exhausted. Then I heard: "Now rest."

Relief washed over me. I was lifted to a beautiful palm-shaded, sun-drenched beach front. I placed my little boy's head in my lap and stroked him on the forehead, while relaxing to one of Mimi's bedtime stories and pieces of cake. It must have been days or weeks . . . It felt like a long time. Eventually my little boy was ready to go.

"Are you ready to be *here*?" prompted the voice.

I sensed a shift . . . something important. Turning to the child, whose presence had solidified far beyond that of imagination, I asked the question. He hesitated with a look of fear and glanced over to Mimi, as if to ask permission. Mimi nodded O.K., along with a few reasons why this would be the best thing to do. Assured, he echoed her signal. I felt lifted, along with my beloved companions, into a realm of light and color that transcended all that I had known before. A rainbow path appeared, leading to a large, elaborate gate. On the other side I found a part of me that had split off and fled the earth long ago.

I don't know how long we took. At times, I felt lost, guided only by his voice. Each time, however, the images came vividly, effortlessly, as I sailed into another part of my memory and experience.

Then, as if awakening from a dream, I fell back into my body. Following a silver cord through the top of my head, I felt a strange grumbling in my solar plexus as beams of light - velvet rays - shot into me from all directions. My fingers, hands and feet - particularly my feet - became anchored to the center of the earth. The voice asked me to keep my eyes closed for a few minutes while I felt someone circle me, muttering something under his breath.

"Now, open your eyes," he spoke calmly, yet firmly.

A few minutes later, I was staring into a face that lit up the room with a vibrant chorus of energy I had not seen nor felt before. The lantern light seemed very pale by comparison. Pachili's eyes were beacons of flashing light. My mouth dropped open. I had nothing to say. I felt it useless to comment. I was *here*, but still felt strangely absent.

"Take a while. Rest. Do not speak. Let yourself come back slowly. Be kind." His words felt as warm as the blanket I used to keep as a child.

I relaxed, looking around. Everything seemed the way it was before, only brighter. It was as if someone had turned up the dimmer switch. I had no urgency; just a remarkable peace, as one who just came through a hurricane fully intact. Being here. Was *this* what my mentor had been talking about?

Pachili got up from his seat, grabbed what appeared to be an empty goatskin flask, and walked out of the cabin, the rustic door swinging shut behind him. I could hear his footsteps disappearing toward the monastery, replaced by the sound of crickets in the woods.

Something was born that night. For no reason, I giggled under my breath, then broke out into belly laughs. I had never heard these sounds coming from me before: hearty, joyful guffaws that brought delight to my new-born spirit. I felt drunk, but not like a dull, alcoholic. This was different. I didn't even know who I was any more. I was alive. Alert. Complete. Feeling totally stupid . . . and loving it!

Within minutes I settled down to check all systems. Eyes work. Ears still intact. Nose smells O.K. Diaphragm works. Jaw moves easily. Can still move my arms and crack my knuckles. Legs O.K. Can stand up and walk. Brain? Currently non-functional, but in reserve. Gently. Not so fast.

I stepped outside Pachili's front door to catch a deep breath of air. The woods beckoned me, and I wanted to explore them in the dark. Before I set out, however, I recalled the bugs, snakes, lizards, and other earth-bound critters that dwelled there, and made a decision to stay on the porch. Pachili returned a few minutes later, carrying his goatskin flask, now filled with water. I had almost forgotten: he had no plumbing.

"Are you ready to go?" he inquired, almost matter-of-factly.

"Go *where?*" I puzzled. "Do you want me to leave?"

"You and I. We go now to World's End." Suddenly my brain popped in.

"You're kidding, right?" I proposed nervously.

"I don't kid," answered my mentor. Although it *was* a beautiful night to travel, there was *nothing* inviting about World's End after dark. I had no desire to return there and spend the night. Besides, I had a deathly fear of heights and couldn't even go near the edge when I was there last time! I expressed these concerns to Pachili.

"This is a special time," he said, shrugging off my concerns. "There is much to learn on nights of the Full Moon. Come. Take us, or I go alone."

I knew he was serious; he spoke with authority and persistence even though I *knew* the 50-plus mile trek to the Horton Plains was more than even Pachili could traverse on foot in a single night. Yet I also remembered - and had this verified with the other monks - that he supposedly walked to and from India several times . . . over 300 miles away . . . just to the long ferry ride that would carry him over the Palk Strait!

"Wait!" I demanded, feeling suddenly insecure. Although I still retain much of my humor and peace inside, outside I fidgeted nervously. Pachili stopped to look at me as I implored him to help me. "I don't understand. Tell me what just happened to me. Tell me about your remedies. Tell me why we have to go to the Horton Plains *tonight. I need to understand all of this . . !!"*

Oddly enough, even as I ranted on, I didn't feel panicky. I felt excited . . . like the rush a kid feels on Christmas morning to open as many presents as he can. My logical mind could make no sense of it.

Pachili, in a gesture of pity for my tortured brain, ambled over and sat next to me on the bench. He spoke softly, yet firmly. "You have concerns," he said patiently, "I understand. Come with me. You will see them clearly when the time is right."

His words satisfied me. I just needed some acknowledgment. Pachili headed back inside and started throwing a few items into a back pack. I followed him and asked if there was anything I could do to help.

"No," he answered curtly. "Is your car ready?"

"Yes. . ."

"Good. Let us depart."

With that, he blew out the lantern and headed out the door toward the trail and the monastery.   I followed him, unable to shake the feeling I was going on a roller-coaster ride: exhilarating and fun, but dangerous.

Chapter Fourteen

"I *still* don't understand why you want to make this trip to the Horton Plains *tonight,*" I said, whining at Pachili for choosing what I considered to be a wild goose chase. I wanted to be angry, but couldn't. It was all too surreal.

He just sat in silence, sipping a small bowl of soup he brought with him. I knew the journey would take at least two hours, traversing a grand arch before getting us in position to ascend the mountain. Although we could almost see the Plains from Balangoda, the actual route was very circuitous and inconvenient.

"You want a cure for your headaches," said Pachili matter-of-factly, "You must wake up; tonight is best for waking."

"Awake to what?" I asked, trying not to sound so naive.

"*Chi,*" he said, adding "Wakefulness has its own quality." I waited for a follow-up explanation. When none was forthcoming, I pressed him for a definition.

"Are you talking about the same *'Chi'* or *'Qi'* I know about?" I interrupted, ". . . the *Qi* of Chinese medicine and acupuncture?"

"*Genau* . . . Yes," he affirmed. "*Chi. Qi. Ki. Mana. Prana. Life force.* No matter . . . It is the substance of life, that which flows through all the cells of your body, into the world, and through all worlds and dimensions. The more conscious you are, the more *Chi* you gather within you . . . around you.

"Your life is a collection of *Chi.* When *Chi* is dispersed, you are dead. But *Chi* remains. It comes again in another form, just as the ocean creates another wave when one dies down. *Chi* is a verb. Not a noun. Not a thing. It never begins. It never ends. It cannot be killed. Cannot be destroyed. It defies capture.

65

It cannot be held in fences . . . boxes . . . *festhalten* . . . What is the English word?

"Containers . . . Containment?"

"Yes, that's it. *Chi* defies containment. If you look deeply enough within yourself, you will find nothing. You and I don't exist! We are only different selves: faces, masks, or qualities created by *Chi* acting on itself, much like a spinning fan can give the appearance of a solid disc." His descriptions reminded me of something I read in a quantum physics book.

"Could you make that a little simpler?" I asked, hoping to grasp something he passed off as very basic.

"You want it *simpler . . ?*" he countered, simultaneously amused and irritated. "Forget Chinese Medicine! There is no such thing! There is no such thing as Western Medicine. There is no such thing as homeopathy. There is no such thing as acupuncture or chiro-praterism . . !"

"Chiroprac*tic,*" I corrected him, suddenly feeling both irritated and confused.

"Chiro-prac-*tic* . . . some such thing," he continued, "There is no such thing as *The* Way! *There is only Chi,* and this *Chi* will present itself to you in *many* ways, all of them unique, *but you must be awake to it!*" I recoiled from Pachili's sudden intensity as if this were my signal to shut up. Although I was driving, I suddenly felt like a prisoner again . . . or a player in some dark comedy. I could hear the bedraggled Buddhist rubbing his beard stubble, conjuring up more insults to hurl at me. I wanted to joke, but our ideas about humor were too far apart for me to try. I just waited, focusing instead on the road ahead.

"Pachili . . ." I ventured a question.

"*Chi* escapes from you like a waterfall," interrupted my tormentor with a deep, dark laugh. "It leaks out through your brain and nervous system. You have a leaky container!"

"Wait a minute," I pressed him angrily, "Just answer a simple question. *What* Chi are you talking about? Is it the same as the subconscious or *Id* of Freud?" I braced for a flurry of insults. Instead, he surprised me.

66

"Freud was onto something," stated Pachili nonchalantly, "He just didn't take it far enough. He didn't know it is as a separated spirit . . ."

"The subconscious? A separate *spirit?*" I exclaimed, braving a request for clarification. Pachili confirmed.

"Hawaiians called it the *ku*. Egyptians, *Ka* Only, in the west, we have difficulty to accept these various qualities as spirits. We think we are *individuals* . . . one person in control. This is a complete myth! Mind is never in control. It's not even present. Mind is always dwelling in the past, or projecting into the future. Creating meaning and fantasy with everything seen or experienced. This leaves room for all kinds of mischief: insanity, struggle, division . . . suffering."

"Is the *ku* or *ka* the same as the inner child of Transactional Analysis and cognitive therapy?" I asked, flaunting my limited knowledge of psychology.

"Yes. Some inner child thing . . . too limited. But same thing. Same idea as *ku* and *ka*. Different than subconscious, but still based on somebody's philosophy. It's all garbage. But, a good start.

I like the word *ku*." he continued, "It's simple. Direct. Probably another Chinese word. Then Hawaiian. Anyway, the *ku* never dies. It is the individual expression of *Chi* . . . remembers everything, and takes these impressions when it leaves the body."

Pachili was exhibiting a side of him I had not seen before. He was familiar with cross-cultural religious and historical events, a fact belying his simple status. Here was not merely some isolated, ignorant hermit, but a well traveled, educated person. I was effortlessly drawn in.

"So how do I get to know my *ku?*" I asked, feeling suddenly like one of those TV kids asking Captain Kangaroo for Mr. Moose. Dr. Matt? Meet *Mr. Ku* . . .

"Silence," he continued, "No thinking. No talking. Just let go totally. Fall in."

"You mean surrender?"

"I don't like that word; it implies you must still *do* something . . . hold onto some mood or something. That doesn't happen. *Chi* is always balanced, *yin* with *yang*. There is nothing to surrender *to!*

"*Ku* - the heart - does not *learn* from ideas. It only *knows*. It is life itself. A vast collection of so-called opposites. If the mind says happy, the *ku* remembers sadness. If the mind seeks love, the *ku* remembers hate. Fear-trust. Connect-disconnect. Light-dark. Loud-soft . . . all life is a paradox. Not to life itself . . . only to the mind." The older man spoke almost hypnotically.

"The ego-mind cannot take this. It only chooses one; it seeks only the world of appearances - the outer world. It will deny all that *ku* feels and *knows* on the inside."

"You mean my *ku* both loves *and* hates my wife at the same time?"

"If one is there, both are present. It can be no other way."

"But . . ." I started to debate, but he cut me off.

"There is a time for being stupid. This is not the time," admonished my teacher. I felt the familiar sting - the one I felt as a child when cut off by some adult.

"Sorry," I said as my words tapering off. We both sat in silence for a few minutes. I was afraid my question interrupted him . . . afraid I would never get to understand this *ku* thing. Before I could get into feeling sorry for myself, however, he spoke again. This time, I detected no animosity or reproach in his voice.

"There is an old Indian fable about a mouse who was always afraid of the cat. A magician took pity on him and decided to help; he changed the mouse into a cat. Suddenly, the mouse, finding he was now a cat, felt somewhat better. But now he was afraid of the dog. So the magician changed him into a dog.

"Still, this did not help. Now the poor creature was afraid of the tiger. The magician turned him into a tiger. It did no good. Now he was afraid of the hunter. Frustrated, the magician returned him to a mouse and walked away, saying there was nothing else he could do . . . being a mouse was perfect for him.

"So you see, no matter what changes you make on the outside, the mouse is always there. Your being - your *ku* - doesn't change. Only awakening matters. Awareness. Dive into the hidden parts and expose the anger. The fear. The beliefs of who you are. Only then will you awaken. Only then will you *know* . . . *ku* then displays this awareness, this *knowing*."

"The mind, the *individual* - when it ceases to be - will drop the judgments and concerns . . . the arguments, the paradoxes will disappear because only the mind – the *"I"* - creates these things. Just relax into no-mind. Universal awareness.

"I only say these things," he added prophetically, "because it is happening now to you anyway . . ."

I found myself listening closely, even as a part of me struggled to deny him. *Fear* arose from the pit of my stomach. I felt sick. Nauseous. Pachili instructed me to take a deep breath. Suddenly, the car hit another blind hole in the road. It was only a momentary distraction, as I recovered control of the car.

"You feel easier?" he inquired after a moment.

"Only a little," I confessed awkwardly, "It's difficult. Whenever I stop thinking, fear comes up. I've tried experiencing *no thought* a few times during meditation," I explained, "but mostly I could never let go completely. To me that means chaos, danger."

Galle Road came to mind.

"That is the first step," said Pachili, "The magic of *knowing* is only discovered when the ego falls away. Fear is the first symptom. Don't be worried about it; it's only natural. Your feeling is hidden. Covered up. You only *think* you know. This covers up the cover up! But you are not alone; same happens to everyone. Inside we are all whole - a living part of *Chi*.

"There is a fog over the people. Inside they *know,* but their minds are polluted . . . like thick clouds covering an endless sky. But, for some reason, *Chi* continues its endless charade, manifesting as people who choose *thinking* instead of *knowing*. Science. Proof is needed. And religion - so-called faith is needed. Everybody covers up - fearful someone will discover their weaknesses. Afraid of being judged. Robbed. Hurt. Fear and suffering is always there. It's universal. So they create governments to save them, then become afraid of the government! The illusion is complete . . . held together by the iron hand of limitation on all levels!

69

"Don't be worried about thinking," added my teacher, "It's just a game. A cloud. A phantom . . . nothing. The so-called thinker will die. Then thinking will go on playing the game by itself. You as Life simply witness the game. Only then does *knowing* arise."

"Like Socrates said: 'I know that I know nothing.'" I added philosophically.

"Socrates was an idiot."

"An *idiot . . .!?* " I sputtered, half in shock. Of all the great men, Socrates was one of my favorites. "What have you got against Socrates?"

"Nothing."

"Well . . ?"

"He's an idiot, that's all." We both sat in silence for a minute. I flinched, confused and annoyed. The conversation was going so well. Why did he do it to me again?! Before I could ask, he spoke again.

"Socrates was wise. Yes. He was also killed . . . by his own people, no less. By the people of Athens, a so-called enlightened democracy. Even *that* was not so bad; he spoke the truth. Now he is immortal. But where are his people? These 'enlightened' people of Athens who made him immortal didn't want to hear his truth.

"*SCHLOOSS!* He was gone . . . flushed down the toilet, and the people were happy. Especially Plato. He got his chance to write all these wonderful stories about his teacher, a cave, and some piece of dirt called Atlantis. He spawned whole generations of idiots.

"Anyway, Socrates had a death-wish. For some reason we admire people with death wishes. He told everyone he knew nothing. Then he won every debate in the city. The people were angry; defeated in a debate by someone who knew *nothing!* How would *you* feel?"

"Same way, I suppose," I answered plainly.

"'Enlightened' Athenians. Ha! They weren't interested in becoming enlightened by Socrates. They were angry at being disturbed! Same thing happened to Jesus. No one wants to wake up; get the message. So they kill the messenger. Even *you* . . !"

70

The conversation became instantly surreal. I had the sneaking suspicion there was a paradox here, but wasn't sure I would get it this time around. Either he was a lunatic, or he was right. Either way, ignore the messenger; listen to the message. Maybe I *was* leaking *Chi*. Too much clutter. Anger. Suspicion. Fear.

"I'm confused," I said, shaking my head, fully aware he could be setting me up for something. "What do you want from me?"

"Always wanting to know what I think, eh?" said the suddenly strange robed figure. "I *think* nothing. I *am* nothing. You talk to a personality - a mask - and believe it's real! Yet you consider yourself a thinking man . . . a man of science and healing. A man of the world, although you were never good at it. You are always living the past . . . the vision of Superman you had as a six-year-old boy, or the memories of failure and success. Then you go out in the world and your thoughts destroy you. *Ku* shows your *real* intent: to follow your dead wife..."

"How did you . . .?" I shrieked as if confronted by a ghost. I *never* told him about my Paula!

"Your mind is filled with so much *quatsch mit sosse,* you cannot see what your heart *knows*," added the mystic as he hit some deep buttons. It was getting hard for me to think. Or breathe. My head was spinning and my heart, pounding.

Chapter Fifteen

"Then *teach* me, already!" I yelled defiantly, eager to break out of my fear and confusion. I was to the point of tears. I had a sudden longing to enter Pachili's world, to see what he sees. How could he could reach into me and pull out Paula's memory? The *only one* I held sacred?? With a single remark, he stripped me naked. Exposed my sadness, misery, and failure. Plundered my psyche. I knew I couldn't hide anything from him.

"Show me" I pleaded. "whatever truth I need to . . !" I didn't get a chance to finish my sentence. One of the deepest sinkholes in Sri Lanka appeared from out of nowhere. We collided with a jolt.

"*Sh . . . t!*" I cursed as we bottomed out of the first one. It felt like we hit a land mine! I was able to steer the car around most of the eroding portions of this treacherous highway, but only by slowing to a crawl. Pachili didn't seem concerned. But then, why should he? *He* didn't have to worry about wrecking Vimal's car! I kept wondering how the Toyota underbody was holding up; thought I heard something rattle.

I looked for - and avoided - additional potholes. After a few miles of smooth riding, felt confident enough to resume normal speed. Pachili kept talking as if nothing had happened.

"Your subconscious is a faithful servant. It will support you, or fight you, based on its training. You taught it to keep you from waking, from *knowing*. It just obeys."

No sooner than he spoke, we hit another pothole. I swerved to avoid two more. It was eerie . . . like a part of me wanted to fight him at every turn. He just continued, unfazed and deliberate, as if he had to get this knowledge to me before something happened to separate us.

"All consciousness - all *Chi* - is the same. It is not limited by the body. It cannot even evolve. It is here! Everywhere. Eternal. The only thing that evolves is our so-called perception of it. A moment of pure awakening. Trust that this is happening. *Intent!* Allow awareness to happen."

I started to say something, but the older man sighed as he gazed longingly out the window. I let it go. For a minute, I thought I lost him, but he continued: "All this is just a bed-time story for those who are asleep," he said at last. "How can one describe a scene from the mountaintop to someone who is asleep at the bottom?!"

"Is this what is happening to me?" I asked pointedly, "that my *ku* is trying to keep me from waking up?"

"You - or your *ku* - can't help it," answered the monk, "Old programs were set in motion by *Chi* itself, even before you were born. Your efforts to stay asleep will come to no end. Neither will any efforts to awaken. *Chi* will decide the time and place. Your mind just needs to be tricked into it."

"But, isn't there another way . . ?"

"All so-called ways are merely devices. Doing. You think some effort is involved. Only when your mind is stretched to the limit will it release you from this bondage. That is your way."

Pachili turned away, indicating his brief discourse was over. As I sat mulling over his words, I caught myself. It looked hopeless: thinking, figuring things out, seeking to understand was so integral to my life. I couldn't imagine existing without it! I wanted to ask him about Paula . . . how he knew. I needed desperately to understand, to pierce the veil of sadness her memory evoked - to dive once again into the deep longing for her face, her touch . . .

"There are things more terrifying than a tiger, a cobra, *or* a Tamil terrorist," said Pachili, suddenly changing the subject. "These threats can be seen. What can *really* strike fear in you is to be completely disconnected from *knowing*. For example, the water buffalo . . ."

"The *what?!*" I smirked, now considering the whole conversation as something akin to an old Vaudeville routine.

"Very often the water buffalo will not let you *see* him. He is programmed by *Chi* - by existence - to be stubborn. He is also difficult to *know* and can be very dangerous - unpredictable - for that reason . . . the most dangerous animals on the island."

Why on earth was Pachili telling me about water buffaloes? I had seen many of them in Ceylon, but never felt intimidated by the big, lazy beasts. I figured it was because I was blissfully unaware they represented any sort of danger.

My teacher finished off his now-cold soup while I strained to see both his point and the road. His point I couldn't see at all. I saw the road only slightly better, no thanks to Vimal's dim headlights. A nervous feeling jumped into my stomach, but I was grateful for the brilliance of the full moon. Night driving would have otherwise been too treacherous, accented by Ceylon's ever-present bumps and sink-holes.

After tossing his soup thermos into the back seat, the robed mystic settled back and took a nap. I asked him several questions, but never got an answer. Pachili was obviously in a world of his own, while I puzzled over the seemingly effortless way he dismantled my psyche. Resigned to my confusion, I focused instead on my driving, concentrating on just getting us up the mountain.

****

Half-way to our destination, I felt a stirring in the base of my spine . . . something that both excited and frightened me. I was having thoughts about my *ku* as a separate being, unique and alive - like a familiar *poltergeist* with a mind of its own, dancing to old songs . . . or hiding them. Was *this* the one I cursed at when things didn't go right? Or was it Paula's ghost??

I started getting frightened. Was I crazy? How could I blindly follow a man some people considered a *Yaka*? A ghost devil? Pachili was playing with my mind, and I was letting him! Strangely, I felt nothing but love for him. At the same time, abject terror! Something about him . . .

In the quiet of the night, I *knew:* parts of me were coming back! How could I emerge as the same rational human being I was before? I wanted to turn back, to run, to fight this curious process with every rational thought I could muster, but it was too strong. Something had to give.

I didn't know who "I" was any more. Was I one Dr. Cannon? Or two or more spirits bound together during this life to learn from each another? Desperate I turned to my companion, trying to grab onto some sense of the reality.

"Pachili . . ." I ventured, anxiously groping for a beachhead of understanding, "Something bothers me. When you talk about *ku* and *Chi,* are you talking about parts identified as *yin* and *yang* or feminine and masculine?"

"You are lost again," mumbled the older man, stirring in his seat, "Be simple! Let it go. Remember I give you *quatsch* for your mind. *Chi* shows itself without such mental garbage! *Chi* simply *is.* Just watch and witness."

"Watch *what?* Witness *what?!*" I demanded, suddenly feeling trapped by an ignorance that seemingly closed in from all sides. By this time, my pulse rate had risen several notches.

The monk did not respond, leaving me to stew in my own cauldron of fear and anger. I started to say something nasty, but caught myself. What good would it serve? What was I to learn from all this?! Pachili had nothing to do with it. Damn it! Why couldn't I *understand?!*" I looked around me, trying to let it go, to witness what was happening. I really wanted some part of me to get it. After a while, sensing the futility of trying to understand the whole thing, I relaxed.

Suddenly, my mind clicked off. I felt a longing for something I've known all my life, yet never really acknowledged. Subtle feelings emerged . . . becoming more and more powerful with each breath. In the next instant, all my circuits fired at once.

My mind reeled. A wave of intense memories and feelings rushed out of hidden areas. All my fears as a child came out: my father's abuse. The whippings and banishment. The loneliness . . . the hidden monsters under the bed. Death in the closet. They were all bottled up. Tucked away . . . until now! Terror pumped through my veins. I let out a shriek as tears cascaded down my face.

"Pull over here," said Pachili, responding on cue to my sudden disability. I found a widened spot in the side of the road rolled in with my lights off, and shut off the engine. Fortunately, there was very little traffic on Route A4 that night. Scared and embarrassed, I leaned over the steering wheel, crying. I waited for some clue from Pachili as to what was happening. . .

"Take time," he coaxed me reassuringly, "This is good. Awareness is dawning. This is good."

His simple words had laid a trap for me . . . and I fell in. Spine twitching, gut turning, I watched as tears flowed; a tinge of strange new feelings - happiness, sadness, fear, and joy combined - all came riding in on a large wave of bliss. It started behind me, then crashed over the top of my head.

Pachili jumped out of the car and closed the door. I glanced up through my tears to see his figure in the moonlight walking on ahead. I blubbered with fear, sadness, anger, and a dozen other feelings. I watched myself react to every sad thing that ever happened to me . . . trying to put significance on the fact that the person was merely walking away!

I was caught in the midst of something, yet insulated from it. Emotion swirled around me. Thoughts crowded my head and pressured each organ of my body. Was Pachili leaving me? No, he is probably going to relieve himself. Why did I ever come see him? How does he have such power over me? Why am I so unstable? Take it easy. It's O.K. He's not a devil. He's really a nice man. He means me no harm.

Would I ever get out of this country alive? Does anyone in the world love me? Of course they do . . . I do. Am I losing my mind. No. I'm still here. This is curious . . . Were we both going to die? Slaughtered by Tamils? Was there a bomb in the car? Did he get out so his buddies could blow me up? Had my luck finally run out? Probably not. You're O.K. . . I'm watching out for you. GET IT TOGETHER MATTHEW CANNON!!

How? . . . Why?

I felt divided. Schizophrenic. Paranoid. Separated. Like a small submarine: buffeted about in a stormy undercurrent, yet self-contained and self-sufficient. Suddenly, I remembered to breathe. With a strange detachment, I watched myself breathing deeply as if I were facilitating a death . . . or a birth! I felt dispassionate, watching my emotions like a biologist observing growing bacteria in a petri dish.

I continued to cry . . . to watch . . . and to breathe.

Chapter Sixteen

The sobbing finally stopped. I'm not sure when or how. I just feel certain it was soon because nature had given me only a limited supply of body fluid. This crying stuff was getting out of hand!

I felt purged. Cleansed both inside and out. After the crying ceased, my body tingled. All over. I felt lighter . . . the top of my head bubbled, as if someone had opened my skull and released 35 years of anger and fear, then poured in a bucket of bliss. I had no questions. I felt no urgencies. I didn't even care where Pachili went . . . I spontaneously went into meditation.

I immediately noticed the difference in this meditation. Effortlessly drawn to the crown of my head, I flew into the center of a brilliant light space, surrounded by pure energy. This space felt familiar. I embraced it as I would an old friend . . . No thoughts. No concern. No body. No mind.

"We must go now."

His voice pierced the stillness. Pachili's return gradually came back to the world of thoughts. As he hopped in, I reacted instinctively, turning car keys, flipping on the lights, and rolling us onto the highway. I had no idea where I was going . . . and didn't care.

"Awareness flows now," said my mentor as he rolled down his window and leaned out, trying to get a better view of the road ahead.

"Drive. Stay aware. *Know* what is next," he advised, settling back into his seat. I just kept driving, enjoying these rare moments of complete bliss. My trusting would guide me. Just *know* . . .

A few minutes later, I looked up and saw the 102 Milepost and the kilometer distance to Haldummulla. A thought

79

out of nowhere as I pulled over again to the side of the road and turned on the inside lights.

"Wait a minute," I exclaimed as I turned to snatch the road map out of the back seat. I remembered . . . something about a connecting trail to the highlands. With a crisp, jerky motion, I opened the map in front of me and folded back the edges.

"This road is on the map!" I said, pointing to a rustic path crept steeply up the hill on my left, next to an old shack. "I remember seeing it before." My sense of economy had taken hold of me. Not wanting to take two hours to travel around the mountain, I was looking for a way - any way - that would cut our journey shorter.

"Does it lead directly to the Horton Plains?" I quizzed Pachili while still gazing at the map. It looked like it did.

"I can be of no help," he answered nonchalantly. "You decide."

Feeling suddenly empowered, I turned within to ask. The answer jumped right back at me: Yes. Suddenly I *knew!* It was on the map . . . that was good enough for me! I revved up the engine, turned into the rustic road and headed up the steep hill. It was rough. And narrow. The road was also covered in high grass, as if it hadn't been used for years.

"I don't like this," I said softly, rethinking my boldness and sensing some fear creeping back into the space that bliss occupied only minutes earlier. I was able to avoid two potholes, but missed the third.

"Watch out!" I yelled, more out of concern for Vimal's car than Pachili. I proceeded more slowly as the wilderness road gave way grudgingly to our encroachment. My thoughts kept coming back to Vimal's warnings. At the time I gave no thought to the possibility of hurting his car. Now a veteran of numerous sinkholes, I reconsidered. It was time to be extra careful.

"Do you feel it?" asked Pachili, suddenly out of nowhere.

"What?" I responded. "Feel what??"

"*Intent,*" spoke Pachili softly as if we were sitting in his cabin, sipping tea.

"I'm sorry," I added quickly. "But I'm a little freaked out right now about going off the edge, O.K.?" I caught myself getting irritated with his little distractions, and slowed the car down almost to a crawl. Despite my concentration, however, I couldn't shake it. *Intent* kept rummaging through my mind. He was playing with my head again, dammit. It was going to be a long night.

I drove slowly, hugging the ride side of the road as we climbed higher and higher. The moonlight revealed an unexpectedly steep view on the left. As if in a dream, I could see the sharp peaks of the adjacent mountains pierce the hazy beauty. Wondrous, ancient forests of the valley crept up the side, framing the occasional cliff or ragged outcropping. A sudden thrill shot through me. Bliss returned, tempered with the stark realization that one careless move could send us hurtling to our deaths below. Again, I set my sights on the next curve.

My sense of accomplishment at rounding the narrow curve soon fell away. There, in the overgrown trail ahead, munching on some weeds were three fully grown animals.

. . . *water buffalo!*

I stopped and scowled at Pachili as if he had placed them there to frighten me out of my wits. He only laughed. I wanted to hit him, but was too scared to move. Could this man indeed see the future? If so, that would explain why he wasn't afraid. But why didn't he stop me? He never questioned my impulsive decision to take this dangerous road. He even now laughed at my fear of it.

"We could plunge to our deaths and you would laugh on the way down," I said sarcastically, trying to convince myself that the situation really *was* funny. It didn't work. I remained near a state of shock. Personally, I wasn't ready to die, but had I convinced my *ku* of that fact? I closed my eyes and let my awareness go, and soon begun to settle down. Pachili had stopped laughing and also sat quietly. Eventually he spoke.

"Water buffalo are unpredictable," he reminded me needlessly, "but they do respond. They are part of *Chi*."

Somehow I recognized what he was saying. I instinctively focused on my heart and head connecting, and began to feel the fear slowly melt. I found myself asking silent

81

permission of the creatures to pass, then waited. Minutes passed. All I could hear was the pounding of my heart in my head. These feelings persisted until, finally, the fear broke. I took that as a *yes*, breathed deeply, released my foot from the brakes, and crawled ahead.

We hung dangerously close to the edge as the disturbed giants scurried and snorted their way next to the mountain, irritated at having their rest interrupted. Rocks broke off and tumbled beneath my left tires. I kept rolling. One of the creatures bellowed, bristled and rubbed the car door on the other side. The chilling thought occurred that the big buffalo had our lives in his hooves! He could at any moment decide to stretch . . . and send our little car over the edge!

But he didn't. Eternity passed. Then, as in a lucid dream, I found myself with Pachili on the other side of the small herd, still on the road. We looked at each other; neither daring to say a word until further along on the trail . . . to a place far beyond our four-legged friends.

Chapter Seventeen

"That was close!" I said, starting to breathe again. Pachili sat quietly in the semi-darkness. For some reason, I again became agitated.

"How the hell . . ? *Aren't you afraid to die?* " I asked, point blank. He remained silent. Embarrassed to say anything else, I waited. More silence. Finally, I could stand it no longer.

"We could have easily been killed back there! Don't you have anything to say?!" I sputtered, hoping to elicit a response from my mute travel partner.

"Yes, we could have fallen" he said finally, "but we didn't."

"Well, I for one was scared out of my wits!" I yelled, glaring at him.

"It was a device," he added bluntly, "to wake you up . . ."

"*What . . ?*"

I was beside myself. Why did he try to scare the crap out of me? Our very lives were at stake! Furious, I sputtered, fumed, and growled. Pachili, amused by my anger, watched me as if looking at a re-run of *I Love Lucy.* This made me even more angry. Before I realized it, however, I witnessed my emotions pass over like a brief thunderstorm. Suddenly I felt relaxed, almost sleepy.

"Every time you pass fear, a kind of death happens," he said at the end of my tantrum. "then freedom. Feelings of death, then a deep relaxation. All restriction leads to freedom. This is the way of *Chi* . . . crossing points into awakening . . . the *Zone.* You feel it?"

"Yes, but . . ."

"Is it dangerous?" he said, anticipating my question. "Yes, usually. Life can be a dangerous game. *Chi* creates it that way. The ego runs from it. Your tendency is to run and hide. Don't. Relax. Let life come to you. It just happens . . . and never according to plan; always unexpectedly. Life. Death. You get used to it . . . an opportunity for clarity to unfold."

Somehow the meaning of "getting used" to death escaped me. I persisted in my line of questioning.

"I mean, aren't you afraid of *physical* death. You know. Smashed bones. Heart attacks. Falling rocks . . . that type of death."

"Where is the fear?" he asked. "Fear cannot remain unless you hold onto it. You die, it's over. Done. Freedom. The point of death is simply another expression of the gap . . . the Zone. The moment you melt the fear, however, death is transformed. You can enter the Zone while remaining in the physical body. . ."

"Melt the fear? . . . Zone?!" I exclaimed, "With all due respect, Pachili, I don't understand what you're saying. I never stopped the fear! That last episode scared the piss out of me!"

Pachili shrugged. "You understand *too* much," he countered, "This is why you suffer. You refuse to let go; to simply accept *being.* Instead, your mind sticks to its principles like flies to an open sewer. You try to be polite; do good deeds. You want to be a healer, a savior. Make good habits . . . be 'good' without being aware!

"All games. You play these silly games. *Chi* is not interested in your habits. You say you want to awake, but fight to stay asleep!

"Death is not your real fear," he announced surprisingly, "Your friend's car . . . your grand search for Truth. These things you cannot lose; otherwise you would be no longer good or significant. This attachment to the guilt of not being good keeps you in fear.

"Knowing is only in the gaps!" he snapped.

I was stunned; he spoke the truth. I never considered guilt as my hiding place before. But, somewhere in my consciousness, I *knew.* Somewhere I was silently watching . . . waiting . . . testing. But the thinking part of me could only protest - another habit of mine. Release guilt? I even felt guilty about that! Everything he said pushed a different button, and I became painfully aware I was trying to swallow the equivalent of a 2-ton elephant in one bite.

"Focus on the gap," said Pachili. "Follow the paradox."

"Like what, for instance?" I asked, again trying to get a fix on this amorphous subject.

"The so-called opposites," he answered, "Hot and cold. Love and hate. Order and chaos. They are just different colors in the same big picture. Experience everything - all these so-called paradoxes. To existence there is no paradox, just *is-ness* . . . no judgment, just bliss."

"Mind cannot understand *Chi* directly. Only as thoughts, images, or meaning-making mind games. When you have love . . . or fear . . . or sadness . . . what is there to think about? You only feel love, fear, or sadness - pure expressions of *Chi!* You also feel the opposite feelings, if you are open to receive them. There is no *reason* for these feelings; they just *are*. Only your attachment to the mind games keeps you looking for a reason. Just let it go."

"But . . ." I persisted, then paused when Pachili sighed. I could tell my questions were getting a bit thick, but figured this was the best time to get some answers. I noticed that being around him was a kind of stimulant; a deep desire to *know* kept tugging at my heart.

"The minds of most people is non-stop nonsense," he said, pressing on patiently, "They have no *being,* no *intent.* They only want to think, think, think! Or *do* something. They keep busy to try to keep from dying. It's useless. The moment you are born you begin to die. We are all a part of the play of *Chi:* restriction, then freedom. The ego keeps the myth going: 'I will live forever' it says. Then you see death coming in a million different ways. *Chi* - through the mythical story of "you" and "me" - is playing with itself!"

"So, then what is left?"

"Nothing. Awareness. *Chi.* Pure *intent* . . . the shadow of a mind that has willingly dissolved itself. At this level, there is no need for distinction - food, drink, mind, *ku,* High Self, universal awareness, laughter, sadness, water buffaloes, trees, or mountains. Even God disappears . . . all is Oneness." The monk sat silently for a minute as if to let the words sink into my consciousness.

"Follow *intent,*" added Pachili. "Not what you hear from some priest; or what you read in some book. That is not *intent.*"

"Meditate, then live fully," he added. "Bring *Chi* back home. In all your thoughts, your actions, you are divided. *Chi* is divided, driven away . . . punished . . . *in verbannung* . . . What is an English word?"

"Separated? Banished? Exiled?"

"Exile . . . yes . . . The part in exile will fight you. Life is good. Life is bad. How to have both? Existence gives you both, but your mind does not understand. Just accept. These arguments are not even important to *Chi.*"

"So, how do I get more of what I want?" I asked excitedly.

"Existence gives you exactly what you ask for!" he answered simply. "What else could you want?"

"Well . . . more money, for instance."

"Do you see the mind's trick?" asked the monk.

"What trick?" I asked. "It's a simple enough request, isn't it?" Pachili shook his head.

"Not so simple," he sighed. "You say you want more money. Where is your awareness? On not having it! Your silent focus is always on the *opposite* of that which you *say* you want! Otherwise, how could you want it? Again, *Chi* playing through the dance of opposites; restriction. Then your anger or fear at not having something drives it away! Existence is very exact; the game is perfect.

"You can only walk on two feet: left, then right. Existence then gives you both. You make money. You lose it. Back and forth. After time, money loses its attraction. Once there is no inner *need* for it, it may come easily. Maybe not. When you awaken, however, the question is irrelevant. Silly.

"This is why Gautama Buddha spoke of the middle path of desirelessness. He did not mean give up all desire. He simply said exhaust all desire, until there is nothing left!"

"But what about money? And sex?" I huffed, "Wasn't Buddha a monk like yourself? How could he give up something he didn't have? Something he had denied himself?"

86

"Oh, there you are mistaken," added Pachili quickly, "The Buddha never denied himself anything. He was a *prince* before his so-called enlightenment. He was wealthy; he had sex. His father the king made sure he was quite content, had everything. he wanted. In this he failed. The prince, seeing the emptiness in wealth, sought escape from it."

"I didn't know that," I said, "I guess I never thought of Buddha as anything other than an enlightened recluse . . . but why did you say 'so-called' enlightenment?"

"My dear friend," he added, "after a certain shift in awareness, there *is* no one. Only the *awareness* of enlightenment – not an enlightened person. Once the individual dissolves, the person ceases to experience. All is left is *only* the experience itself... Buddha *IS* enlightenment itself."

"This, however, is not the teaching of 'Buddhism.' Every so-called 'ism' is a dead expression of the inner life it seeks to represent but cannot."

I didn't get this one at all, and told him so. "But isn't there *something* to believe in? Isn't there a *process* to follow? A *technique,* if you will, to letting go of one desire or the other? How do I become, so to speak, one mind?"

"So many questions. You have enough of technique. Now you must live. Fully. Awareness is unfolding on its own; there is nothing to do other than what is being done. There is no hurry. Enlightenment has nothing to do with what you do, do not do, or what you think. It lies in the gaps. Let go of the drama of life, the struggle. The praise or criticism. Just watch without judgment.

"Know your deepest *intent.* Then enter the gap . . . the Zone. All desires will be magnified. Then purified. Burned from your awareness. The contrast is so great you feel there is nothing to give up. There is no concern one way or the other."

"I'm not so sure . . ."

"Sure of what?"

"I'm not even sure I'm ready for such a state. I've *barely* committed myself to your damn headache cure! Why should I open up to some mysterious *Zone,* or *gap?*" Pachili then said something that struck me as particularly relevant:

"The question is about trust. Your headaches are only the burden of memory: excess caution, fear, anger. This creates a burning fire in the nervous system and arises as unresolved pain. You hold on too tightly, trying to escape. Your mind and ego is the only part that does not trust. *Until you can trust, existence cannot give.* The headaches are expressions of *Chi.* Remember that and fall into them. You cannot lose anything except the fear."

"So how . . . how do I let go?" I asked reluctantly reassured, still feeling my jaw tighten. I took a moment to relax it and really hear him. Pachili again scratched his beard and ruffled the few hairs on his balding scalp. I caught sparks of moonlight dancing on the smooth surface of his forehead.

"As I said, this is already happening to you," spoke the robed mystic. "You already put yourself under my care. Your ego must be convinced. Tricked. Then destroyed. Your *ku* must be cleansed of all deeply rooted *quatsch.* Brainwashing. Please understand . . . this is major surgery you have agreed to. *Chi* has chosen this time for your awakening." I felt fear rising again, along with the hint of another headache.

"But I . . ."

"*Doing* is not so important as a deeply-felt and committed *intent.* By following *intent*, your *ku's* conditioning will change; purify itself in the pure light of *Chi.* Then the headaches will change; you will see them as *Chi* sees them. Maybe it will happen sooner. Maybe later. It depends, how *Chi* directs events through your mind. That is *intent.*" The fear rose higher in my belly.

"Your mind cannot understand. Let it go," he instructed. "All thoughts and techniques are of the past. Dead. There is no benefit in trying to fix anything. Your *ku* knows all these tricks . . . programmed by the mind, the ego which created them. It will only frustrate you. You are trying to pull yourself out of quicksand; the more you try, the deeper you sink. Let it go.

"Let all experience be a meditation. Let all *Chi* - all pure consciousness - come together. The enlightened mind is filled with *intent* . . . seeks only *Chi,*" he said, repeating himself. "Let go of meaning, purpose. Forget about being a savior. Seek the most subtle level of meaning . . . the gap."

Gaps. I strained, but couldn't quite get it. I figured I would, though, sooner or later. Maybe. Meanwhile I would let go as much as I could. Lulled by the power of his words, I began to relax. I drove the remainder of our upward journey, gazing out my half-open window and marveling at the magnificent scenery unfolding in the light of the rising moon. The sound of falling water had been creeping into my consciousness for some time . . .

Suddenly, I saw it. Rounding the next curve, I gazed upon one of the most magnificent waterfalls I had ever seen. A quick look on the map told me it was Bambarakanda Falls with a total drop of 790 feet! I drove very slowly, taking in as much as I could.

"Whew!" I exclaimed, feeling a tremendous rush of joy. "I got it!" Pachili just smiled.

I felt we were close to the Horton Plains. We had traveled quite a distance and were getting very low on gas. Up ahead, I spied a cut in the mountain.

What at first looked like Greek or Egyptian columns, revealed themselves at closer inspection to be two very tall, solid rock outcroppings that framed the sky. The narrow road slipped between them. Beyond that, I could see no mountains and felt we had reached the peak. Passing through the stony edifices, I had a sense of awe. I hoped this would be the perfect ending to our journey. It was not to be.

As I watched the road descending below us, my heart sank. There, in the moonlit landscape not more than 200 yards away, rushed a stream . . . passing over the road! I eased the car down to get a closer look. There was the stream all right, but no bridge. Mirage? Were my eyes were deceiving me? Unfortunately not; we were trapped.

I suddenly felt defeated.

89

Chapter Eighteen

The road lay ahead of us, totally blocked! My eyes searched in vain for some alternative, some way around the cascading obstacle in the road before me. None were available. Having no answers to the problem, I sat mournfully shaking my head. If this was my first test of *knowing,* I failed. I had no more emotional strength. Pachili didn't say a word, instead looking at me as if waiting for instruction.

"We're stuck!" I moaned, stating the obvious. "How about levitating us out of here!" I said this, half in jest, half serious. If this person could read my thoughts, *certainly* he could do some simple telekinesis! Otherwise, we had nowhere to go but back . . . and we had come so far! I suddenly tired of my teacher's wild goose chase.

"Pachili, step out of the car and go up ahead. Tell me how deep that river is, would ya?" My companion obliged me without comment, pulling up his saffron robe and climbing out of the car. Trotting the 100 feet or so to the river, he kicked off his sandals and waded into the rushing waters. My heart sank further with each rise of the water mark above his shins.

Almost two feet of water! It was more than this poor Toyota could handle. I again tossed around in my seat, then discarded the idea of turning and heading back down the mountain. We were too close! As my mind raced to figure another way across, Pachili started waving . . . motioning me forward.

"My god, he wants me to drive through *that?!"* I questioned the steering wheel as if expecting an answer.

I checked with my *ku;* he was scared. Pachili continued to wave, stronger and with enthusiasm. Figuring he knew something I didn't, I took another deep breath, revved the accelerator, and muttered, "What the hell; I made it through buffaloes!"

My thinking was that, since Pachili was standing next to the drop-off point, and since the water level was about two feet there, I chose to hug the inside corner. There, I figured, I would have the best chance to get across, since it was obvious that the other end was too deep!

Steady. Steady . . .

Suddenly, my partner waved his arms as if to scream "No." It was too late. I careened toward the inside corner, water splashing everywhere as my reluctant vehicle came to a soggy halt.

The fear I had known earlier was nothing like what I felt that moment. The car was sinking! My mind flashed on Vimal. I would have to pay for his Toyota! I would have to explain why I was so stupid . . . why I got us lost in the middle of nowhere, thirteen thousand miles from home!

This fear was keen; cutting deeper than . . . *death!* Pachili was right. Fear of death is not the strongest! My body shook uncontrollably as I yelled a few obscenities and shuddered. THE CAR WAS SINKING!!!

Then, suddenly, it stopped . . . *The car stopped sinking!*

I opened the door to jump out, pausing long enough to see the water rushing under the door's threshold, with not more than half an inch to spare!

"Why did you not drive where I was waving?" yelled Pachili, rushing to my side as I waded onto dry land. I tried in vain to explain my warped logic, but fell into gibberish . . .

"It doesn't matter," said my companion matter-of-factly. "We make it on foot." He sighed, grabbed the nearest large rock, and sat down.

"What?!" I said incredulously, "Leave the car??" I still half expected Pachili to levitate the thing out of the river. "I have to get the car back to Vimal!" Pachili just sat, looking at me as if I were part of the evening's entertainment. This made me livid.

"Well maybe *you* don't feel a sense of responsibility, old man, but *I* do," I yelled, then stormed defiantly into the river to check on the car.

92

Observing the passenger's side, I discovered the two right wheels had gone over the edge, into what appeared to be a three-foot-deep eddy pool. The car itself was sitting on the wheel rods, shock absorbers, or some other solid thingama-jigs. I gave thanks to all the deities I knew for saving Vimal's car - and my pocketbook - from a watery grave.

Resigned to my fate, I dragged myself over to a rocky seat next to Pachili. I wanted to cry again, but had no more tears. I took a drink from his goatskin instead.

Chapter Nineteen

"Full moon." announced Pachili, redirecting my attention to the now-brilliant orb that lit up the evening sky and landscape like a small sun. "You know today is *Poya* Day?" My mind was still swirling, trying to come up with a solution to our current dilemma. Finding none, I sighed, then answered mechanically.

"It happens every month doesn't it?" I said, admitting my acquaintance with the Sinhalese holiday.

"Yes, it does. This day is also significance for the union of opposites. It is a time when *yin* and *yang* are at their greatest attraction, and when all levels of *Chi* have their greatest connection."

"Splendid," I said sarcastically, but slightly intrigued. Now that I got us into this ridiculous jam, Pachili was not only forgiving, he expressed no concern whatsoever. We were at least 30 miles of rugged roads from anywhere and all he wanted to talk about was the moon! This surreal scenario jolted me into another Deja-vu experience. I had been here before!

"Is my *ku* mad at me?" I whined, "Trying to teach me a lesson?"

"Actually not," he said, surprising me. "*Chi* is quite strong for us here. That's why we were able to get this far."

"Well, thank goodness for small favors!" I exclaimed sarcastically. I expelled a deep breath, wishing I'd had this *Chi* thing figured out, but realized I didn't know anything any more!

"Is *Chi* - or my *ku*- *that* destructive?" I asked, pressing Pachili for an answer. "Does my *ku* really want to experience fear and sink Vimal's car?"

"Sink the car? No. Otherwise it would be totally underwater! Your *ku* is a part of perfect existence . . . takes care of the details. Perfectly." Pachili spoke with such certainty, I felt compelled to question him.

"How . . . *why,* then, do things go wrong?"

"Come now, doctor! Surely you remember being a child?" admonished the monk. "Tell the child he has a wonderful voice; then tell him to be quiet. Two suggestions. Two decisions. Which does the child make? It doesn't really matter. He just grows up.

"It's a paradox, remember? *Ku* is a child. Give him - yourself - an opportunity to go beyond his programming; a chance to be awake, more intelligent. This will happen almost automatically. *Ku* can do no wrong unless you decide it is wrong."

"So, what have I decided wrongly today?"

"Nothing."

"Nothing?" I asked incredulously.

"Behind the silly request for a headache cure, your real *intent* is to *know.*" I immediately took exception to his implied insult that the search for a headache cure was 'silly.' I thought it best, however, to hear him out.

"*Knowing* - acceptance of life and all its paradoxes - just happens. *Intent* guides your *ku,* even as your mind fights you. This, too, is inevitable. But *ku* remembers; it simply follows *intent.* Time - and belief - is irrelevant to *ku.* Only experience.

"You *think* you need a wise man to teach you . . . a healer to save you. These are all ghosts. Wake up! I cannot do it for you. *Intent* - and awareness - is the only key.

"All the things you think you want are parts of *knowing* you have discarded at one time. You threw them away! Now you want them back? So be it! Simply align with *intent* . . ."

"By *knowing,* do you mean God?" I asked to clarify.

"Forget God," spoke the older man in a firmness of tone that seemed out of proportion to the question. I squirmed uncomfortably. "You're an adult now. Leave God alone. He has enough to do!

"Drop this myth!" continued Pachili, waving his arms in the air, "God doesn't care about your petty affairs! Why? If there were a God always doing, always judging, what would you learn? How could you evolve? You couldn't. God becomes an excuse to stop growing - an invention of *Chi* as the ultimate restriction.

"You started as a child by praying to your father and mother to get something. Now you bother God instead. *Knowing* is within you, around you . . . the whole of you. You cannot pray to *knowing,* only live it."

"Well, then, who . . . *what* is God?" I pressed, strangely eager to solve all theological problems in a single evening. There wasn't much else to do at the moment.

"Why be concerned?" added my teacher. "*Chi,* undoubtedly. But some great, big person that holds everything? Creates everything? Nonsense! Just put a white beard and robe on him . . . Father Christmas was good for that.

"If you want something done, simply *know.* Meditate. Then act. Pray if you wish, that all so-called parts of *Chi* connect with one another."

"Pachili, we might need a prayer here tonight," I sighed, figuring I had bothered him enough. He chuckled, then delivered a curious message.

"You have already prayed . . . and your prayers are answered."

The man said it with such a straight face and glint in his eyes, I broke the twig I was fondling in my hands. My mind buckled, losing all reason. Biting my lower lip, I looked off into the distance, wanting desperately to believe him, but taking note of my inbred cynicism. I decided to follow his advice; let go of finding hidden meanings. Just *accept.* Nothing happened.

"I give up," I said at last. "Tell me when this miracle happened. I missed it."

"You didn't miss it," he hissed, wrinkling up his prominent nose in mock anger. Pachili's eyes and forehead glistened in the moonlight as he pivoted on his rocky bench to face the valley below. "You just don't *feel* it. Wake up. Take a walk. *Know!*" Under ordinary circumstances, I would have called him a loony or fanatic and walked away. Tonight, I was his captive audience. I figured the best way to survive this was humor him.

Picking myself off the ground, I headed for the clearing at the top of the road, where the curve gave way to the clear sky beyond. Ambling slowly and in no hurry to run away or get lost, I consciously settled into a semi-meditative state. I had no concerns other than rescuing Vimal's car. And even *that* was falling away. Clearly there was nothing I could do about it now. I just walked, searching inside for some feeling, some confirmation that what Pachili said was right. My mind was still.

The full moon hung like a Christmas ornament before my weary eyes. I stopped to look at it, then look beyond it; to feel the night, connected with the sky, the emptiness of space. It was a clear autumn evening, with the coolness of the mountain air settling into the stillness of valley below. Other than a few crickets, I heard nothing. I stood, totally silent. Stillness. Peace.

The bliss returned. I had a feeling of being in the womb again, fully nourished. The fullness of the night grew fuller and I suddenly felt a strong presence: the precession of silent beings walking this road. Some were strong; wise. Others felt sinister. It was eerie, but I'm sure I felt some brush against me! The hair on my arm stood up as I turned to watch moonlight dancing in the road. This was their place. I was a part of their story. Were these the other parts of my being? Denizens of the *Zone*?

Then . . . a subtle thought arose from the center of my awareness. It became a sound: a subtle vibration at first, then audible . . . up ahead. I opened my eyes.

Headlights! My heart jumped. Something felt right. Almost as if I had been expecting them, I greeted the oncoming vehicle with a wave of my arm, and a song in my voice.

"Hello! Do you speak English?" I cried, not knowing, nor caring which language they spoke.

"Ah, yes . . . hello!" greeted the large, jolly man in the jeep as it came to a stop. He was Sinhalese, and accompanied by two others. "I am Ravi Coomsay and this is my wife Sonji and good friend. We are from Colombo . . . returning late from Holiday . . . But what are *you* doing in this forsaken place? *No one* ever drives on this road!" I explained our plight and desire to reach the Horton Plains sometime tonight.

"Oh, *no*, my friend." he admonished, "You don't want to go any further. I'm surprised you made it this far in that Toyota."

"Isn't the Horton Plains straight up the road ahead?" I persisted, eager to rest for the night.

"No . . . no!," said Ravi, waving his hands in a motion of denial, "This road does *not* lead to the Horton Plains. Believe me, friend, you don't want to go where we came from! I won't even go back there myself . . ."

Curious, I asked him why.

"Because, you see," he explained, "I like to drive on mountain roads. I often take the most difficult ones to test my jeep. We just came from such a high, narrow, winding mountain path - much worse than the one behind you. Surely, you would have fallen off and been killed . . .

"This road is called the Devil's Staircase *and is the most difficult road in Sri Lanka . . !"*

Chapter Twenty

My body glowed for hours. I had a feeling of grace I had never known before. For the first time in my life, I *knew* the connection between my mind, body, and spiritual self. It was so clearly tangible: everything - including my body - bathed in a golden aura. I neither laughed nor cried, though I wanted to do both. I carried instead a pervading sense of ease and thanksgiving. I experienced soft, persistent stillness, a connection with everyone and everything around me.

It took about two hours for our new-found friend to go for help in his jeep. Meanwhile, Pachili sat under a tree in silence. I took a short walk, enjoyed the air, the view, the feeling of the road on my feet, and the slight breeze blowing in my face. All the while, my mind and ego had fallen off as if shedding a large winter coat. How *differently* I felt . . .

I was happy.

Our friend Ravi eventually returned. Some local Tamils were with him, along with a jeep full of ropes and chains to haul us out; and a jug of gasoline for our empty tank. Around midnight, after two hours of painstakingly removing Vimal's vehicle from its watery trap, we finally crawled back down the mountain. This time I saw no water buffalo.

The Toyota was still in good shape - a minor miracle in itself - except for the muffler jerked loose during the rescue operation. In my blissful state, I could only laugh. *Whatever* the cost of repair, it would be a trifle.

We said our good-byes to Ravi and his crew at the base of the mountain. My heart went out to this moon-faced individual from Colombo - my beautiful messenger from *Chi*. He flatly refused my offer to pay him for his troubles and quickly sped off toward the city. After the turn-off to Balangoda, we were on our own.

"Did you know these events were going to happen?" I asked my new-found *guru* and confidant. He smiled.

"I saw only that which *Chi* had solidified."

"Solidified *Chi*?" I exclaimed, realizing I had stumbled onto yet another road of his seemingly endless maze of insights.

"Yes. It only happens with awareness of the gaps: the Zone. This is where *intent* solidifies. Where so-called free will intensifies, then disappears. This process pushes away every block to *Chi*, like a . . . what's the name of the device on the front of old railroad trains in America?"

"A cow catcher??"

"That's it, a cow catcher . . . it pushes aside all blocks to the flow of *Chi.*"

"And if I am *not* aware?" I asked, ever on the lookout for options.

"Your *Chi* train hits a cow, people scream, and everything goes off the tracks!" said Pachili, eyes rolling and sparkling with mischief. He broke out into such a roaring laughter, I too started chuckling. After the laughter died, we drove for a while in silence. The experience on the mountain had completely squelched my mental chatter; I felt little need to talk.

As the night flew by, so did the mountain road. I knew we had another half-hour or so of driving, and the feeling of bliss had diminished somewhat. Thoughts returned. I looked over at Pachili, who sat quietly staring out the window, and wondered if he were in the mood for conversation. There was a nagging question that had been on my mind, but I never new quite how to approach him. There was always the danger he would release some weird emotional specter from within me. Finally, I spoke up.

"Pachili, what is the Zone?" I could see the older man in the softening moonlight as he turned in my direction. He sat quietly for a long time, then spoke:

"The Zone" he stated, "is a realm of open possibilities . . . where anything can happen. Is this what you wish to know,

Matthew?" This was the first time he said my name. Apparently, I had awakened him from sleep.

"Yes . . . go on," I prompted Pachili as he stopped to adjust his seating position.

"In the Zone you can be completely free, or completely *geistesgestört! Verruckt."*

"Pardon?"

"You get sick in the head . . . disturbed."

"Go insane . . crazy?"

"Crazy. Yes, this is what I mean. Mad."

"But, how can I go mad in a place of freedom where anything. . ." I suddenly stopped, getting the picture. "O.K., like, be careful what you ask for; you just might get it . . ?"

"Simple, is it not?" Pachili asked, chuckling. "Quite simple, this Zone. You have not yet released your so-called free will, but you come face-to-face with pure *intent.* Then . . ." Pachili paused, as if to reflect on the negative side of this picture. "The rules change. The will - the ego - disappears; only freedom remains. For a while comfort disappears. You experienced this, yes?"

"On the mountain, yes."

"It was time."

"You mean," I queried anxiously, "I no longer have free will?"

"Free will is virtually irrelevant," he answered calmly. "So-called free will has never existed anyway! It is part of the illusion of ego: *Chi* hiding from itself."

"How is that?" I countered.

"Think!" he chirped, "Most people will do *anything* from knowing they are truly free!"

"Why . . . ?"

"There is an old Sufi story," he continued patiently, "about a very pious and orthodox dervish who taught in one of the religious schools in Arabia. He was one day walking along a river bank, thinking about some moral issue.

"Suddenly his thoughts were disturbed. Someone was shouting in the distance, repeating a familiar chant - a dervish call - in a way that was wrong to him. The teacher shook his head, not believing that someone would chant 'OO YA HOOIE!'

instead of 'YA HU.' He, of course, had to correct the fellow because, as a teacher, he felt a duty to show this ignorant fellow the right way.

"So he hired a boat and rowed to the island in the middle of the stream . . . this was where the sounds came from. He found a poorly-dressed man sitting in the middle of a reed hut, rocking back and forth to 'OO YA HOOIE!' Over and over again.

'My good fellow,' he said, 'you are saying the words wrong! I am a teacher of such matters. Please let me give you the proper way.' The teacher then gave him the right sounds, and the poor man humbly thanked him.

"With that, the teaching dervish climbed into his boat, satisfied he had done his duty. After all, it was written that correct repetition of the sacred formula would the speaker to even walk on water . . . and this was something the teacher had never seen, but always hoped to achieve. Silence. The teacher could hear nothing as he rowed away, but was sure his lesson was well-received. Then he heard 'OO YA HOOIE! The idiot started repeating the phrase his old way.

"The teacher sat reflecting on the stupidity of humans when he suddenly saw a strange sight. From the island, the other man was coming towards him . . . walking on the surface of the water!

"The dervish stopped rowing. The second man walked up to him and said: 'Oh great teacher, I am sorry to trouble you, but would you tell me again the right way to say the mantra? I find it difficult to remember!"

I giggled happily, delighting more in Pachili's telling of it than the story itself. "I like that," I said truthfully, "But what does it mean?"

"Ask yourself," continued the monk, "Am I ready to be alone? Completely free of all things? All thoughts? Beliefs? All attachments? Most people need rules, guidelines. Things. If I am truly free, then who am I? My masks disappear. *Chi* is all there is. What do I think? *Who* is doing the thinking?! Why? The moment the answers fall away - as they do in the Zone - your

104

feeble mind and ego rush in to take over, then . . . *du bist geisteskrank."*

"Mad?" I echoed, getting somewhat used to his teutonic inflection

"Genau. This is why *intent* must be strong while in the Zone. Otherwise, *ku* takes over with old memories. If I am free, who is running the show? Anything can happen . . . like you want to wake up from a nightmare, but cannot. The shadow of your former 'free will' is creating chaos." Pachili spoke the last words with such urgency, I felt a charge of energy rush up the back of my spine.

"Intent makes its own freedom. There is no free will in the subconscious or *ku.* It's all programmed. However, because of the illusion of free will, you experience sameness from one minute to the next . . . never broken . . . what is *Fortsetzung* in English?

"Uh . . . sameness . . . Repetition? No. Continuity?"

"Continuity! That's it . . . a programmed *ku* helps the ever-changing world look the same from minute to minute, and day to day. To know the Truth of no-mind is to drop all concern for change altogether.

"Is that why I appear to be slipping out of this . . . this feeling of . . ." Words escaped me for the moment.

"Bliss?" he said, finishing my question. "Yes, surely, but it depends. While you drive this car, you have programmed your *ku* to ask for a continuous road."

"You bet!" I said, watching the road carefully in case he pulled any of his tricks.

"In the Zone, that could change. In choosing bliss, the road might truly disappear . . . or turn into a snake!"

"But, Pachili," I asked, trying to clarify, "what happens when somebody wanders into the Zone who is not prepared for it?"

"Now you are talking myth, right?"

"No, I don't think so. What if . . ."

"If doesn't happen. Those who are not prepared to enter the Zone will not find it . . . will not even look for it."

"Never?"

"Well," relented my friend, "*IF* someone entered the Zone who was not prepared for it, as you say, he would become *geisteskrank* . . ."

"Go crazy . . . mad."

"That's what I said. But, again, he will not go near it. His *ku* will know where the Zone is . . . and avoid it. It has been programmed to do so. These people will not be attracted to areas of the Zone."

"But, you said earlier . . ."

"I know what I said. You will find the Zone when you are ready. Then you have the option to go crazy or not. Free will, remember?"

"But you said there *was* no free will . . !"

"Going mad already, are you?"

I glared at the shadowy figure before me who, it seemed, was quite earnest in his attempt to drive me nuts. I resisted, knowing full well I was being set up again, but for what?? Hadn't we both been through enough for one day?

"Why would I *want* to go mad?" I asked, finally recalling my earlier bliss.

"Because," answered the older man, "going mad is - if you wish to believe this - safer for your mind and ego. You don't have to be responsible."

"I can't quite grasp that going stark, raving mad would have any safe value to it whatsoever."

"Think, you idiot!" he snapped rudely. I was in my head again. "You are put in the asylum. You are fed. You are clothed. You don't make any major decisions. Mad people don't even take the responsibility for their own madness. They think they are sane, that they still have free will and can walk through cell walls! *Chi* is just playing with restriction again. Enough?"

"Excuse me, Pachili . . ." I asked, changing the topic of conversation, "Is the word *Zone* from some religion, philosophy, or metaphysical teaching . . ?"

"I made it up."

"You . . . made it up?"

"The gap is there. I didn't have a name, so I made it up. Now, do you want a lecture on philosophy?"

"Oh, sorry . . . please continue," I said, still amazed at his tendency to be so blunt.

"Will becomes truly free in the Zone," he said, picking up where he left off. "It is so free it disappears! No rules except the ones *Chi* has put there for its special entertainment. Fantastic things come to your mind. Images so bizarre, you question your sanity . . . but *intent* allows you to flow through it.

"You experienced some of this free flow of consciousness after taking the first remedy, did you not?" My memory flashed on the weird sensations, the 3-D images, my distorted face in the mirror, and . . . yes . . . my questions of sanity!

"Tell me the truth, Pachili, was that a hallucinogenic drug you gave me . . . like LSD? Is that what this so-called Zone is all about?"

"Sorry to disappoint you, my friend, but no," sighed the older man. "The remedies - there will be time to tell you about them later - they are different.

"With LSD, the mind is under the influence of chemicals. It is impotent. Free-floating. The mind stays bound to the disjointed fears and impressions of the *ku* and ego. You feel loved, jealous, paranoid . . . whatever. You can also feel these things with the remedies, but differently. They do not influence, only open up. These remedies allow an awareness of *intent*. They awaken the *Chi,* the *gestalt,* the *spitzfindig* . . . subtle?. . . qualities of the mind and nervous system."

"Yeah?" I pressed, "So, how did you discover these remedies? Are they in the Materia Medica?"

"Some are. Most, I created. But the makeup of the remedies is not important," he continued, again frustrating my attempts to get the formulae. "Only the result is important. Superficially, the remedies subtly stimulate the endocrine system - especially the pineal and pituitary glands in the brain - and open the door to ancient memories. They bring out more strength, but can also be deadly if taken improperly. The remedies are only a window to the Zone. You must then use *intent* to walk through the door."

"What do I learn from the Zone?"

"You wanted a cure for your headaches, *gell?*" asked the monk.

"Yes."

"These headaches are painful reminders that you live in a world of paradox and try to deny it. The Zone contains a network of realities, all created by your *intent*. If your body is strong enough, you will *see* and *know* all sources of this denial."

"Sounds scary," I whispered.

"It is," echoed my tutor with a knowing smile.

Chapter Twenty-One

Friday, November 6, 1987. 2:30 A.M. I had been driving for one and a half hours, but wasn't very tired. Pachili had abruptly ended our conversation twenty or so minutes before, leaving me to question whether or not I had offended him. As the last few miles unfolded, my mind started to wander.

I thought of home - Georgia - and my father, the carpet salesman whose fortunes rose and fell with the industry. I missed him. His death two years ago left me both empty and relieved. I missed the stories about his boyhood, like the time he went to New York to see Lou Gehrig and The Babe. I remembered his gripes about lost sales, and trying to make ends meet. I missed his swings, misses, and "attaboys" every time I got a fastball passed him. I missed the proud look on his face when our high school baseball team won the state championship . . . with me pitching.

I felt relieved that he died quickly. Heart attack while watching a football game. Falcons lost to St. Louis. Dad fumbled too, but got six points off St. Peter. I guess it all evens out.

I had to admit - part of me was glad to see him go. Very strict. Whipped me badly as a boy. "For my own good," he said. I had a lot of anger about that . . . felt I could never please him. I always came up short. Even after we won the state title, he pulled my cap down over my eyes and said, "Don't get too cocky about this thing now, y'hear?"

Although I laughed about it at the time, deep down I felt hurt. I wanted him to be proud of me, but he never allowed me to celebrate my success . . . to "show off" as he put it. Somehow, that stopped me later when it really counted. I always came up short: Money. Love. Success. I *did* manage to be a good pitcher and later graduated chiropractic school . . . but only after busting my buns to do it. Inside, I was angry. The bastard was still with me, haunting me at every turn. I even saw his face when I looked down the table at those damn Ethics Committee doctors who tried to block my use of acupuncture.

I felt bad, not having the money to help him and Mom out those last few years. I got over it after Dad was gone. Mom remarried a fellow with retirement benefits. I was happy for her. Nice man, too, that Roger . . .

"You will stay the night at my cabin, yes?" asked Pachili suddenly, dispelling my cloud of thoughts.

"Why, yes. Thank you," I said, surprised he would even ask. *Of course* I would stay there, I thought quietly to myself. Go back to Colombo this time of night? Forget it!

I continued to focus on the road. A few minutes later, I watched as Pachili rolled down the window, mumbled something, then tossed out his goatskin water flask!

"Why did you do that?!" I asked in amazement, wondering why he would throw away such an expensive container. Besides, I was getting thirsty.

"You are asleep."

"O.K., Pachili, what's the lesson this time?!" I asked sarcastically, feeling patronized and slightly fearful, as if I'd done something wrong. "What's new? It's late."

"You are sleep walking, sleep driving . . . even sleep *thinking!*" I guess I was too sleepy to understand what he was telling me. I just mumbled something, as I used to do to my mother when she gave me a list of "to do" items.

"Awakening can happen at any moment. What is your *intent?*"

"Whaddaya mean, *intent?* To get us to your place, O.K.?" I said, irritated with the man. He kept on talking.

"You lost your *intent,*" he stated matter-of-factly. "It has nothing to do with going anywhere or doing anything." The old man seemed determine to twist my mind into a pretzel. I started to bite, then decided to just sit and listen. My jaw tensed as he

110

continued. "Focus on *essence*, not form. Pure *intent,* not appearances.

"But, what about . . ?"

"Relax your need to understand. It is a trap for you," interrupted the bearded, robed figure beside me. I tried to relax, loosening my jaw.

"Your mind seeks to understand. Just feel. Your thoughts distract you. *Intent* is lost. That's why you look to me, or some other *guru*. You have to trust someone else to show you the way, to brush away the clouds. You get lost in them. Otherwise, you make it on your own."

Now I felt lost, confused. Was he saying I should do it own my own? Do *what?!* I suddenly felt deserted.

"You want to know what I'm thinking? Ridiculous!" said Pachili. "You even doubt your own thoughts," he added, getting more personal. I tensed up again, my heart rising into my throat. All bliss disappeared as I felt suddenly enraged. I didn't deserve this abuse!

"My so-called personality is a cartoon," he prodded mercilessly, "A shadow. Yet, you cower, beg, and pretend to be friends with a shadow. You suffer from feelings you attach to me, then push me away to stop the suffering . . . a pitiful comedy.

"You cannot see me. You see only your mother. Your father. Your grandmother! You cannot see *me* because you cannot see your *Self.* Your awareness is dust. Dead. *Intent* is lost in the shadows. *Wake up,* you stupid dog! You are wasting my time!!" The tyrant attacked harshly, tearing at my ego like eagle claws ripping the heart out of its prey. I gasped for breath . . .

"I'll have nothing more to do with you," he added coldly.

This last brush-off seared me like a hot poker. The lump in my throat swelled as the sudden pain in my solar plexus rose towards my head. Pain quickly mixed with rage; I wanted to run the car off the road, killing us both. Tears welled up inside me. My heart pounded. My head ached. I clutched the steering wheel, bracing for an act of violence. Then I remembered . . .

He did this before! I had forgotten . . . the stupid old fool was pushing me - *again* - beyond safety. I was skirting the gap again. Beyond my normal senses; facing into the Zone! I knew this, yet still felt helpless to stop it. My *ku* was on a rampage.

I managed to pull of the road, then sat stunned, still clutching the steering wheel as I did the day I met the Tamil. I *knew* . . . and waited. There was only silence from Pachili. I closed my eyes, witnessing a flood of emotion washing over me. The steering wheel became my only anchor in this swirling sea of uncertainty. I was going over the edge again.

Did Pachili mean what he said? Or was he just testing me? Forget it! Let it go. I couldn't. It was another trick. A test. Remember the peace . . . the bliss . . . I couldn't. Try as I might, the rage swelled within me like molten fire. I wanted to kill the bastard! I wanted to shred him from limb to limb! I wanted to . . .

I gripped the steering wheel.

****

I gripped . . . the edge of the bed . . . tighter. Tighter. I didn't want to give him the satisfaction of seeing me blow up. I didn't want to let him know I hated him for beating me. I tried crying before, but learned my mother never came to help. What could I do? The belt came down. My exposed legs and buttocks withered in the onslaught, more from the anger than the pain itself. There was no escape!

Suddenly, I had a flash of insight. I turned to my father and looked him in the eyes . . . those eyes burned with an intensity I had known for ages. I turned and said fearfully, but with intent: "No more!" He continued beating my body, whose feeling, strangely enough, melted and disappeared. I simply said again, "No more." Then he stopped.

This was my cue. I leaped on him . . . trashed him . . . tore him from limb to limb. I cut him with knives . . . threw him down ten-story buildings and stomped the life out of him. I tortured, killed and burned my tormentor until he was a smoking mass of ashes beneath my feet. I had never felt so powerful, so . . . different! I continued stomping, cursing, and fighting until all his beatings, all his physical insults purged themselves from my memory.

****

All darkness. I drifted again, then a dull blow across my temple. I fell out of the car onto the dusty ground. An awful pain seared through my body. Someone pulled my head back by the hair and yelled something in my ear I didn't understand. Others yelled. I was alone, hurting, and bound like a sheep for the slaughter among an angry crowd. My heart beat as if it were coming out of my chest. I spit out some dirt.

I felt a blow to the head. Another kicked me in the stomach and I gasped for breath. I sobbed as someone ripped off my blind fold. Tamils. They appeared wild-eyed . . . crazy. Their eyes expressed a kind of hate I had seldom witnessed. Their bodies seemed almost animal - muscles glistening in the torch light. One of them held a knife and came closer.

I froze . . . then relaxed, knowing I was going to die.

Chapter Twenty-Two

Time disappeared. I just floated for what seemed like an eternity. The fear and anger lessened. I became aware of something being sealed from my awareness, like forgetting a dream upon waking. I also noticed that I didn't care! Again aware of my surroundings, I sat quietly, but with strangely no feeling at all.

The flood of anger was gone, and I wasn't dead! My grip on the steering wheel eased as I leaned back in the seat. I had no idea how to act, nor was I concerned. I just sat there, listening to an owl in the distance and thinking how wonderful and peculiar that owl sounded . . .

I was also thirsty.

"I would like some water. Wish you hadn't thrown that goathide flask away," I said flatly.

"Here," came the older man's voice. I didn't even bother to look at him.

"Take the water, blind boy." I glanced in Pachili's direction. There, extended from his hand toward me was the goatskin flask! I accepted, too emotionally drained to question. I took the flask and downed a few gulps. It seemed real enough to me.

"How . . ?"

"Later," he said. I drank some more and soon felt refreshed, but surrounded by a mixture of raw feelings floating around me: anger, awe, fear, and humor. As I watched the feelings, they disappeared like a morning fog in the sun. Without thinking, I pulled the car back on the road and continued towards our destination.

We drove for a long time in silence. Pachili was first to break the silence: "Hold the *intent*. Hold . . . your body is starting to open."

"What's my *body* got to do with it?" I responded, "I thought my *head* was the part I wanted to heal!" The older man just nodded and answered with a renewed crispness of tone.

"*Chi* is divided. Your head is clear, but your body is still shut down. Almost dead, but coming back. *Chi* flows more. You must be willing to enter the Zone awake . . . to stay awake even if you are afraid, angry or sad.

"Hold your *intent* until *Chi* is united. Complete. This can take one second," he said, adding ominously, "or it can take lifetimes." I listened without comment or question. My mind and body were emerging into a newer, fragile space.

"What happened to me?" I asked.

"You became the killer." Strangely, I felt something, but mentally drew a blank.

"Me, a killer? Me, the one who couldn't even kill a fly or an ant? Ridiculous."

"You are not complete yet, " added my companion. "The killer part of you is still dormant. You shut it down and will remain a slave of it until you fully accept it. Your *intent* has been to kill, but you hide it with false love . . . false compassion."

"So, what do I do?"

"Doing is not so important as being . . . *intent*."

"Well, how do I recognize my *intent* then?"

"Just watch and let go. Observe. Accept."

"Accept what? Watch what? Killing?!" I pressed my teacher.

"Others. Events. Feelings. Results . . . all will mirror your *intent* completely."

"Completely?"

"Absolutely completely," declared Pachili without hesitation. "You want to know your *intent*? Look around you. The world dances to your song. When awareness is clear, the song is harmonious, melodious. Celestial. Interconnected. When you are asleep, there is much noise. Clamoring. Strife . . . all trying to wake you up!

"You are a killer. Therefore you will find this quality in others . . ."

"What quality?" I asked, still not seeing, "Please explain."

116

"Very well," continued my companion, "Know this: a killer is involved with the going out and the coming in. Death and sex. This is your focus: all the mystery of dying and conception. Death and rebirth. You seek this naturally. But in an unopened state of awareness you are fixated on it - confused and afraid of it. You try to hide it, but your tendency will not stop because of fear. Just like a dying plant sends out billions of pollen seeds, your consciousness seeks stability everywhere, but finds it nowhere. It just keeps going on, and on, and on . . .

"You want to deny it? No problem. Life will give it to you through others. Through circumstances. You will run against it over and over again - death and sex - until you have enough. Until you become aware and let go. Let it go. Forgive."

Part of me suddenly wanted to prove him wrong. Shut him up. But the sad truth was . . . he was right! There was no hiding from it. Brutal as it was, I couldn't run away. I was even powerless to stop his speech. I devoured every word as if it were food for a starving prisoner.

"The main thing is," he continued, "do not deny anything. Embrace everything. Even sex. And death . . . until you can see the awareness - the *Chi* - hidden within each. You will find the quality of each is the same."

"How do you know this," I questioned, "being a Buddhist monk and all? I mean, aren't you a celibate?"

"Celibate simply implies a state of self-sufficiency. Most people think it only applies to sex. No. In awareness, all is perfect. Self-sufficient. Free. There is no need to avoid sex. You cannot deny sex - or anything - anyway! If celibacy is to be real, one needs accept this and more. Then *Chi* decides. Otherwise, its simply a farce, a denial of life.

"My own life? That is not important. I don't ask for your approval, belief, or respect. Don't be like me. Don't act like me. Find your own way. The feedback you get from me is pure; I have no motives. I don't seek disciples. You may either listen or ignore. This is your privilege.

"But soon," added my mentor, "you must devise a way to navigate without me. You must do away with me; I will not guide you for long." Suddenly I felt sad. Do away with him?

Drained though I was, he was still able to play on my emotions like a violin.

"You must trust, even when faced with danger. Trust even when there is no reason to trust. *Knowing* reveals itself to you at all times. Through all things. But it is tricky. You can be fooled, just as you were so easily fooled by that stupid trick with the goatskin. I never threw it out. Reality is never fixed. Watch your thoughts."

I wondered about the goatskin . . . How did he do it? I couldn't help wanting to know. I swear I saw him toss it! Yet, he didn't, obviously. My mind completed the picture; must have been hypnosis!

"Be aware when you are about to enter the Zone . . . *know.* Your *ku* will obey *intent.* Your mind will be useless. Besides, you cannot row the boat in two directions at one time!" laughed the old codger, apparently pleased with his little joke. I wondered about this Zone business; also about some words he used.

"What's the difference between *knowing* and *intent*?" I asked, trying to clarify.

"*Knowing* is universal; *intent* is personal," he said. "The whole purpose of *intent* is to reunite with *knowing* - or vice-versa; just like a wave falls into the ocean. Or the ocean rises to become the wave! Clear?"

"I think so . . . But doesn't *intent* involve thinking?"

"No. Thinking arises out of *intent.* As is your *intent,* so are your thoughts. *Intent* lies at the most subtle level of feeling; near the bottom of the ocean. Thoughts - like waves - are near the surface. Thoughts constantly change while on the surface. This implies weak *intent*, or non-awareness of it. True awareness of *intent* is rare.

"For example, your *intent* now is to go beyond time, space, sex and death, but your ego-mind is not yet done with them. You go into your hiding space. Your pity space. Your fear and anger spaces. You think these places are safe. They are not. They are actually self-contained and self-defined cancer cells floating within the Zone . . . that vast ocean of *Chi,* or consciousness. The disease is only there as an expression of your

118

petty thought processes. The remedies act to strengthen *intent,* loosen the cell walls, and free the individual awareness."

"Each remedy allows your awareness to dive into the Zone in its own special way . . . to connect with pure *intent.* Be aware of this transition. Be awake. You will *know.*" Pachili paused to take another swig of water from the goatskin.

"The first remedy stimulated your body awareness," he said, wiping his mouth on his sleeve, "opened you up, like surgery. Gave you a *taste* of the Zone. I was with you. The seed remains, however. Your deepest killer still lurks. It was aroused and will grow again. You will experience pain and torment. It may take days, weeks or months. Maybe years."

"How can I root out this so-called killer?" I asked, already fearing the answer, but determined to get over my persistent agony.

"As I said before: watch. Observe. Accept. Strengthen you intent, then dive into the Zone." I winced, figuring he was going to tell me something like that. He continued: "Stay awake; the Zone is more potent than anything you have ever known. I will not be there. You alone.

"But," he added reassuringly, "you can come to me if *intent* is strong enough. Trust."

"What was the second remedy you gave me?"
"One for trust."
"Obviously I needed it . . . I never trusted you enough to take it," I said frankly, waiting for his scolding. It never came. Instead, I could feel him smile.

"That's right," added the bearded sage, "The remedy was meant to arouse in you a paradox. It started the process of purification. Started you towards *intent* . . ." Pachili paused for a moment, then emphasized the importance of the point he now made by tapping on the car window.

"It was sugar."
"Sug . . . just sugar? A *placebo?!*" I exclaimed in mock outrage. "Why?"

"It made no difference whether you took it or not. The important thing was to bring up feelings . . . a paradox. The *real* second remedy will take you into the Zone . . . when you are ready." A ripple of anger rose, then settled in me. Normally I would have cried foul at such trickery. Not this time. He was right again. I wasn't ready.

"Are there any more remedies after that?"

"One more," he added without hesitation. "The third remedy . . . it allows continuity to return, while awareness remains."

"Why is that necessary?" I asked.

"Because," said Pachili with a sigh, "the second remedy will drop you into the Zone. You may be blinded by appearances - unlimited possibilities - and never get out. Even if you get out, there will be a time of instability: after your mind goes, but before pure consciousness dawns completely.

"The third remedy allows you to rise out of self-pity and self-concern, relax into being, and unite with the rest of humankind. Once beyond the drama of the Zone, you can drop all your desires and just *know* . . ."

"Even the desire for enlightenment?" I added.

"Even that," he echoed softly.

SECTION II: THE SECOND REMEDY

Chapter Twenty-Three

Morning came with the rooster. I awoke with a start and looked around for something familiar. I recognized Pachili's *avasa,* yet it seemed stark. Raw. Crisp. As if I were seeing it for the first time. I looked at my watch, surprised. I was wide awake at 7:45 a.m. I remembered it was three in the morning when we finally arrived. Exhausted, I fell on his mattress and into a deep sleep. No dreams. No thoughts. Just peace and stillness.

Pachili was not there. I noticed a pitcher of water and bowl on the table and took the liberty of washing and shaving. Next to the bowl I found a packet where Pachili had scrawled my name on the front. Curious, I open and found it contained a folded tissue with powdered sugar in it, and a short letter:

"Second Remedy. Take under the tonge (sic)."

A shudder ran through me as I had a moment of fear. Although he said it as an afterthought, I never forgot his caveat: *"The real second remedy will take you into the Zone."*
Was this the *real* remedy this time . . . or was he still just testing me? I wondered why Pachili didn't wait to tell me himself when he returned. Why . . ? Figuring it was useless to speculate, I carefully re-wrapped the remedy and placed it in my pocket. I would take it later when - or *if* - I had more resolve.

Venturing outside to attend my other needs, I observed a large dark cloud closing in from the northeast. Unexpected thundershowers were not uncommon in Sri Lanka, but still I never liked getting caught in them. I finished my business and hurried back inside, finding myself witnessing a torrential downpour so complete that water was misting its way through the cracks of the cabin.

The rain lasted about thirty minutes. Meanwhile, I amused myself by recounting the horrors and blessings of the previous day. I made a few notes in a journal I always carried with me, then sat to meditate. It was quiet in the cabin, and I felt very safe from any outside disturbances.

My mind was calm and my head clear, a welcome relief from the previous chaos. As I sat quietly, I noticed a new layer of consciousness unfold. Unaware of it until now, I observed a subtle pull towards the top of my head, the area of the crown. Suddenly my head opened up, spontaneously encompassing my surroundings: the room, the field outside, the monastery . . .

Although my eyes remained closed, I *saw* the movements of the flies on the windowsill. The subtle creaking of the floorboards, then the silent murmur of the cabin itself. The dripping sway of the banyan trees and bushes outside. The flight of birds. The roll of the clouds and persistent sunlight on the upper canopy of the forest . . .

Then total silence. No thought. No feeling except a warming bliss that seemed to permeate everything. I fell into a pool of silent awareness. Hours went by . . . or so it seemed. I lay down after meditation and rested in the warmth of this bliss for as long as I felt the need.

Feeling the stir of thought and activity again, I sat straight up and opened my eyes. The same crispness I had observed earlier seemed more so. I again saw the familiar golden luster surrounding everything in the room, then realized it was emanating from me! I looked lovingly at all objects in the room, overwhelmed by a sense of gratitude - at just being alive. I could feel the tears again, this time of great joy.

Blissful as I felt, there remained something inside I could not explain: a strong urge to leave. I did not know why. It was as if someone were telling me to pack my bag and go! I wondered if this was because of my doubts about the second remedy. Should I take it? Or wait? Or just leave? Pachili had been absent a long time. Suppose he left town?

My mind wanted to intercede and argue the merits of each action. My strongest desire was to leave. But why? It made no logical sense. My host had not yet returned, and I had more questions . . . unresolved issues. My thoughts fluttered with doubts, fears, and hollow rationalizations. I made an attempt to quiet the mind, to understand and follow the inner urging.

All I could hear and feel, however, was . . . leave. Rightly or wrongly, I made the decision to go. I stuffed my things in the overnight bag, left a note thanking Pachili, and walked out the door into the heat of the noonday sun.

The rain storm had long moved on. In its place settled an ocean of muggy air, populated by dripping trees and bushes. They glistened in the sun and a haze spread out like a blanket in the valley barely visible below. I noticed the colors as never before. The different shades of green. The soft gray of the cabin itself, the rich brown and red hues of the earth. Sweet aromas from the multi-floral vegetation hung in the air. I inhaled deeply and savored each breath and each step.

I still wasn't sure why I was leaving, but it didn't matter. I was quickly learning to follow this inner prompting. Was it fear? Or inner longing? Whatever it was, refused to be ignored. I just listened. And followed.

On the way to the monastery, I passed a clearing in the woods and heard voices - Pachili's voice! I moved closer and came within viewing distance. I heard the laughter of children. Curious, but not wanting to slow my exit, I squatted behind a clump of trees to spy on events taking place.

In the clearing sat my friend and mentor. He was surrounded by perhaps a half-dozen children, giving them something - remedies perhaps - and talking softly. I couldn't make out what he was saying, but the tone was very loving and full, very unlike the son-of-a-bitch he often projected onto me.

Sitting not far from the homeopath was a striking figure: an old man of about seventy, with a long, ashen beard and an old weathered cane. His eyes sparkled in the sunlight. He didn't wear the robes of a monk, but a traditional Sinhalese *sarama,* or sarong, a simple buttoned shirt, and sandals. He did not speak, but gave loving attention to both Pachili and the children.

Neither did he appear to be a patient; more like an older associate of some sort. I thought to walk out and introduce myself, then changed my mind. I knew this would involve me in their activities . . . I would end up staying. I would have to take the remedy. I decided to just observe for a while, then move on.

Then it struck me; I recognized the old man! I couldn't remember if it was from a dream or what. . . He bore a striking resemblance to Pachili, except he was of native - not German - descent: darker, with the characteristic body frame, high cheeks, face, and lips . . . and he was looking at me!

I ducked, my heart beating rapidly as I sat there. Thoughts darted through my head. Why was I so afraid of showing myself? Who was this old gentleman? Maybe he didn't see me. Why didn't I just stand up and admit I was spying? I didn't do anything wrong . . . surely it would only be for a short while! I resisted the obvious and polite thing to do. Instead, I listened to my fear - the powerful urge to escape.

Crawling on all fours for about fifty yards, I was finally able to stand up and jog softly toward the monastery. I couldn't shake the feeling that I was guilty of something. I forced myself, however, to dismiss the whole incident as trivial, got into my car and headed off down the road. I stopped only to snatch a bite to eat.

****

Other than the constant rumbling noise that resulted from the sudden loss of the muffler and tailpipe between Ratnapura and Panadura, the trip back to Colombo was without incident; easy and enjoyable. All residual fear had disappeared. In its place was increased awareness of my surroundings that became more and more evident with each passing mile. The richness of the countryside, the people and even the carts, goats, and water buffalo in the road - sent waves of pleasure through me.

I arrived before dinner at Vimal's house, happy to see him and his lovely bride Sita in spite of the expected scolding I received for losing his muffler. I promised to have it repaired the next day, then threw myself on his couch and slipped off my shoes. I related stories of attacking Tamils, evil monks, invading hordes of water buffalo, and dramatic rescues from the jaws of death. I spoke with such flair and exaggeration that my friends, of course, didn't believe a word of it.

This was typical for Vimal and Sita. They were like a worn pair of shoes. Everyday friends. Comfortable to be around. Loving and warm. And superficial; a marked contrast from the grueling intensity of a Pachili. Their cook prepared the usual fare - curry and rice - making allowances for my aversion to the hot stuff.

The meal they prepared for themselves and Ama - Vimal's elderly mother - was extremely spicy. I watched with amazement as they engulfed the chow - like witnessing a flame-eating spectacle. Between bites, Vimal told me about events of the day, the usual troubles with his employees, and more gossip about the hospital and our good friend Alfred.

Ama was an old, loving individual; squat and fat, with a penchant for her rice, *pittu, roti,* and *sambol.* As she exchanged gossip with Sita, I asked her casually how she was doing. Her response was predictable.

"I'm not long for this world," she uttered so matter-of-factly, I could only smile. Somehow I believed her . . . this deadly curry could strike at any time! Chuckling quietly at my own private joke, I thought it but never said it.

****

My mind felt clear for days. Thoughts would come and go, but much of the worry, duty, fear, and anger I had based my previous life on disappeared. I was quite relieved to find I could exist without them.

I moved to Mt. Lavinia, south of Colombo. No reason. I just felt it time for a change of venue. It all happened so easily: Dr. Goonilike, one of the clinic doctors had a room for rent that was reasonable, so I took it. His guest house was a nice place, with eight rooms opening to a common courtyard with a front gate. My room was second from the end, near the road. No one was renting the spaces on either side of me, so it remained quiet.

The most attractive feature of my new place, however, was its location. The guest house was only a block from the beach, and three blocks from the luxurious Mount Lavinia Hotel. I loved to spend Sunday afternoons sitting by the hotel pool, or picking through their sumptuous buffet.

In Mount Lavinia, I felt rich on a limited budget. Although it was a small town catering to tourists, there was much there to enjoy. Besides the hotel - used in the film *The Bridge Over the River Kwai* - there were restaurants, gem shops, fax and telex facilities, and a small artist colony.

I continued to work and teach at Kalibuwila hospital, but came and went as I pleased. Life was good.

"Any news about the Seattle SeaHawks?" I turned around to greet large gentleman with a big smile. He was waiting for a chiropractic adjustment.

"What's that?" I asked, rather puzzled. "Sorry, but I'm more of a baseball fan."

"Well, the Mariners didn't do much when I was there, but I always followed the team."

"Why do you think I'm from Seattle?"

"I don't; but I knew you were American. Spent two years there myself . . ." said the man who introduced himself as Johannes Vidkun Olafson, a Norwegian photographer. He told me he also lived and worked in Mount Lavinia, and asked me to call him Jon.

He was a big man, with the arms of a blacksmith and the legs of a horse. Jon was slightly older than me, about 38. That day, he filled me in on the gossip about local expatriates, and gave me tips on island happenings, such as the best places to eat, swim, travel, and photograph.

Every day for two weeks I saw him at the clinic. Said his neck was a problem. I didn't care; it was good to have a friend. Often we got together evenings at a local beach pub, eating, drinking and laughing until the early hours of morning. We tossed out stories about the Superbowl, Asian women, European beer, and other shared experiences. Anything that crossed our inebriated minds was fair game.

I was reluctant, however, to share some of my more esoteric experiences with him. Our relationship was, strictly speaking, a guy thing. I enjoyed it immensely as something I had not experienced since adolescence.

With friends like Jon, and patients at the clinic who seemed devoted to me, I forgot much of the fear, sentiment, and anger I had accumulated over the decades. All my stress magically dissolved. Somewhat disturbing, however, was the fading relationship with my wife. In the beginning, Cheryl and I talked daily on the phone. To save money, we decided on a weekly conference. Then we barely talked at all. Whenever we did, we seemed distant, as if starting to forget who we were together.

As the weeks turned into months, my other life slowly disappeared altogether. The island lived inside of me.

Chapter Twenty-Four

On Friday, November 20, I awoke with a start. It was dark. Although I often arose earlier since my return, this was too early. I looked at the clock; it was still hours before dawn. Full moon light filtered through the thin curtains, revealing the shadows of my clothes discarded the night before. I also noticed the vase of now-wilted flowers given to me by a grateful patient.

I sat up in bed, unsure what to make of this sudden awakening. There was no sound other than that of a cricket outside my half-opened window. I had not been dreaming. There was nothing to attribute my waking at such an hour. As I sat wide awake, I listened for some sign of movement. I neither heard nor felt anything for several minutes.

Figuring it was nothing, I again lay my head on the pillow and closed my eyes, but couldn't sleep. Something was ringing in my ears, subtly at first, then with an increased roar that ebbed and flowed with the energy of an underground dynamo. I had read brief descriptions of the sudden rise of Kundalini, and immediately wondered if I was experiencing it.

Not able to sleep, I decided to sit up and meditate. I fell into a familiar clarity of mind, but stayed poised as if something were about to happen. It did; very subtly. I felt and saw a faint light arise from within my heart and began circulating throughout my body. Slowly it rose and fell, rose and fell, like waves caressing a rocky shore. I continued to watch. And wait. Rise. And fall. Back and forth . . .

Suddenly, my mind reeled as a burst of energy emerged at the base of my spine, connecting with the top of my head. Although my eyes were closed, I could see everything in the room as clearly as if it were daylight. I then became keenly aware of something I was unprepared for: a presence in the room!

In my mind's eye, I saw a figure standing at the foot of my bed, but couldn't make out his features. I was afraid; afraid to open my eyes; afraid of the unexplained onslaught to my senses. Afraid of going crazy. I felt a swirl of something - a tangible force - that became more solid as the seconds ticked by. Someone - or something - was trying to appear . . . !

I forced my eyes open and caught a glimpse of a shadowy male figure before me that disappeared before my eyes could focus. My hair stood erect at the back of my neck and I shivered momentarily as a rush of adrenaline shot through me. There was no earthly explanation for this experience - an eerie event that soon had my heart pounding as if I had just run a mile.

I jumped out of bed, turned on the light, and threw on my T-shirt and shorts, as if preparing to flee from a fire. The presence was still there. I listened, but could hear nothing, feel nothing. My eyes strained to catch any movement while I focused on trying to stop the pounding of my heart.

"Who are you and what do you want!?" I demanded, not really expecting the intruder to answer. My heart still pounded. I asked again, then exhaled forcefully. Then, as suddenly as it came, the apparition disappeared . . .

Silence returned. My vascular organ never ceased its pounding, however, even as peace once again prevailed. I was suddenly aware of being vulnerable to forces beyond my comprehension. Instinctively, I surrounded myself with light, threw on my walking clothes, and hurriedly dashed out of my small apartment.

I ran the two miles to the beach, then continued pacing up and down the coast until morning. Finally feeling relaxed and exhausted, I found a gnarled tree trunk on the beach and sat down. Silence prevailed once again - at least for the moment.

As the welcomed sun emerged from behind the trees, I witnessed the ocean bathed in golden light, revealing the majesty of soaring seagulls and distant clouds. Not even the long walk on the beach, however, could dispel my deeper feelings of uneasiness. Some ethereal force had attached itself to my head and solar plexus, and I feared as if the life force was being drawn out of me! I shivered to try and shake the feeling, to no avail.

The beach was deserted except for a few early-morning fishers and wandering beggars. I stood up, resolving to visit Jon who lived not far away. Although it was early, I felt I needed his strength and advice. I decided to skip clinic that day and try to sort out and clarify my experiences.

Chapter Twenty-Five

Jon was not there when I arrived at his small apartment. A neighbor informed me he had headed towards the south beach at dawn with his camera. I thanked him, turned as directed towards the south, and spied a distant figure approaching. I knew it was Jon. No one else could be that large! I trotted toward him, waving. He saw me and responded in kind.

"Hello, my friend! What brings you here so early?"

"I need some advice, Jon," I responded obliquely. I had never talked with him about such matters, and suddenly felt afraid and embarrassed.

"Oh? Come inside. Let me make you some tea and eggs." Jon liked his tea and eggs.

He showed me to the sofa while he prepared breakfast, then served us on bamboo trays. I gorged myself with an appetite I thought I had lost over the last several weeks since my return from Balangoda. I then started to relate my experiences, prefacing them, however, with a caveat that what he was about to hear was not easy for me to say.

"Just tell me what you can, my friend. I have no fear for your honesty or sanity," he said reassuringly.

Feeling bolder, I began telling him everything, starting from the beginning. I revealed details on my trip to Pachili's: the attack at Panadura, the remedies, the Devil's Staircase, the hallucinations, and the old man. I ended my narrative talking about the latest scare in my room that morning.

While listening attentively to my confession, Jon finished his tea, leaned forward, and lit his pipe. He took a few puffs, then slumped back into his favorite lounge chair. I continued while holding nothing back. I knew he would be honest with me; report whether my stories were the ramblings of a madman, or the experiences of everyone who lived on this strange little island.

I sat back nervously, waiting for his response. The big Norwegian said nothing for a long time. He continued to puff on his pipe, sometimes staring at the ceiling, then bringing his eyes back on me as if trying to piece together bits of a very large puzzle. When he finished, Jon emptied his hand-carved pipe into a small tin he always kept beside his chair, then laid the pipe on the table in front of him. He leaned back in his chair and placed his folded hands behind his head.

"Tell me more about the old man," he boomed in his deep voice that resonated across the room.

"There's not much to tell," I explained. "I only saw him once in the clearing . . . saw him looking at me. I then quietly slipped away."

"What was he wearing? What did he carry? How did you feel immediately after making eye contact?"

I described what I saw and felt in detail, curious why my friend chose to focus on something so seemingly insignificant. I described his cane, his beard, his shirt and sarong . . . his eyes, and the feelings of guilt I carried away with me.

Jon leaned forward at the mention of the old man's eyes, stared blankly at the coffee table for a minute, then spoke. "You know I've lived on this island about three years, don't you?"

"Yes, you've told me that," I said, trying to follow him.

"Do you remember the time I told you about the *Veddhas,* the ancient tribe that lives in the highlands that do strange things?"

"Yes, vaguely. I think we were drunk then," I said, laughing ". . . doing strange things ourselves!" Although I was half-joking, I also remembered something about a little boy in Ratnapura . . . something he said . . . something about "Vittas."

"Well, the stories are true," proclaimed my friend solemnly, "and I suspect that old gentleman is one of them." That said, Jon again leaned back in his chair and folded his hands.

"I don't mean to be argumentative," I said, "but he seemed cultured . . . didn't at all look like a *Veddha,* at least like any pictures I saw of them, or descriptions I've heard about

134

them." I said this, recalling the images in my guide books of half-naked primitive tribal members: aboriginal hunters and woodsmen.

"That may be true," Jon confessed, then added, "But remember, they can change clothes too! Some *Veddhas* have left their traditional villages and blended with the Tamils, Sinhalese, and even Europeans. Though many choose to remain the so-called backwoods primitives, others have kept their ancient knowledge while becoming adept at blending with other cultures. I even met one at a spiritual gathering in Nepal."

Jon surprised me. Besides making sense, he revealed something about himself I had not known before . . .

"I didn't know you went to spiritual gatherings," I remarked in amazement. "What kind of gatherings?"

"This one was a gathering of Zen Buddhists," he answered matter-of-factly.

"A *Veddha* at Buddhist gatherings . . . *in Nepal?!*"

"Oh, yes. He actually was just passing through on his way to China."

Amused, I let out a chuckle. I never thought of a *Veddha* as being able to leave the village, much less travel the world! Yet, if Jon's words were correct, I was learning something quite new and profound . . .

"So why would a *Veddha* want to haunt me?" I asked, still concerned for my safety and sanity. I hadn't taken the second remedy yet. This was not a Zone experience, so far as I knew . . . or was it?

"I don't know," admitted my Norwegian friend. "so I can't say for sure. . . perhaps he was testing you. Perhaps he wanted to give you something."

"Well, he could have called, for Chrissakes!" I blurted. Surprised at my own rudeness, I took a deep breath, then apologized to Jon for interrupting. He continued.

"That's O.K. . . . You see, from what I've learned - and it's not been very much actually - a *Veddha* is not bound by social graces, but they do have a strong sense of fair play. If you spied on him, he may feel perfectly justified to drop in on you.

"If he wants something, he asks. If he sees something that interests him, he will pursue it. The most interesting thing of all, however, is that because of their self-reliance and relative isolation, the *Veddhas* have developed remarkable psychic powers and use them regularly."

"What kind of powers?"

"Well, you probably experienced one this morning. Mr. Old Man, or whatever-his-name-is, decided to visit you, scared the bloody hell out of you, then left when you asked him to. I've heard stories of them doing those sorts of things." I felt a little better knowing I was not crazy, but still apprehensive.

"What else can you tell me about these *Veddhas?* And what can I expect?" I asked, pressing Jon for more details.

"Let's see. . ." Jon said, pausing for a moment. "Now keep in mind, much of what I'm telling you is just hearsay . . ."

"Hey," I acknowledged laughingly, "I'm the last one to judge you! Please. No disclaimer. Go on." I urged. I could tell Jon was uncomfortable talking openly about such things.

"Well the *Veddhas* go way back, before recorded history. They go back even before the myths and legends. They are probably linked somehow to the aborigines in New Guinea and Australia . . .

"Anyway, are you familiar with the *Mahavamsa?*"

"Sort of," I confessed, "Isn't that the story of the founding of Sri Lanka and the enlightenment of Prince Vija-somebody?" I knew it was a great work, comparable to the *Bhagavad-Gita* and the *Mahabharata* of India, but couldn't remember the specifics.

"Well," he continued, "this is where fact and fiction become blurred. There is a passing reference in the *Mahavamsa* to tribes of *yaksas* and *nagas.* They lived on the island long before the arrival of the Sinhalese or the Tamils, between about 500,000 BC and 5,000 BC . .

"You see, these *yaksas* and *nagas,* were not human. They were spirits. Despite that, however, they actually carried on trade with foreigners, and eventually evolved into the stone-age Balangoda people who lived until about 500 BC. Then they spread throughout the island. The *Veddhas* are believed to be

136

descended from these people . . . and from the *yaksas* and *nagas!*"

"What does all this mean?" I inquired, "That the *Veddhas* are not human?"

"Oh, I don't know," shrugged Jon as he stuffed more tobacco into his pipe, lit it, and took a few quick puffs. "They are probably as human as the Sinhalese who are supposed to be descended from lions! Or you and me, for that matter, who are supposed to be descended from monkeys . . . or ancient astronauts!" I could tell Jon was being facetious, although the whole subject captivated me.

"I tell you one thing, though," he added more sincerely, "the *Veddhas* I met are amazing people. They have a way of seeing right through you. Their ties with the natural - and supernatural - are beyond anything I've ever seen. That's why I perked up when you mentioned the old fellow's eyes."

Jon and I continued our conversation until about noon, covering such diverse topics as haunted houses, herbs, devil masks, and spooky natives. We eventually carried our discussion outside, gravitating towards the beach to a small thatched-roof visitor's tavern that served alcoholic beverages and tourist snack items. There we sat, drinking *Ceylon schnapps* - his name for a mixture of wine and coconut juice - and laughing about the new level of kinship we discovered in each other. After a while it seemed easy to share my deepest experiences with him.

We never did solve the mysteries of the ghost in my room, the *Veddhas,* or the Old Man. After a few typical days and evenings had passed, I figured that whoever came to visit was not coming back, and set out to enjoy life in its fullest.

Chapter Twenty-Six

Late November was beautiful. Although it was not cold, there were some signs of seasonal changes: the rains came less often, the skies were clear and crisp, the sun more colorful, and the shadows deeper.

It had been more than a month since the others had left and I had gotten used to my new routine in the clinic, which only took up the mornings. The rest of the day I spent exploring whatever life threw in my path - a path often littered with opportunities to learn and grow, but mostly just enjoy.

My stay in Mt. Lavinia had been pleasant. I still gathered with various friends in the afternoon at tea time, and occasionally went drinking with Jon. My knowledge of Sinhala was growing daily, thanks to my friend Prannam. He insisted on teaching me the language even though we both knew I would never use it outside Ceylon.

This particular November day held a strange emptiness. A thunderstorm had swept through, taking the dust and leaving a freshness in the air. Although my world was beautiful, I sensed of loss of something. I felt uncertain about my purpose for being here. Slightly adrift. I followed Pachili's advice to just witness and not be concerned.

For some reason I chose to visit my old neighborhood - RamaKrishna Road - before going to clinic. It was a nostalgic affair, with the usual exchange of hellos and gossip with the owners of the Brighton Hotel. Afterwards, I set out toward the Hospital. It was a familiar route, with large mud puddles dotting the landscape next to quaint houses and cottages. Everything seemed in place. Familiar sights and smells were everywhere, even the blackbirds, or crows.

Crows were quite a presence on the island. Visions of Hichcock's horror classic about birds often came to mind whenever I saw them. They were the size of small chickens, glossy black, with flattened heads and an unusual look of foreboding. When I first arrived on the island, I was fearful they would attack, later deciding the fear was unfounded. No one else was concerned, and so far they had left me alone.

This day, a couple of crows perched themselves on a nearby fence, staring at me. At first I didn't notice, but became increasingly uneasy as I passed them. Without gazing directly, I made an attempt to study them more closely. These particular creatures were larger than usual. Different. Was it their heads? Something about their eyes . . .

I shot them a direct glance to make sure. They were looking . . . staring directly at me as I realized . . . these eyes were *human!* Choking on the idea, I quickly averted my eyes and scurried around a wide puddle. The hairs on the back of my neck stood up. I developed an intense headache. Suddenly, my *ku* was yelling at me. Danger . . . Danger . . . !

Out of pure instinct, I ducked. One of the crows whizzed overhead, releasing a hideous sound that likened more to a wounded panther than a crow. He just missed me!

They were attacking! The first assailant landed in a tree across the street and continued squawking as if sending coded messages to his partner in crime. Sure enough, I turned around long enough to see a massive flapping black object hurling itself at me. I dodged it without a moment to spare.

Then, another hit - this one from behind! I fell forward and passed out . . .

Regaining consciousness . . . I don't know how much later . . . I took a minute to regain my composure, and soon felt a throbbing pain on the back of my head, and something else. Something wet. I touched it and looked at my fingers. Blood.

A small crowd had gathered around me, but not too close. They seemed fearful, I suspect, of more crow attacks. I raised myself slowly from the muddy road and stood up, not feeling too steady. More pain. My head throbbed, my hands muddy, and my face and hair felt like they were a mess. My clothes were streaked with blood and mud.

Someone eventually came forward and handed me a handkerchief. I thanked the gentleman who offered, and began wiping off my face and hands.

"I'd like to pay you for your handkerchief," I said in English, hoping he understood. I stood there, embarrassed to be the center of attention. The man appeared to be middle-aged, one of the many European descendants called Burghers that populated the island.

"Please. No worries about the handkerchief. That's a nasty bump, Sir," replied the Burgher in perfect English. "Would you care to tidy up here before continuing on your stroll?"

"Yes . . . Yes I would. Thank you very much," I acknowledged, managing to stagger to the side of the road and in the door. I was a mess . . . but grateful.

Inside, my hosts, a Mr. Percy Colin and his spouse, offered to wash my clothes while I took a shower. I thought their offer extremely generous, given the fact they had no washing machine. I declined the clothes wash, but readily agreed to use their bathroom facilities.

Relieved at the opportunity to clean up, I quickly washed the mud off my hands and the blood from my forehead. In the mirror, the cut didn't look too bad, but my head throbbed with a constant pain. Mrs. Colin offered me a small bandage, which I gladly accepted.

Once revived, I agreed to sit with them for the customary tea and cake. This time the "cake" was a piece of local fried bread, or *papadam*.

"Did you see those crows?" I asked the Colinses after dispensing with the usual formalities and introductions. My head still hurt, and I felt a recurrent dizziness to accompany the sting of the blow.

"Yes, but not very well," answered Mr. Colin. "We just saw them fly off after the last one attacked you from behind. Very strange, indeed."

"Indeed!" I echoed. "I've never had it happen to me before. Why did it happen now?" I asked the question, not really expecting an answer. Mr. Colin, however, presented something startling:

"Those crows were probably *Veddhas* or shamans."

I stared at him, flabbergasted. Where did he get *that* from? I had said nothing to him about their eyes, or that I had encountered a *Veddha* recently. Yet he seemed to know something I didn't. That little boy in Ratnapura wasn't telling me some wild story. He pointed to some birds . . . "Vittas". . . Apparently this was common knowledge to the locals. I pressed my host for details.

"Well," continued the Burgher, "I've seen them here before. They have human eyes. They think like humans. They act like thieves and hoodlums. They are all evil. Bring bad Karma. I have even heard them talk."

"You heard them do what?!" I interrupted, rather skeptically.

"Talk," he repeated. "One time - about two years or so ago - I was going to work when I, too, was attacked by the bloody beasts. I actually knocked one out of the sky with my umbrella. The bugger came down with a thundering crash and started to curse at me . . ."

"In English or Sinhalese?" I asked, rather amused at the whole thing.

"In Sinhala. Very clearly, I mean to say!" he insisted adamantly.

I didn't know whether to laugh out loud, or pretend this was just a normal topic of conversation. I had a strange feeling, albeit a scary one, that he was telling the truth.

"What did you do?"

"Nothing! I just stood there, amazed, as the black fellow got back on his feet and just flew away."

"Is that all he said?" I persisted.

"That time, yes . . . although I recall hearing them frequently when I was a lad. My wife will tell you of times she has heard them as well. Others - mostly in the countryside - tell many stories, mostly about these birds and their link to the Devil. Being Catholic myself, I believe their stories are true."

I tried to put all this is perspective. The reference to talking birds by the boy in Ratnapura, irrelevant at the time, seemed suddenly pertinent. I was familiar with the stories of Native American shamans taking the form of animals, witches and warlocks merging with their *familiars,* but this was my first actual encounter with such a phenomenon.

"How . . . why . . . does a human being become a bird?" I asked Mr. Colin, hoping for some clue.

"That I'm not quite sure. There are several ways, according to legend. He could be reborn as a bird. His past life as a man was too sordid or wicked to come back as a man. So he became the form of his thoughts. Stories also have it that these birds are forms the *Veddhas* took to travel great distances.

"Or," he added, "for mischief . . . to teach you something."

"Teach? Teach me what?" I inquired anxiously.

"That, I do not know. I have heard this from others who had *Veddhas* follow them - fellows they knew - that were connected to them in some way." His words fell on me like a thud. For some inexplicable reason, they felt true.

"Again," added my host, proffering his pitcher, "it rarely happens. Those fellows who hit you are probably just crows with a sour stomach! Pray that is all it is . . . Would you like some more tea?" I didn't respond, suddenly caught in a mental whirlpool. *Veddhas*? My curiosity was burning at a fever pitch.

"How can I . . . how can anyone tell . . . who these creatures are?" I interrogated further, ignoring his offer for beverage.

"I tell you, Sir, I do not know," he said, growing more irritated with my persistence while pouring tea into his own cup. "I avoid such devils. I have told you what I can. More than that, you will have to ask a *Veddha,* or the devil himself.

"And that," he added sternly, "I do not recommend!"

With that last remark, Mr. Colin made known his intention to end the conversation by getting up to help his wife clear the table. I muttered an apology, profusely thanked my hosts for their hospitality, and said something about having to be at clinic. I was soon on my way, feeling more fresh physically, but more puzzled about this *Veddha* thing.

Were there any accidents on this strange little island? Or did someone - or something - set me up for this cosmic spoof? Even the original name of the island - *Serendib* - the root of

143

Serendipity - meant "discovery of desirable or valuable things accidentally or unexpectedly."

Undoubtedly, I was being set up. The messages at Ratnapura, kamikaze crows, a chance meeting with Mr. Colin, and the sudden proliferation of *Veddha* stories - all were too strange and coincidental to dismiss as trivial. Besides, I couldn't forget it. My head throbbed for several days after visiting the hospital. They treated me for a scalp laceration . . . told me these things were fairly common.

Chapter Twenty-Seven

Tuesday, December 1st. It was raining when I awoke. The back of my head pounded with the memory of the crow attack more than a week earlier. My dreams had been so vivid I wrote them down in the book I kept handy for such occasions. It was about Pachili, Ruth Graham, and the old man.

In the dream, I was sitting around a campfire with the three of them. Pachili was talking, the whole time I was staring at Ruth. Suddenly the old man got up from his seat, slowly came over to my side, and clobbered me over the head!

I woke up, throbbing. Somehow, Ruth was there to show me something, but I got hit before she had the chance.

"Weird," I muttered to myself as I put my book away. I knew somehow life was preparing me for some encounter with them. I knew this because I had the same, familiar feelings come over me . . . ones I knew as at the Devil's Staircase. *Chi* was playing mischief again.

I rubbed my pulsating head. Interestingly, the pain was different. I could handle it, unlike those horrible attacks that started at the base of the skull and spread throughout the head, ending behind my eyes. They were a mystery, whereas this pain appeared to come from my wound. I gave myself some acupuncture to help the pain.

"There, that's enough!" I reassured myself after grudgingly slipping a single needle into the web of my thumb and gently stimulated it. Although my head felt better immediately, I still wasn't sure the treatment was worth it. I also felt a touch of nausea that subsided after five minutes.

It had been almost a month since my last visit with Pachili. I recalled he *did* mention something about headaches coming back . . . different ones. Was this the kind he was talking about? Surely not, unless he knew I would be hit by a crow! I laughed at the idea while nervously studying my face in the mirror, using oriental-type diagnosis for signs of *Chi* imbalance. I looked fine, other than a few gray hairs and something else . . .

As I fingered the dark spots under my eyes, I reminded myself I really should do something about treating my liver and kidneys!

****

The walk and bus ride to the clinic were relatively uneventful. It was a dull, cloudy day, but the rain had stopped and I managed to tag a ride in a bus with room to spare. Arriving earlier than my usual time, I set up my table and began working on the line of prospects. I had no worries and looked forward to a whole day of easy routine.

Then *she* walked in.

Her safari clothes were the same bright khaki she wore the last time I saw her. Ruth's absence for almost two months led me to believe I'd never see her again. But the dream! My *ku* was connected with hers . . . I knew she was coming!

She stood at the entrance of the clinic, smiling and waving at Lola Premadesa, Dr. Alfred's assistant, and some others. I froze as I watched her walk over to Lola. They were laughing, sharing stories like two long lost friends. What was this? I felt jealous that she didn't look for me! I tried again to focus on the job at hand.

"Take a deep breath," I told my patient, "Now, let it out. Esthuthi . . . Thank you."

I caught myself stealing glances at her, and berating myself for being so taken. My heart betrayed me, leaping around like a starving hamster in a cage. I went from glad to sad, anger to jealousy . . . then to fear. Will she notice me? Does she even remember? I felt like a little kid on Christmas morning, trying to ignore Santa . . . and could barely shake the desire to run over and embrace her.

After what seemed an endless conversation with Lola, the object of my affection turned and started to walk out, but

146

suddenly stopped and glanced in my direction! I quickly looked down, pretending to be engrossed in my work.

"Well aren't you going to say Hello, sport?" she said as she approached. Her words sang in my ears. I looked up and smiled in fake surprise. Playing hard-to-get was not my style.

"Oh, Hi Ms. Graham!" I gushed, "I wanted to say something, but you looked rather involved with Lola. Besides, I didn't know if you remembered me . . ."

"Oh, don't be silly, Dr. Cannon. Of course I remember you!" she said, gushing back. "I just came to say hello to Lola and, you know, talk girl stuff."

"Oh . . ."

My mind screamed at me mercilessly. "Can't you say something decent?! Something more profound than a stupid 'Oh!??'" Ruth didn't seem to notice.

"I just got in from Thailand and Burma. I'm here for two days. I must say, Doctor, Sri Lanka feels more like home to me than anywhere else. In all honesty, it's good to see you again! I thought you would have left for America by now. I'm actually glad you didn't."

Suddenly I felt bold.

"Would you wait for me?" I asked without hesitation. "I would like to talk with you some more, if possible. I'll be through here in about ten minutes. Is that O.K.? We can go downtown and I'll treat you to lunch." I held my breath, waiting for an answer. I actually needed to stay another half-hour or so, but didn't want to pass up this opportunity.

"I'd be delighted, Doctor . . ."

"Please call me Matt," I said stiffly, trying not to sound too much like an over-eager schoolboy.

"O.K., Matt," she added, "If you will excuse me, I'll continue my conversation with some other friends while I wait for you. N'est pas?" I nodded with a smile. With that, Ruth spun around and melted into the small crowd, laughing and talking as she went.

Chapter Twenty-Eight

I was able to sneak out while Dr. Alfred was busy with the crowd and hailed one of the ubiquitous three-wheel taxis waiting on Hospital Road.

"I'm staying at the Galle Face Hotel downtown," announced Ruth as climbed into the rickety vehicle. I eagerly offered to take her there after lunch. Meanwhile, our taxi driver plunged into the chaos of Galle Road and fought our way north toward the bowels of the city. We soon arrived at one of my favorite spots, a little Bengali restaurant on Slave Island. Alfred once told me about it, saying their spice was so mild and flavor so great, I would become a regular customer. He was right.

Ruth and I devoured *samosas, chapatis* and chicken curry while exploring the wonders of travel, healing, and music. That afternoon, we leisurely meandered through the hot and humid streets, sharing bottles of soft drinks with each other and the beggars. At a local dress shop, I gave her my opinion of some saris she wanted to take back to England. I did little things for her, like opening the door, holding her chair, and brushing the beautiful auburn hair away from her face.

The feelings of love I once tried to deny myself rushed forward with each passing incident. As I decided to just relax and enjoy it, the initial awkwardness gave way to a feeling of freedom . . . We talked about our travels, our fears, our childhood experiences, and our marriages. I discovered Ruth recently divorced Claude, a French import-export merchant, but still went on shopping trips for his company.

"Oh, he doesn't like to travel," she announced.

"But isn't that odd?" I queried, "that an import-export person hates to travel?"

"It *is* funny, isn't it!" Ruth responded with a laugh. "Actually, he doesn't mind traveling . . . it's just that I *love* to

149

travel, so he still sends me to all these places to bargain with the locals for the best deal . . . and I usually get them! My trip to Thailand netted us a profit of twenty thousand francs on a silk flower deal."

I was happy for her, but indifferent to the subject matter. I only wanted to look into her eyes. The woman I once saw as proper and reserved turned out to be a genuine human being, with a broad smile and heart-warming laugh. Sitting with her, whether at a restaurant or on a bus, gave me a sense of belonging, a feeling of timelessness.

As we got off the bus near her hotel, I offered to extend our visit and buy her dinner. She declined, but wouldn't say why. There was a long moment of uneasy silence.

"Was it something I said?" I asked while we sat at the edge of Galle Face Park, watching a local urchin trying to launch a stubborn kite in the stiff breeze.

"Not really," she said, "I must admit, however, that I like you . . ."

"I like you too . . ." I replied. The awkwardness returned.

"Well . . . you're married." she said with a look of sadness, I gazed down at my fingers, picked off part of a loose nail, then grimaced into the wind. I was beginning to wonder how far to take this.

"I tell you what," I said, trying to set us both at ease, "Let's be friends and not worry about this boy-girl thing, O.K.?" She smiled and grabbed my hand. I suddenly knew this "friends" idea wasn't going to work.

"I'd like that," she said, then rose to her feet. "Walk me to the lobby?" I obliged while feeling a bit sad. The warmth of her palm electrified me as nothing had before.

"Can I see you again?" I asked.

"In a few days," she responded without hesitation. "I've got a trip planned to Kandy, but I should be returning by Friday."

"That evening then?"

"Yes. I'll be at the Ramada."

"Good. I'll pick you up at 7:00."

****

The days dragged on. I hated to admit it, but I was deeply in love - grabbed in the gut like a force as strong as a grappling hook. My stomach churned every time I tried to eat. My head throbbed with every thought, and I developed a rash on my forearms and abdomen. Ruth's memory consumed me.

I made only one appearance at the hospital, staying only an hour. My focus was lost; my heart wasn't into it. I just spent my days skipping rocks on the ocean, or pacing up and down the beach. Jon kept leaving messages, which I never returned.

Chapter Twenty-Nine

Friday, December 4th. I spent the afternoon circling and studying the Ramada like a hawk. By 6 p.m. I knew every nook and cranny, window and door of the place. I went in and surveyed the lobby, hoping vaguely to get a glimpse of Ruth. She wasn't there. I settled in one of the hotel's finer leather chairs, sipping a Piña Colada and counting the minutes when I would approach the desk and ask for her.

The Colombo Ramada was huge, modern, ornate monument to the Japanese and their status as the world's nouveau riche business leaders. I checked my watch: it was 6:20. I handed my glass to a waiter and walked out to the pool deck to check out the swimmers . . . something . . . anything to keep my mind occupied for forty more minutes.

"Matthew!" chirped a familiar voice.

I glanced towards the deep end and smiled. As Ruth climbed out of the pool, grabbed her towel and glided towards me, I couldn't help admiring her body, seemingly poured into the modest bikini. She was thin and firm, with a slightly angular build. The tops of her ample breasts glistened in the late afternoon sun. Her legs and feet moved with a softness that bathed my senses and aroused my sensibilities. My heart jumped.

"What are you doing here so early?" she asked.

"Nothing else going on right now," I replied truthfully, "Thought I'd come down and see the place."

"Well, I just came down for a quick dip. You bring a swimsuit?"

"No."

"That's fine; I've had enough anyway," she said while slipping on a T-shirt. "Wait in the lobby and I'll be down quickly."

I started to say something, but couldn't; she was already out the pool gate, quickly disappearing through one of the many side doors.

That evening, we went to a little Italian place, not far from downtown Colombo. Her favorite, she said. As we drank wine before dinner, Ruth filled me in on her buying trip to Kandy for spices and exotic plants. I listened, enchanted by her eyes and the sound of her voice.

"Now, enough of me, Matt," she bubbled, "Tell me what you did this last week."

I told her something; lied about having a busy week trying to find gems for export. I wanted to tell her about my strange adventures: the crows, the ghost, and Pachili. I wanted to shower her with exotic tales of Tamil attacks and psychic little boys. I wanted to open my heart . . . I wanted to, but didn't. Somehow, I felt obliged to avoid these subjects; felt it wasn't the time.

Adroitly, I shifted the conversation back to her. She didn't mind . . . chatting away about other deals and friends and family back home. Finally, as the evening wore on, the candlelight became softer and the conversation more intimate. I shared with her the story of Devil's Staircase.

"That's amazing," she said after hearing my story. "That same day - full moon day - I had a similar experience happen to me in Thailand!"

"You're kidding."

"No . . . It happened near Chiang Mai. My Thai friend and I were traveling along a deserted mountain highway when our car just died . . . couldn't get it started. Thirty minutes later, a bus comes by and saves us . . . said they never travel that way!" I listened, enraptured by her story and the growing love within me. She and I were connected somehow, and I found it hard to restrain myself. I had to say something.

"I hope you don't mind me saying so," I said, "but I'm captivated by your eyes." There was a long pause as she looked away. Her eyes darted around the room, as if looking for a hummingbird.

"But what about your wife?" she asked, repeating her earlier concern about my marital status. "Isn't she helping you

154

with the gems . . . looking for markets back in America for them?"

"That's the plan," I sighed, discouraged about a part of my life that wasn't working. "But the last time I talked with Cheryl, she had made no progress in lining up any buyers."

"That's a shame," continued Ruth, "There's money to be made in them, you know. But you won't make any." I must have looked puzzled. Ruth explained.

"They can't work . . . the deals, that is. The energy is not right. Your heart is not into them. Every time you mention your wife, your face drops like a rock. With that kind of feeling, it's a wonder you are still married to her!" My jaw tightened.

She continued curtly: "I'm sorry, but I care for you. I must tell you that's where you're headed. Listen . . . you've seen me only a few times, yet you act like you're in love with me . . ." I started to protest, but we both knew she was right. I'd been caught with my hand in the cookie jar. All I could do was sit there quietly and weather the storm.

"I'm quite fond of you too, but as I see it, I've got three options. One. I can play the usual 'Oh-you-poor-man-your-wife-doesn't-understand-you' role and be your mistress. Two, I can tell you thanks, but no thanks. Bugger off. The third thing I can do is simply tell you the truth and hope for the best. Which would you prefer?" I mumbled something about the truth.

"The TRUTH is," she announced all too eagerly, "you are not really connected to this woman, BUT you are married to her. And the TRUTH is, although I am very attracted to you, I'm not mistress material . . . I've been down that road before. So please, wake up so we can both learn something from this, O.K.?"

My lips tightened, shoulders cringed, and my brain went into a tailspin; southern women *never* talked like this! I felt like I was with Pachili again. I wanted to disagree, but couldn't . . . afraid of what she might say next, while hoping for some relief.

"You see, it's like this . . ." she continued. Her voice felt like blows from a rubber hammer: soft, yet persistent. "When you are with your woman, her love surrounds you like a warm blanket. You feel secure. Loved. Other women are aware of this and feel attracted to you, but in a different way. They sense your love for that woman, your bond. And, unless they are neurotic, they can still love you and respect that bond.

"With you and Cheryl, I feel no bond. You are not connected. You don't have a woman, although you speak of one. This makes me sad because you are a powerful man who needs that balance. I am attracted to you sexually, but can do nothing about it. You don't allow me to love you with respect.

"I don't know where your wife is in all of this," she continued, "but until you get clear about your marriage, you will never get clear with me . . . or your life!"

"Now, wait a minute . . ." I snapped firmly, trying to stop this female juggernaut from igniting every emotional tender spot I had at once!

"Yes?" She cooed while staring me squarely in the eyes, waiting for a reply. I was suddenly speechless. Her words were raw truth. I knew it. She knew it. I had the same eerie feeling come over me as when I'm scared and have no place to hide. I felt naked. Vulnerable. And angry.

"I'd really rather not get into all that right now, if you don't mind . . ." I protested meekly, trying politely to stem the tide of my own anger and uneasiness. Ruth was no help.

"Certainly," she responded crisply, "And what would you rather talk about, the weather? O.K. I can do that. Nice weather we're having isn't it. I wonder if it's going to rain tomorrow. Or my eyes? Yes, I have lovely eyes. I got them from my father." She said, glaring at me with those large, penetrating eyes while batting her bold eyelashes.

"SHUT UP, DAMMIT!" I exploded as I threw down my napkin and stood up. "You have no right to cut into me like that! I just wanted to be friends with you . . . sorry if my stupid *heart* happens to get in the way!!" Feeling hurt and afraid, I launched into an obscene mini-tirade, incensed by what I considered her insensitivity and sarcasm.

"Forgive me. I was rather abrupt," mumbled Ruth, suddenly relinquishing the position she had captured during this last raid on my feelings. Her tone softened as she smiled, then held her hand out and gestured for me to sit down.

"Abrupt?! Lady, you blow my freaking mind, you know that?" The dining room became quiet, punctuated with a few whispers and stares. I looked around, embarrassed at my show of temper, then returned to my seat with a scowl.

"Anyway . . . You're right, dammit!" I confessed into the my plate of half-eaten lasagna, arms folded tightly across my chest. I suddenly lost my appetite.

She reached over and silently touched my arm. As she squeezed it, I felt somewhat reassured. Although I was waiting for her apology and confession, I never got one. She was too strong for that. I felt like a hurt child conniving to get his mother to change her mind . . . to love him. I also felt embarrassed that those buttons were still pushed so easily.

"It's the truth," I confessed, my eyes almost in tears, "I'm in love with you. But I'm having a hard time right now accepting that my marriage is over. I still love Cheryl." I tried to sound convincing, but somehow, I wasn't. "I just don't understand . . ."

I didn't want to cry. Not again. Not here! Yet I couldn't help it. Ruth just sat silently holding my shoulder as I dowsed the tears.

"What the heck. Tears and Italian food go well together, don't they!?" I blubbered, looking for comic relief. Ruth motioned the waiter to bring me another napkin. He arrived with several.

"Should I bring a mop to wipe up the wet floor?" asked the waiter earnestly. We both broke up laughing.

Tension dissolved, the rest of the meal went much easier. I finally told her about Pachili and other things I was reluctant to share before. She listened. She didn't even think I was crazy. We also shared funny stories. I told her about the time I almost set my neighborhood on fire. Ruth confessed her visits to Scotland as a child, hoping to find out what was underneath the kilts . . .

We stayed at the restaurant until closing time, then strolled for a block or two along the beach. I didn't want the night to end. It was very late, though, and I reluctantly caught us a cab to her hotel. I suddenly felt awkward again, but decided to let events unfold on their own. Pulling up to the Ramada, I told the driver to wait, and walked Ruth to her room.

"It's a little funny, isn't it," she said as we got off the elevator. "Here we are alone, together. I would make love to you, except that you're married." I took a deep breath, suddenly wanting to encourage her . . . then exhaled. I simultaneously felt pure excitement . . . and utter defeat.

"I'll hold that thought," I smiled as I kissed her hand gently, looked deeply into her sparkling eyes. "Will I ever see you again?"

"I wish you could," she said, "I've been talking with Dr. Jayawardene about some deal, and may come back to Sri Lanka next month." My heart sank when I realized I would be in America by then. I conveyed my regrets.

"I hope you will at least drop me a line; let me know how you're doing," I implored, slipping her one of my cards. We stood there looking at each other for another minute before I finally took her in my arms for one last embrace. And kiss. Her lips were the sweetest I had ever tasted.

I let go quickly, unable to handle the bittersweet moment for too long. Although her eyes begged me to stay, I forced myself to turn and leave - go back to the waiting cab. Each step towards the front door filled me with an aching desire to return to her room, embrace her in my arms, profess my love, and spend the night in blissful union.

Holding back the tears I let her go, knowing I may never see her again. Much as I desired Ruth, I also knew she was right; I had some things to work out first.

Chapter Thirty

The cab dropped me off at the entrance to my guest house. Because it was fairly late and I knew others were sleeping, I carefully closed the gate as walked quietly to my room.

Exhilarated as I felt this day with Ruth, I felt only emptiness upon entering my room. Stark loneliness. Sadness. She was right: my marriage was over and I didn't even know it. Worse, I couldn't even be with her. My sense of duty tormented me as I tried to convince myself it was all a dream: Things don't happen this fast! Settle down. Go home. Go back to work. Be happy. What did I *really* experience today anyway? Nothing! A temporary hot flash. Puppy love. Hormones! The rush of a new adventure. A wake-up call. I don't even *know* this person . . !

Feeling intense conflict, I screamed into my pillow for a while, hoping it would pass. It didn't; I couldn't even cry. Or feel. I resolved to lie still and take whatever was passing through me. I turned off the light and lay on my back. Slowly the sadness came. It was stronger than I had anticipated. It came in waves . . . tidal waves. Large swells of emotion rolled through my gut and into my chest and throat. I felt a deep sense of urgency as the waves rose in me. I had no idea where to turn . . . could do nothing but just feel it.

"Trust even when there is no reason to trust."

Was it, I wondered, part of the Zone experience? I still hadn't taken the second remedy. Whatever it was, all I could do was take Pachili's advice and trust. I lay there with eyes closed, watching . . . waiting. I anticipated the onslaught of something more terrible than I had experienced to date, but resolved to let it come.

Suddenly it hit.

I clutched my heart. My head felt like it was being ripped from my body; I thrashed around bed in a way that must have looked to an outside observer as a choreographed death scene. A tidal wave swept over me. I held my resolve. Let it come . . .

Horror - and an old woman's image - came to me as I reached for my pillow, afraid of waking the neighbors. I screamed until my chords felt they were bursting. My eyes widened and my throat swelled. My bladder emptied and my spine jerked and rolled with the force of someone being torn apart!

****

I awoke to a writhing in my stomach. It felt like a convulsion. Horrible, bitter. This was no love-sickness! I doubled up and screamed. I heard the voice of the old woman yelling something in Sinhala as a large man ran over to steady me on the edge of the bed. I felt a ripping in my bowels . . . a burning. They guided me over to a large bedpan. The stench of the massive stool made me vomit. Afterwards, I collapsed back onto the bed, feeling more relieve than I had felt in weeks.

****

I had no idea how long I passed out. The first wave had subsided. My *ku* was not too happy about losing Ruth, but there was something more. A thrashing in my body as if something were trying to escape . . . trying to find some other body more suitable to his liking. I felt a growl rising from deep within my throat. Dropping to the pillow again, I watched as the low, guttural sounds escaped in violent fashion, taking with them a fair amount of saliva . . . I was going again . . .

****

A candle flickered in the distance. No watch. No sense of time. When the flickering flame went out, I was plunged into total darkness. The only sounds I heard were my own breathing, heartbeat, and the brush of my hands on the stone floor. I struggled to the wall in search of a secure spot in which to curl up.

The fear arose more strongly as time went by: was I dying? Was this a tomb? Had they buried me alive?! A strong cow odor. It was not easy to get comfortable . . .

****

It was him! . . . The old man! As he approached, my heart spontaneously unfolded. I knew I was not one of his group of followers, but it didn't matter. He showered me with love: intense, unconditional and unremitting. I fell to my knees.

He stopped as I saw his sandals turn to face me, his white robe rustling softly. He paused then got to his knees in front of me. I looked up and saw those loving, fiery eyes . . . burning into my very being. I became transfixed. He leaned closer. Closer, until his forehead touched mine. I closed my eyes, thoughts spinning wildly . . .

****

I was pulled back . . . as if by a giant, invisible hand . . . I could not escape!

"Your intent to is to kill..."

The dagger came down. Bright red blood oozed from his deep wounds, quietly onto the dark marble floor . . .

****

The pain, visions, and nightmares came and went all night. As I struggled in vain to get some sleep, I watched helplessly as deep sobbing arose from within me, bursting to the surface in strange forms. Sometimes it came in deep sobs, sometimes jerks . . . and sometimes it forced its way through the pores in my skin! I felt as if fishhooks were being pulled out of me!

161

Mercifully, about four or five o'clock, I fell into a fitful slumber. When I awoke, the morning was still. I glanced over at the clock. It was ten . . . I overslept, but didn't care anymore. I fell back onto the bed and noticed I had no energy. No desire to get up or go anywhere. I felt nothing except exhaustion. Worse, I reeked with the odor of body fluids. The aura of toxic release permeated the room, as if I were coming off a week-long drunk.

Forcing myself awake, I rushed to the bathroom to take a shower. I scrubbed myself vigorously, hoping to wipe off the fury of the night. After bathing, I changed all the bed sheets, then lit some sage and carried it throughout the room to drive away my evil spirits.

The sage treatment hardly made a difference; I had to escape the room. I quickly grabbed some things, slammed the door behind me, and walked out into the common courtyard area. There I encountered a surprise sitting at a patio table: it was Jon. He was drinking tea, but quickly put it down when I ventured toward him to shake hands.

"I went to the clinic looking for you - again - this morning, but they said you weren't there," explained my friend. "So I came here . . . You're harder to see than the Pope these days!"

"Sorry, Jon . . . I haven't been myself lately."

"I was a little worried about you; tried to reach you for days. Your friend Ali told me you were here - I spoke to him as he left for work this morning."

"Ali?" I queried, experiencing a brief lapse of memory. Then it dawned on me. "Oh . . . you mean that short, nerdy - looking guy who works for an insurance company downtown," I shrugged, almost talking to myself. I barely knew him, except as a rabid collector of newspaper clippings . . . and gossip. He always walked with a tight shuffle reminiscent of one who had just been kicked in the crotch.

"He said you spent the day yesterday with some pretty lady, coming home late last night . . ." added my Norwegian friend.

"Boy, are some people nosy!" I sighed, shaking my head in mock anger.

162

"It's an island, my friend. Everybody here knows everybody's business. Besides, I heard no criticism from him. I suspect Ali's just reporting on your whereabouts . . . Anyway, you want to tell me about it? You look like something that got chewed up and spit out."

I muttered something about being sad, Ruth, and my conflict about marriage with Cheryl, but didn't go into detail. Sad and embarrassed, I was reluctant to rehash it all . . . didn't want to exert the energy it took to explain.

"I see you've had a rough evening, my friend. Did you sleep at all? You look drained . . . as if something has sapped the life out of you."

"Some," I shrugged, still uncomfortable talking.

"Would you rather be alone right now? My treatment can wait . . ."

"No, that's all right," I interrupted. "I don't want to go into a long session, but I'll be happy to adjust your neck."

"That would be marvelous, buddy," said Jon as he sat in the chair. I palpated his neck, looking for uneven muscle tone as I rotated vertebrae. I found two.

"This is the spot; Now drop your head," I instructed. Jon relaxed his head as I quickly reset a couple of spinal segments gently into place with a slight 'pop.'

"Fantastic!" exclaimed my willing patient, obviously buttering me up for something. "I don't know how you do it, Doc, but that move works every time!" Jon stood up, rotating his head and shoulders. I noticed I was feeling more energy just working on him.

"Now, Dr. Cannon, do you want to tell me your troubles willingly, or do I have to drag you to the pub to get answers out of you?" Jon had a way of disarming me. I laughed and confessed that I had been afraid of rehashing all my pain and embarrassment.

"Welcome to the human race!" added the big guy. "That's what friends are for!" I smiled broadly, then accepted his offer for a mid-morning snack.

Chapter Thirty-One

The food tasted like rubber. I could only nibble a few bites of bread and egg.

"Shakti!" commented Jon with the calm precision of a surgeon asking for an artery clamp. He had just finished hearing my confessions about Ruth.

"Did you feel tossed about all night? Ancient memories coming up?"

"Yes." I muttered, thinking it didn't take a Sherlock Holmes to figure that one out.

"This woman just gave you a blast of *shakti* energy. You're not in your body," explained my wide-awake companion. He seemed thrilled to share his wisdom.

"You said I was not in my body?!" I queried, "What . . . How did you figure *that* one out?"

"It's actually quite simple," added Jon, reminding me of a cocky professor I once had. "You told me about this *ku* - or subconscious - part. Remember?"

"Yes," I responded cautiously, wondering where he was taking me.

"And you consciously made decisions that went against what this *ku* was feeling, correct?"

"But, I didn't have much of a choice . . ."

"Aaaah , but you always have a choice," he nodded wisely, "You just refuse to acknowledge it!"

"So, what if that's true?" I said, nodding wearily.

"You feel empty, right? Void of feeling right now. Spaced out. Not quite together."

"Yes."

"Well, if things really are like this Pachili said, then maybe your *ku* took a hike. Left. Your feelings, memory, and emotions separated. Your *ku* . . . he mutinied!" Again, I affirmed half-heartedly. "Apparently our *ku,* by not being in the body, is subject to all kinds of bizarre experience.

"But . . . just a thought, that's all," he added. "After all, *you're* the doctor!" Maybe Jon had something. I *did* feel awfully strange, as if my *ku* had staged a bloody coup. Visited different dimensions. Feelings and sensations whirled about me. It was true; they were not connected.

"Let's go for a walk," I suggested, not knowing what else to do. "I have to clear the cobwebs." That said, I dragged myself out of the chair and headed for the door, curious on how to resolve my out-of-body dilemma. I turned to ask Jon to hurry up when I noticed him paying the bill. I felt slightly embarrassed at being so disconnected. Forgetful.

A cool breeze whipped up some sand on the beach as we headed north towards the nearest landmark - Mt. Lavinia Hotel. A dark storm cloud appeared to be heading westward from the interior to the ocean a few miles north of us. I watched the mass of dark clouds form above us as if someone were rolling out a mountain of moist, black mud. It was eerie.

"The thunder god is paying us a visit," I remarked to my Scandinavian friend.

"Ja, it appears," he countered, then walked with me in silence as if to allow my shifting moods some leeway. I remained stuck on the idea I might be out of the body. I had always thought out-of-body experiences were of the Hollywood kind: exotic, glamorous . . . looking down on everything, flying, going through tunnels, and the like. It never occurred to me that being shocked or hit with a bolt of *shakti* was a similar occurrence.

"You know, Jon . . ." I mused aloud, "I remember seeing something on TV some time ago about a lady in Mexico who healed people after major earthquakes. She did some sort of shamanic ritual and helped bring people's spirits back into their bodies . . ." As I rambled, Jon glanced at me from time to time. We continued walking, hands behind our backs.

"I wonder if the process she used could also cure my condition?"

"Mexico is a long way," replied my companion.

"I know, I know . . . I bet we can discover a way to do it. Will you help me?"

"I'll do what I can."

"Great!" I said, "You can start by helping me think. I seem to be stuck in no-man's land . . ."

"Let's head back to my place," spoke Jon as he took the cue and turned us around.

We made the half-mile jaunt to his apartment just in time. The moment we turned off the beach and headed down the last block to his house, the storm hit. This rain was the heaviest I had seen in several months on the island. The wind whipped along at with a fury of small typhoon. We ran.

"Come in and close the door, quick!" He ushered me in after beating me home in the foot race. I was glad to oblige. As I entered the warm confines of his modest apartment, I could hear the wind and rain pounding on the door behind us and the window screens rattling in their frames.

"Is this part of that shakti energy you were talking about?" I queried, half in jest. I could hear branches breaking outside, but figured we were safe here.

"Could be," he said while changing his shirt and offering me a replacement to my soaked cotton Nehru pullover. I accepted without comment, even though his University of Washington sweatshirt swallowed me as I put it on. I sat on the couch, still feeling lost. I recognized this feeling: the one Pachili constantly warned me about.

"Jon. Please help me . . ." I said in a whimper, gathering as much strength as I could before my *ku* dragged me unconscious into the Zone again. Jon said something about putting on the tea first.

"Your body is still shut down; almost dead, but coming back . . . be willing to enter the Zone; to stay awake. Conscious.

"Knowing . . . total acceptance of life and all its paradoxes . . . opposites . . ."

Ruth! She presented me with the strongest paradox I ever faced: an irresistible wave of fresh love crashing head to head with a sworn duty to my marriage. It felt like an impossible situation! A paradox I could not - or would not - resolve. I struggled . . . My *ku* would not return to a divided awareness!

"Close your eyes. Listen to my voice."

My eyes fell as the sound of my friend gently drifted into my waning consciousness. Although I knew he was not a healer, to me it didn't matter. His words seemed perfect for the moment; I hung onto them like a lifeboat to reality.

"Wherever it went, just ask your spirit to come back. No need to make any decisions now. No need to fight. Just wake up. Be aware. Be here. Accept whatever is . . . as it is."

Slowly. Almost imperceptibly, my inward fading stopped. I felt something come in from the top of my head, rushing through my body like warm water running over frozen body parts. Same as with Pachili . . . ! Eventually the fog melted away, as my eyes opened to a world of crisp colors and sounds. Jon was sitting across from me, eyes closed, steam rising from his cup of tea. I felt suddenly awake, and waited for him to open his eyes.

"I really felt that one!" exclaimed the big guy. "Are you here yet?"

"Yes, I'm back," I acknowledged, "Thanks to you . . . It was too simple. Just ask? That's all there was to it?"

"Did it work?"

"Seems to. I feel more alive - free of that dullness I kept slipping into. Apparently, my *ku* leaves quite often. I only notice it, though, when the shock is bigger . . . Jon, you're a genius!"

"I've had a good teacher, my friend."

His words were ironic. Whatever I taught him was passed on from Pachili. Where the old monk learned it, I couldn't say. Suddenly I could see the pattern: we were all casting seeds onto fertile ground. Some seeds sprouted; others waited for another season. Those that sprouted continued the re-seeding process . . .

I shook my head, realizing I was resorting to trite rationalizations to explain feelings of emerging bliss. Pachili's words gently drifted into my head:

"Be still . . . Come back slowly . . . be kind."

Chapter Thirty-Two

"Now what about this female energy?" I asked. Although familiar with *shakti,* my knowledge had thus far been academic.

"You had it last night."

"Had what?"

"Haven't you ever been in love before?" he asked blithely while reheating the tea kettle and warming some biscuits.

"Yes, of course."

"That's *shakti.*"

"That's all there is to it?" I mumbled incredulously as I squirmed to peak out over the collar of his overgrown sweatshirt to grab my cup of tea.

"Are you sure you have been in love?" asked my companion a second time. "I mean LOVE, where you can't sleep, you can't eat, your heart feels like it's going to crack open, and you nothing else in the world matters . . . ?"

"*Besides* what happened to me last night?" I asked stupidly.

"Yes. Besides that."

"Well, yes . . . I did have this thing once for my third cousin when I was thirteen; moaned and groaned for weeks; thought I was going to die."

"That's it!"

"What's it? Moaning and groaning?" I quizzed, playing with him.

"No, you bugger. The feeling that came before the groaning."

"Yeah? My parents called it puppy love and laughed at me."

"It's more than puppy love, friend. It is the spark of life that happens when two people get together under very special circumstances . . ."

"You mean, like, with me and Ruth?"

"Bingo."

"It was special, all right . . . but I'm a married man. I can't go around hopping on every woman I fall for!" I protested, still feeling the pressure of my duty to Cheryl.

"All the more reason for this *shakti* energy to be so strong. Do you think *shakti* cares whether or not you are married? Do you think it asks permission first?! That it cares about your petty concerns? Let me ask you," he continued, searching for an example, "did you sexually consummate the relationship with your cousin at age thirteen?

"No, of course not."

"Well, you're in the same situation here. Frustrated. In love. Impossible situation. *Shakti* is the feminine sexual energy. Both males and females have it . . . it starts at the base of the spine – Hindus call it the 'Root Chakra.' Then it either travels up the spine, is discharged . . . or both. Unlike when you were young, however, now you can at least understand it. When a person blasts you with his or her *shakti,* you can sit on it and die, or else use it to transform yourself, like in the basic principles of alchemy." I pondered where he was going with this. He continued.

"This happened to me. Didn't have sex for a year, then met this person who absolutely turned me on. We expressed love, but didn't consummate our relationship for weeks . . ."

"Then what happened?" I asked, anxious to see a way out of my dilemma.

"We made love."

"Then what?"

"Two days later? Nothing . . . except an easygoing friendship. That's the way it is. You can let it go, or it can drive you crazy. *Shakti* is peculiar like that. It comes and goes. Let it transform you; enjoy it while you can, and give it little thought."

I didn't know what to say. Parts of what he said made sense, but other parts sounded a little contrived.

"Either you make love to this woman, or use the energy some other way. It's your choice," he continued between bites of fresh biscuit. He appeared to be making love to his food.

"What choice did I have at age thirteen?" I protested.

"Didn't matter then," he shot back. "You were young. Even if you *did* have sex with your cousin at that age, there is so much *shakti* in youth that it wouldn't have mattered . . . except you were brainwashed by society and the church to think it was a great sin or something." Jon paused for a moment.

"Your body and mind needed that energy to transform you into an adult - to grow and evolve. Now? Apparently you need it for some other great change in your life. Something big is happening to you; otherwise, why would the energy be there?"

Jon sat back after putting the finishing touches on his philosophical masterpiece. Although I was more alert, I began to get irritated with my friend without knowing why.

"I confess I am going through a major change in my life, but it's also been more than three months since I've been with Cheryl. Is that what you're saying - that its a simple matter of mechanics? Biology?!" I grimaced, continuing to protest.

"Why not?" he countered, "Diet, exercise, and acupuncture all have basic laws, don't they? Look at it another way: *shakti* and *kundalini* are both energies . . . like electricity. There are volts, amps, and watts. If you add too much to a small appliance, don't you blow the appliance, blow the fuse, or both?"

I quietly stared at Jon; letting him know I was weary of this line of thought. His mind was getting more excited, while mine was settling. I appreciated his growing enthusiasm, but the ordeal of the previous night was catching up to me. Much as I wanted to hear him, I couldn't focus on Jon's words. The storm was abating outside, and I felt the effects of the change lulling me to sleep.

"May I rest for a while?" I asked him as my arm dropped limply to the couch. My eyes strained to open.

"Certainly, my friend," spoke Jon softly as he moved closer to where I was sitting. There was a long pause. I opened my eyes and saw him staring at me.

"I've got a confession of my own," he said hesitantly. I felt a slight chill rising from the base of my spine.

"What? What is it?" I inquired, rather concerned.

"Well," he continued, eyes downcast, "I was worried you won't like me anymore and . . ." I noticed a knot forming in the pit of my stomach. Whatever he had to say seemed serious to him. I decided to maintain my composure, no matter what the news.

"No, it's all right. Go ahead," I said as calmly as I could, sitting up. "What is it, for Chrissakes? Did you *murder* somebody?" There was another long pause.

"No, nothing like that . . . You know I'm in love with you."

"That's fine, buddy. I love you too," I said, trying to keep the knot in my stomach from exploding.

"You don't understand," he said, "I mean to say I want to make love to you!"

For the moment I was in shock. I made an effort to drink some tea, but there was no taste. Funny. The little things I notice; the cold, calm way I look at them at times like this: the curve in the teacup handle, the texture in the napkin. I thought it rather odd . . . I had no interest in him sexually, but had to admit there was an attraction. I'd received two emotional shocks in the space of twenty-four hours. I just remembered; I left my apartment and forgot my key. I was locked out . . .

"I mean, I don't want to pressure you or anything," said Jon, obviously trying to smooth things over, "but I think it would be a tremendous release of *shakti* for both of us . . ."

I tried to speak, but the words stuck in my throat. I wanted to tell him I felt betrayed, deceived, tricked, and taken advantage of. I wanted to tell him I felt hurt; that I didn't want a lover. I just needed a friend. I wanted to say how *stupid* he made me feel for not revealing his motives before now.

I also wanted to embrace him and say I still loved him as a friend . . . still needed his gentleness, his wisdom. I wanted to tell him it didn't matter that he was gay. Or bisexual. Or whatever the hell he was. I wanted to ask him what it was like . . . how was I attractive to him? Did I have *that* much to learn? Was *this* part of enlightenment? Was I missing something? I could barely fathom the idea. Did I find him sexually attractive and not know it . . ?

Suddenly, Pachili's words echoed in the back of my mind like some timely advice from an old high school teacher:

"Death. Sex. You try to hide it . . . will run up against it over and over again until you have enough. Let it go. Forgive."

I put the tea cup down, staring into the coffee table.

"I . . . don't know what to say," I mused.

"I see," responded the big guy. We both sat silently. My eyes were glued to the tea cup; his nervously darted around the room as he rocked back and forth in his easy chair. My *ku* was gone again. I felt void of any life at all, but strangely at peace.

"Give me a minute," I said, then closed my eyes.

"Take as long as you like, friend." Suddenly the word *friend* grated on my nerves. I chose to let it slide; to forgive. I sat, eyes closed, trying to bring awareness back into my body.

Another minute or so passed . . . I don't know. Time seemed to take a holiday. I sat there, feeling more empty than I ever felt before . . . wondering if it was worth it . . . worth coming back at all. I felt like I was dying.

Was there *anything* or any*one* I lived for? I wondered. If so, I had to somehow find a way to straighten out my life. Wasn't life itself a miracle? Even if I felt none of it this moment? But whom could I *trust* anymore? Mimi? She was dead. My mother? Yes. Cheryl? Ruth? Pachili? Maybe. Dr. Alfred? My father? Jon . . ? You must be kidding.

The last thought did it. I came back . . . angry.

"Damn it!" I shouted, bursting out into tears. "Why'd ya have to go and *screw up everything,* Jon?!"

"Sorry, I . . ."

"Don't give me that . . !" I let go a volley of expletives and threw my teacup against the wall. Porcelain and tea splattered in all directions. "Why? You could have told me *weeks* ago, you stupid bastard! Why *now??!*" Jon opened his mouth, starting to speak, but froze.

"You want me to release *shakti* with you??" I bellowed as if possessed. *"I'll* release some *f--king Shakti!!"* Big as he was,

175

the Norwegian was no match for my rage at that moment. I felt powerful . . . in control . . . *possessed!* I knew I had to get out of his house before I did some real damage. Was this *forgiveness?* I was capable of . . . murder!

In my moment of realization, the energy shifted. Jon - sensing it - took control.

"Stop!" he commanded, holding his large fists as if ready to knock my lights out. "Drop it, buddy, or else you won't be leaving here standing up!"

We had tangled before - playing around of course - after a few beers. This time, however, he wasn't kidding. I knew it was over. Whatever had taken possession of me had gone. I dropped my arms to my side and plunged back onto the couch like a sack of old melons. I covered my face and sobbed gently. I could tell Jon wanted to comfort me, but respectfully held his distance.

"I couldn't live with a lie, Matthew," he said, "I'm sorry if I wasn't honest . . . if I hurt you. Please forgive me." I knew he was sincere, and tried to speak after clearing my throat and wiping away some tears.

"I do," I said at last, "Forgive me too . . . as you can tell, I'm not used to these situations." Jon smiled and held up his hand in a gesture of peace.

"You can still call me a friend, you know. I won't try anything. Promise."

"Thanks. I needed to hear that," I sighed, growing weary of this whole series of events. I told him I felt very tired and needed to sleep.

"You're welcome to stay," he said, then asked if I preferred the bedroom to the couch. I agreed. "I may leave here myself . . . I'm feeling rather sad - you know what I mean. I may be gone for a few days."

I had no comment, but offered him a respectful salute. I really did love the guy . . . but not *that* way. I also felt distant. Cold. Was this my killer? Suddenly I felt a kinship with Ruth.

"We both socked it to 'em, didn't we, old gal!" I muttered snippily to myself as I staggered, eyes half-closed, into Jon's small back room. As I fell on it, I noticed the bed was hard, but inviting.

I was soon fast asleep.

Chapter Thirty-Three

"Sweetheart, I'm home!" I yelled into the darkened hallway. Our cat jumped from the top of the refrigerator and scrambled wildly out the open front door. My wife's car was here, but no lights were on. She's probably asleep, that lazy thing . . . I flipped on the living room light.

"Are you here? I've got some more medicine for you!" My voice just echoed in the silent eeriness as I edged towards the bedroom. Something was not right. I was hoping this new medicine would help Paula pull out of her latest depression. I saw her shadow on the bed and flipped on the light . . .

She was asleep. No . . . red ink all over the bed. . . She wasn't moving . . . breathing . . . gun on the floor . . . .
gggggggnnnnnnnnnNOOOOOOOOO!!!

****

I sat up, dripping with cold sweat and an aching, pounding headache . . . in the middle of another nightmare. It was dark; my watch said 2:30 a.m. on December 6th. Why was I living this all over again? Paula is dead! Why was my *ku* tormenting me with these memories? These *damn headaches?!*

Much as I tried to distract myself, the gory dream images persisted: Paula's once beautiful body sprawled fitfully across the fully made bed, soaked in blood from a gunshot wound to the head. But *why* did I sit there and study that macabre scene as if I were an art student of looking at a still life? What sickness dwelled within me that kept rehashing this over and over again?! I thought the nightmares had stopped years ago! Not so. Now they were back, stronger and more vivid than ever!

I groaned as I rubbed my eyes, then got out of bed to wash my face. Flipping on Jon's bathroom light, I ran some water into my cupped hands and spread it gently over my forehead, eyes, nose, mouth, and chin. Suddenly I stopped, captured by the look in my eyes. *Those* eyes! I studied them in the mirror, going deeper and deeper, even as his voice danced through my head:

"You are a killer . . . Sex and death. Let it go."

"Willing to be here?

Reluctantly breaking contact with the mirror image, I returned to the bed, not sure if I should go back to sleep, leave and go home . . . or take notes. I chose the latter, but remembered I had not brought my diary. Looking around in the dim light for some paper, I spotted a pad and pen on Jon's desk. Grasping the implements in my awkward hands I settled back on the bed, turned on the light, and began to write. As if taking dictation, words poured into my aching head . . . crisp as a morning snowfall:

"You live in paradox and deny it . . .."

"Chi will show itself to you . . . be awake!"

"Until you can trust . . . receive . . existence cannot give."

"There is no one . . ."

I wrote furiously as the thought-voices layered themselves in my conscious mind. Feeling an incredible rush of energy, I became aware of my personal passion play . . . the *Gestalt* of what was happening to me! All the agonizing pain, indecision, fear, and painful memories magically diminished as I pursued my task.

It seemed so simple! Be conscious. Awake. Make decisions . . . No! Allow possibilities to *come* . . . and trust. By *allowing* the possibility to be here - no matter what happened - I retained my power and connection with *Chi!*

I suddenly understood. *Intent* was clear: embrace *Chi* . . . *knowing.* My headaches had been a tool to get me to this point! I had to enter the Zone . . . whatever that meant. No more fighting it. For the first time in my adult life, I felt single-minded. Calm. Fully resolved. I had nothing else to lose.

But, how to begin this unknown journey . . . this suicide mission? As I sat silently in meditation, *knowing* hung in the air like some tangible mist, urging me to leave. I figured the details would come when needed.

Memories flashed before my eyes like a million sparkles of light, beaming into my head and unfolding patterns so vivid as to be unmistakable. There was something deep within me, something *immortal.* There was also the seed - the killer. I would trust, face him, and survive. I would not back down . . . and I would change. Lose myself perhaps. I would never be the same again.

As these thoughts flashed before me, I stopped writing and, for some mysterious reason, jumped out of bed. As I stood there, still wearing Jon's big sweat shirt over my pants, I felt a slight crinkling in my left pocket and dug to retrieve the small envelope inside. It was the remedy . . .

The *remedy!!?* I had almost forgotten I put it there over three days ago - "just in case" I'd thought. *Intent* had prepared me for this day!

"Ku . . . takes care of the details. Perfectly."

"The <u>real</u> second remedy will take you into the Zone . . when you are ready."

Ready . . . ? I felt a sudden wave of fear crashing over my head. I made more notes on the paper:

"Trust, even when faced with danger. Trust even when there is no reason to trust.

"The seed remains. Your deepest killer remains. It will grow again. You will experience pain and torment . . . days, weeks or months. Maybe years.

"Enter the Zone completely. Trust. Witness. Transcend the killer."

Tears came to my eyes. Trust. Without it, my life would only be as Pachili indicated - "a snail leaving slime marks." I stopped writing, put the pen down, and went to Jon's kitchen, flipping on the light. I was suddenly thirsty. Finding a glass, I poured half a glass out of his bottled supply. I found his note:

> Sorry I bummed you out. I never meant to. I've gone
> away for a few days. Can we have lunch together
> when I get back? Maybe next week? Take care. -
> Jon.

I scribbled "O.K.- I'll call when I get back" on the bottom, then left it on the table. Somehow, my relationship with Jon had become a distant priority. My marriage was on the rocks. I was thousands of miles from home. Even Ruth was fading from my consciousness. I had nothing else to lose No reason to even be alive, except to follow the mystery laid out before me.

My whole focus now was the remedy. As I held the packet before me, I paused, savoring the intensity of the moment. I knew however, if I hesitated too long, I would never take it. Three gulps took care of my thirst. I put the remedy under my tongue. It dissolved slowly.

Time stopped while I waited . . . expecting strange things to pop out of the walls. They didn't; nothing happened. No lightning bolts. Nothing. If anything, I felt calmer, almost bored. Maybe Pachili was just testing me again. Maybe he was just trying to scare me. Most likely, however, this remedy - like most others - took time to kick in.

It was 3:15 A.M. and I was fully awake. I had slept only six hours, but felt supercharged. I wanted to move, to exercise. It occurred to me to return to my room, but I still didn't have the

182

key. Dr. Goonilike would *not* appreciate being awakened at this hour. The night obviously had something else in store for me.

I needed to take a long walk . . . or run. Because I hadn't run in weeks, I was beginning to miss my old routine. I ran some in the beginning, but Sri Lanka was just too damn hot! Maybe nighttime running was better. Much cooler.

I went to gather my few belongings: a slightly damp shirt, some change, and my watch. I exchanged shirts, figuring the old one would dry faster on my body. While pulling the sweatshirt over my head, I noticed the old crow-wound was throbbing slightly . . . the first I'd noticed it in several days.

I went to the back room, tore out the notes I scribbled, thrust them into my pockets, and ran out of Jon's empty apartment into the night.

SECTION III: THE WORLD OF SPIRITS

Chapter Thirty-Four

I ran for miles on the beach without knowing my destination. Somehow, it didn't seem to matter; I knew I was headed in the right direction: further south. Between strides I glanced to the eastern sky and saw the moon hanging over the trees. Full and brilliant, it tossed soft, golden rays over the ocean. I stopped to take in the glorious sight.

"Poya Day!" I exclaimed to myself, remembering the Sinhalese full moon holiday. It then occurred to me why most of the shops looked closed earlier on Saturday. Pachili's words again echoed in my consciousness:

"Much to teach us on nights of the Full Moon."

Although the cluster headache appeared gone, the back of my head still pulsed with a methodical rhythm, the memory of the crow attack. I was curious: someone - or some*thing* - was trying to communicate with me! I slowed my run to a soft trot and waited for the next thought.

I heard a commotion. Up ahead I could see a large fire, torches and flashlights. Getting closer I observed a group of perhaps fifteen people in a wooded clearing, engaged in what appeared to be some ritual dance or festivities. Curious. It was very late at night - or early, almost 4 a.m. - and I seldom saw anyone outside, even during the regular night hours. Curfew had been the rule since the Sinhalese riots a couple of months ago.

I sat on the beach at the edge of the woods behind some fallen trees and observed the action. The crowd consisted of all males, most in their twenties and dressed in the traditional sarong. In the center was a dancer wearing a noticeably gruesome devil mask. I strained to get closer to see what he was doing . . . closer . . . closer . . .

I caught glimpses of him through the crowd. He appeared to be twirling and stomping in circles. Chanting. I began to feel sensations as I watched - something tingling in the back of my spine - rising to the back of my neck and skull. The pain in my head increased . . .

Fear clutched my heart.

As if struck by a bullet, I felt the pain of something grab the back of my neck. Instinctively, my arms reached back to ward off the attacker. I felt nothing, flailing at empty air. But *something* - it felt like a metallic band drawing tighter and tighter - cut off my circulation! . . .

I awoke to noise and darkness.

Whatever grabbed me had gone, but something had tightened over my eyes . . . and my hands were behind me, tied by some fiber cord. I was in the back of what I sensed was a slow-moving, horse-drawn cart. From the sounds, I deduced a smaller crowd - maybe six or so - and could barely make out some torch light against the forested background. I heard no sound of waves. They were taking me somewhere towards the interior . . . !

The fear grew stronger. For the first time in my life, I felt totally lost. I had no frame of reference. My thoughts raced and my heart beat with the fury of a doomed man:

"Every time you pass fear, a kind of death happens . . . crossing points of consciousness . . . the Zone.

So *this* was the Zone . . . or was it just a stupid mistake on my part? A late-night jog turned sour? Why didn't I go home when I had the chance? Why did I take that remedy? Why did I run this way alone? What did these people want from me? Were they even *real??* Or was this another phantom scene staged by my *ku?* Suddenly, I didn't want to die.

"Stop!" I commanded my *ku,* whose fear was compounding the trouble . . . trying again to leave.

186

Remembering the exercise with Jon, I asked it to return to the body . . .

I took a deep breath and waited. The fear was still there, but also a feeling of surprising calm. There was, I reasoned, obviously nothing I could do at the moment. *Chi* would not have brought me this far just to kill me! . . . or would it?

"Let go of meaning . . . all experience a meditation."

Explanations would have to wait. Still, doubt crept in, as I struggled for my conscious mind to take the reins of my heart.

"You want to know intent? Look around you. There is much noise . . . trying to wake you up!"

I focused on staying centered . . . and *here*. The awful buffeting of the dirt road and a strong aroma of curry reminded me I was not in Georgia any more!

After what seemed like an eternity, the cart stopped. The talking did not. Although I was able to make out a few Sinhalese phrases, the bulk of the group's language was of a dialect I found indecipherable. I figured I was among Tamils.

"Namaste," I said aloud, hoping for a second miracle. I felt a dull blow across my temple, falling out of the cart onto the dusty ground. The awful pain seared through my body as I realized - this time - my luck may have run out.

Someone pulled my head back by the hair and yelled something in my ear I didn't understand. Others yelled. I was alone, hurting, and bound like a sheep for the slaughter among an angry crowd. My heart beat as if it were coming out of my chest. I spit out some dirt.

I felt a blow to the head. Another kicked me in the stomach and I gasped for breath. Visions of my mother passed through my mind, as I wished for nothing else but to see her again . . . I REMEMBERED . . . but felt helpless to change the script. *I had been here before . . !*

I sobbed as someone ripped off my blind fold. Finally I could see the faces of my tormentors. I remembered them from my vision: young natives . . . maybe Tamils. They appeared

187

wild-eyed . . . crazed. Their eyes glared with a kind of hate I had seldom witnessed. Their bodies seemed almost animal . . . muscles glistening in the torch light. One of them - apparently the leader - held a knife and came closer. I froze . . .

Then relaxed. I knew what was coming, and resolved to die quickly and easily. No anger. No remorse. Maybe this time I got it right . . . maybe I learned something. Time moved as in slow motion. I found myself again with Pachili. His little cabin. His voice guiding me through my first fears. They all seemed so childish compared to my current dilemma. Or would I wake up again? No. This time it was not a dream. I *knew* . . .

Pachili! I still felt his presence. I would not die alone . . . But suddenly the presence faded and disappeared!

"The Zone is more potent . . . I will not be there."

The man's knife plunged into my left leg. I cried out as he pulled the blade out as if to examine the blood. A fierce pain rippled up my thigh, through my solar plexus, and into my brain. This time the feeling intensified because of my desperation. My God! They going to eat me!! I started to jump out of my body, straining at the tether held by my soul. "Be here!" I commanded myself . . .

"OH MY GOD . . . *NO!"*

"NO!!" I screamed, hauling my conscious mind back in. *I will be here, BY GOD* until I was through with this body. Suddenly I jumped out of my body, watching the wretched being strain himself violently against his tethers, lost in mortal fear and anger. I watched as I cried out:

"YOU STUPID SONS A BITCHES! YOU HAVE <u>NO RIGHT</u> TO DO THIS!!" I screamed, as blood continued to stream from the open wound in my leg. Suddenly, the talking stopped. I watched, both in and out of the body. One of them approached me closely, whispering in my ear . . .

"Yes. We have the right. You gave it to us."

I felt it strange hearing English . . . for no particular reason, I looked at the sky. There was a hint of daylight. I heard the sound of a crow and knew the dawn was near. Then, all became blurry . . . I watched my body go limp. I passed out.

"Hold your intent until Chi is complete. This can take one second . . . or lifetimes."

Pachili. The presence was there, but distant. For some inexplicable reason, I was awake. No more sound or sight. No pain. Yet, I was awake.

"The killer. . . you will be a slave until you fully accept it . . . Just watch. All will mirror intent completely."

I remained calm and awake. Perhaps this was the death I sought. No movement. The thought came through, like a beacon through the fog . . .

"Will becomes truly free in the Zone . . . No rules except Chi . . . Fantastic things . . . you question your sanity."

Nothing else came. What to think? Who is doing the thinking? I just have to feel . . . Open my eyes . . . Open. I'm in a softly lit room, looking up at the blue ceiling. I could hear my mother's voice approaching, talking to another person. I strained to hear, but cannot move. I'm too small. I see the form of a woman above me. Mimi.

"Why, you're awake, sweety-pie!" I could feel my grandmother's hand gently caress my forehead as her voice rolled across my body like a warm massage.

"My precious little boy!" said Mimi, as she leaned over the table to see if I was awake. I cooed as I looked into her eyes. It was Mimi, but somehow the eyes were flat . . . something was wrong with this picture!

"You cannot see me. You see only your mother. Your father. Your grandmother. Intent is lost . . . Wake up!"

189

An illusion! Fear arose in me, then subsided as the image of Mimi disappeared. I fell into a flatness, a twilight, surrounded by a pale nothingness that stretched out forever.

This time I was lost for good!! Unable to get out, this twilight world of magpies and monsters would torment me forever!

"You have the option to go crazy . . . or not."

Stop. Look around. Flat. Was this death? Everything was a blank slate. I would write my own story. But what to write? For whom . . . ?"
"Pachili!" came the answer. Felt nothing except a still, soft presence . . . at a distance.

"You can come to me if intent is strong."

A gentle thought . . . a faint desire arose within me for the truth. I asked for the truth. No change. I pressed the thought, harder and more deliberately than before. Finally, I SCREAMED it . . . as if to pierce the veil that kept me bound in an endless twilight.

"Be awake, you stupid pig!"

I felt a finger pressure between my nose and upper lip. Suddenly, my head swirled and my body twitched. I snapped into the body along an elastic chord that quickly diffused into a deep breath. My chest heaved outward as air filled the lungs.

Chapter Thirty-Five

Eyes still closed, I moved instinctively to feel my left leg. Surprised I was no longer bound, I felt the torn tissue and matted scar and knew my body was intact. Yet uncertain about opening my eyes, however, I resolved to accept whatever happened; to release the fear.

When I no longer felt afraid, I cracked one eye, then another. My body shivered as I lay on the ground under a thin blanket. It appeared to be early morning as I lay by myself next to the dying embers of a campfire. Lifting my head slightly, I looked around. I was in a clearing surrounded by dense forest on all sides. There was a path to my right that led into the thickness. I could hear the revel of crickets and night beasts dying out, replaced by sounds of morning wind through the trees, bird songs . . . and crows.

I was alone. Bruised, and hurt, but alone. I lay there and continued my mental survey of body parts and systems. My leg felt cut, but no longer bleeding. A sharp pain in my left temple now accompanied the recurring pain in the back of my head. My stomach and back hurt, my neck was killing me, my chest felt tight, and my arms and legs felt cold as ice.

And . . . I was alive!

Then again, maybe I *did* die. Maybe this was just the stopover place. Maybe the place they were taking me was too full! How crass, I thought, to leave me unattended. I might escape! Ha!

I mustered as much of a laugh as I could, then tried to sit up. Pain shot through my neck, back and leg. I lay back down, taking rapid, shallow breaths and wondering what to do with myself. The thought occurred to me to wait - that I would be O.K. I lay there, taking in a view of the life around me. I never really thought I would see it again. I felt blessed.

I heard a sound through the underbrush, but quickly discarded the thought to run and hide. I couldn't even move! Perhaps my momentary rebirth would end - cut short by the return of my attackers.

Out of the path on the edge of the clearing emerged four young men. They appeared to be the same ones who attacked me the night before, but I wasn't sure. I detected no sign of violence or craziness in them. Apprehensive, I watched as the individuals walked straight toward me, carrying what appeared to be a banana-leaf and bamboo stretcher. They looked tame enough, at least for now. For reassurance, however, I held open the palms of my hands and asked, "O.K.?"

There was no response from any of them. No hint. No smile. I thought to myself: I'm either O.K., or doomed. Either way, there's not much I can do about it now! More curious than scared, I relaxed as they rolled me onto the stretcher and hoisted me to their sides, sliding into the opening in the forest.

My caretakers carried me for about a mile, maintaining their silent expressions. I watched as the forest unfolded around me. We were on a footpath, barely wide enough to accommodate the width of our silent procession. Because all things were strange on this adventure, I dropped all worries. I didn't even fret about our destination. As I lay on the stretcher, gently bouncing to the rhythm of my carriers, I felt detached and centered.

I had learned to harness something. My *ku* was no longer the unruly child of my past. No longer throwing out useless doubts, my mind fell silent . . . simply observing the path, the motion, the faces of my attendants . . . the trees, the birds . . .

The sky. It was unfolding and I realized we were coming to a clearing. I could see the mountains in the distance as the path opened into an area of rolling hills, dotted by bushes and small trees of every description. The path proceeded on an incline, as my carriers made every effort to see I didn't fall out of my makeshift bed.

We soon reached a plateau. I could see almost to the ocean; I detected what appeared to be several sailing ships anchored offshore. Before I could speculate, my hosts placed my stretcher next to a clump of bushes and ran off.

As I lay there wounded, staring at the morning sky, I regarded the whole scene as too strange to forget. But, how was I going to tell others what happened? I could muster no thought on the matter. My fate was still tenuous.

Suddenly, I heard shots in the distance. These were not ordinary rifle shots. They sounded dull, like old single-fire shotguns . . . or musket fire! I made an effort to raise my injured body above the bushes to get a better look.

Barely managing, I was able to catch a glance at what appeared to be a battle going on in the distance. I saw what looked like native peoples being gunned down by soldiers dressed in 18th-century armor and helmets! The soldiers carried muskets and bayonets and, although fewer in number, vastly outgunned the simple weapons of the natives. Either they were filming a movie here . . . or something was radically wrong with my senses!

I collapsed onto the stretcher, exhausted from those few minutes of watching the contest below. A short time later, I again heard footsteps; my so-called friends had returned. I noticed there were now only three of them. The shooting had stopped. Before I could say anything, they roughly jerked my bed into the air and trotted further down the path. I winced in agony. The swelling in my leg was getting worse.

We traveled for miles. How many I couldn't tell. My hosts seemed tireless, even with a heavy load. This impressed me. None of them were over five-foot, six, or carried an ounce of fat on their bodies.

Eventually, I observed the mouth of a cave. My handlers carried me straight for it. As we got closer, I was able to see more details . . . the mouth of the cave stood there, surrounded by ancient stone carvings of the Buddha and other deities I didn't recognize. Once at the entrance, they set me down, made some kind of offering to an altar, mumbled something in Tamil - or whatever language they spoke - and bowed for several minutes. When they finished their ritual, my captors again hoisted my bamboo stretcher to their sides.

As they roughly lifted me again, I cried out with pain. My leg, still throbbing from the stab wound, had swollen to about twice its original size. Suddenly, a hand reached over my face and I smelled a strong, pungent odor - one that forced its way up my nostrils and into my head. Soon I felt a calmness . . . and a fatigue. Stay awake! I can't . . . I just drifted into a twilight space of no pain. So far I was groggy, but not totally out of it.

Light turned to what appeared to be total darkness as we entered the cave. My hosts, obviously familiar with the interior despite the blackness, carried me through a very long, narrow passageway. I don't know how long. I couldn't remember much of what transpired, or even how long we it had been.

Eventually, we came to some kind of open space. Although the blackness was almost suffocating, I could tell by the larger echoes that we entered a large cavern, or cave room. I then saw a faint light . . . and traced it to a candle. It was at the far end, on top of a ledge near the ceiling.

Without saying a word, the four men set me down in the center of the room and returned through the long, dark corridor from whence they came. I was alone again, and my thoughts returned. Why was I here? Was this some sort of hospital? Were they preparing me for something?

After several more minutes, the candle flickered, indicating that a large door had closed somewhere. I was *really* alone now, and set about the task of finding my bearings.

Chapter Thirty-Six

My eyes eventually grew accustomed to the pervasive darkness. The light of the small candle slowly revealed a view of my surroundings. I was lying in the middle of a circular chamber about eighteen feet high and thirty or forty feet in diameter.

Every inch of the walls and ceiling appeared covered with something: intricate inlaid carvings and glossy oil paintings showing the Buddha and others in unusual poses. Of particular interest to me were deities and their consorts, either in scenes of lovemaking or engaged in battle.

I had seen cave temples before, but this one portrayed a kind of stark reality I had never seen in the others. Strange Buddha poses? Lovemaking? Depictions of fierce battles? *Theravadin,* the branch of Buddhism most common in Sri Lanka, had no place for such ideas. Unlike Tibetan Buddhism, it's northern cousin, conservatism was the rule.

Everywhere in Sri Lanka, temples were very simple and conservative. The only place I was aware of similar erotica was on the walls of Hindu temples in India . . . or in the ancient Ceylon mountain city of *Sigyria. Kasyapa,* the city's founder in about 500 AD, was the only ruler in Sri Lanka's long history to embrace *Mahayana*, or Tibetan-style Buddhism.

"The Buddha never denied himself anything . . ."

But, I thought, why was I rehashing ancient history? How or why did I even *remember* all this? Was my mind so useless now it needed something to do, as Pachili said? Thoughts of exotic history were nice, but I soon grew weary of waiting.

The awful, throbbing pain in my leg reminded me that I could still be in mortal danger, most likely from infection. Looking for more clues, I attempted to raise myself off the bamboo-leaf palate. After a great effort, I was able to prop myself up on two elbows and look around. The candlelight flickered again, no doubt from my movements.

Then it occurred to me: they were holding me for ransom! The only glitch to that idea was that no one knew who I was or where I came from. I wasn't carrying any ID or passport when captured, and no one asked. They seemed too eager to rip me up.

The ordeal was not over yet. My assailants might just be waiting for an interpreter . . . or someone who would extract information to give to the American Embassy. I didn't feel safe with the idea of going without medical attention for more than a day. Infection from these jungles was setting into my wounds, and I would be a goner no matter who paid up, if any!

I measured time by the candle. My watch, ripped from me during the struggle, was miles away. By the time the flickering flame went out - five hours by my estimation - I was plunged into total darkness. The only sounds I heard were my own heartbeat and the brush of my hands on the stone floor as I struggled to the wall to find a secure spot in which to curl up.

My emotions welled up as in a well-rehearsed play, the memory of future events. The fear came back: thoughts that my so-called friends left me here to die. Or was I even in a temple? There were no bones, coffins, or other evidence of a tomb . . . then again, maybe I was their first victim! Whatever, I resolved to wait it out, happy to still have the thin blanket despite its strong cow odor. It wasn't easy getting comfortable. In the total darkness, however, I tried to get some sleep . . .

Dark. Still. No sound at all. My thoughts came, pounding like a sledge hammer against the side of my skull. My breathing appeared much louder in the absence of other stimuli. Dreams came. I drifted in this isolation for what seemed like an eternity . . . then awoke to a hissing sound! Was this still a dream? Maybe, but it wasn't over. Maybe it would *never* be over . . !

"You will experience pain. It may take weeks . . . maybe years . . .

"You want to know intent? Look around . . . the world dances to your song."

There was a soft, dull light permeating the room; enough to illuminate the fact there were now other candles in the room, all lined up against the wall. Some matches lay at my feet. I rushed to light one.

In the flashing blaze of light, I cringed . . . a large cobra! Not more than ten feet away! My heart jumped into my throat and I froze. The reptile also froze, displaying the characteristic fanning of his neck. I stared at him for what seemed like an eternity . . . neither of us making the first move.

Suddenly he struck . . . My right leg recoiled in sharp pain.

"My God!" I cried out. The serpent continued striking me: my arms, my shoulder, my legs . . . I endured the needle jabs for what seemed like ages. Fear and venom coursed through my veins. It was like a scene out of a Stephen King novel. I knew I was a dead man . . .

I felt numb. I knew I had absorbed enough venom to drop an elephant, and resolved to drift away quietly. As I spread my mangled body on the stone floor, the blackness returned. Silence. Ageless. Timeless. Only one desire . . .

Pachili.

Chapter Thirty-Seven

The master sat before me in what appeared to be a soft lavender room, edged with rich golden embroidery and satin curtains partly covering a window to a garden terrace. Pachili looked as much at home in this environment as he did at his small hovel.

"Why do you suffer so much?" he asked, shrugging his shoulders. "Why can you not let go?" Although I had no mind and no frame of reference, the question seemed somehow appropriate. I mumbled something about his insensitivity . . . feeling I didn't have much of a choice in the matter!

"Oh, you've quite a bit of choice, you idiot," he emphasized in his unique vernacular. "Drop the suffering. Don't you know you can change *intent?*"

"I wasn't even aware my *intent* was to suffer."

"To suffer for your so-called enlightenment," he said. Wake up!"

I squirmed slightly, feeling suddenly awkward. How was I supposed to wake up when I never knew which scene was real and which was the dream?!

"It's *all* a dream!" said Pachili, answering my thoughts. So much for so-called reality. "From the moment we are born, we begin to die," he continued, "Your *intent* can take you *beyond* death . . . beyond suffering. Or *intent* can kill you slowly, painfully. Focus on *knowing*. This is your only task."

"But," I queried, "How will I know when I'm on the right track?"

"Take nothing seriously . . . even enlightenment."

With that, he picked himself up and headed for the door. I tried to follow him, and found I couldn't move.

"When you're ready to follow, change intent."

Another minute saw Pachili out the door. Feeling helpless and confused, I watched him circle around behind the garden and head for the floral-laden hills behind it. A light breeze pushed the satin curtains aside as everything went blank for a moment. Another dream came. My little boy's body felt stuck . . . wooden bars blocked my access to Mommy. All I could do was watch . . .

I was hungry. Thirsty. Couldn't move out of this crib. Lonely and scared, I waited for my salvation. It never came. Intense fear overwhelmed me as I beat my head against the bars, rolled around, and screamed. Tears later, Mommy came. Food at last . . .

Falling . . . pain. Hurt my arm. Broken. Screams. Cries later. Attention came. Mommy and Daddy no longer angry. Love. Food. Attention . . .

****

I sat up in bed, sweating. My god, what a dream! I was swimming in terror. I waited for someone to save me from this terrible nightmare that crept into my waking consciousness. I looked around and prayed for someone . . . anyone to extricate me from the evil shadows that lurked behind each piece of furniture in my room . . . It was my old room on Fernwood Avenue! Jesus came in and sat at the foot of my bed. He stuck his hand in the air to give me blessing, then disappeared . . .

I floated in the blackness without end. Aware that consciousness remained, I sought to bring it to a place of peace. I waited.

****

The fire started small - at the end of the room - then spread. Someone had poured kerosene on the floor of the dark temple and lit it. They intended to burn me now, thinking I was dead. Just as well. I was nearly dead . . . Come on. Do your worst.

"Life can be a dangerous game. You get used to it."

I waited for the flames and smoke to engulf me. They did not. I gagged from the smoke as the fire went out and blackness returned. My breathing had grown more and more shallow as my body seemed to slip away into eternal numbness. Welcoming death as a friend, I felt a warmth of spirit I had not known before. I gave thanks for the numbness, silence and darkness. In the timelessness, I forgave all those who ever angered me, and asked for forgiveness from everyone else. I was at peace.

Suffer? Pachilli's words struck me as peculiar in this space. Yes, I had chosen to suffer. But now that death was here, I released that decision. No need for it anymore. Go quietly, I said to myself, smiling inside. Slip into a place of no pain. No pleasure. No drama. No attachment to anything . . . no suffering.

****

I left the body and almost floated through the temple and down the now softly lit corridor. Coming to the mouth of the cave, I could see in all directions. A thousand souls lined the hills of my view, as I felt a love that flowed freely among us. The brilliance of light permeated my body as I soaked peacefully in the bliss of the moment.

A thought. Pachili was nearby. I began to fly. Higher . . . as if attached to a large balloon. There, not more than 300 yards away, was the path leading to his small house! I saw him. Isn't that odd. I was so near . . . but now I'm dead! He turned to me, seemingly irritated.

"Intent!" he said.

Before I could fully remember, I tumbled into a large flaming cavern where thousands of beings lay dead or in pain. Horrible faces of death were everywhere as I struggled to understand my fate amidst the choking fumes and rotting limbs. I tripped over a corpse. It was . . . *Paula!* She smiled at me . . . hideous smile. I cried out. No help; no response but the sound of ripping flesh and bones . . .

This was not my *intent* . . .

****

Blackness returned. The searing pain in my left leg reminded me I was no longer out of the body. No other pain . . . just that. I sat up, straining to see something - anything at all. Nothing. Yet, I was alive! After all those snake bites? I wondered.

Minutes before, I was ready to accept death. Now I wanted to survive . . . to *live!* That meant leaving. That was all I needed to do. Leave. But how . . ? I could barely move.

"Listen to intent . . . then act."

I focused on my new *intent.* Soon I could feel a surge of vitality, starting in my heart and spreading throughout my trunk and into my arms and legs. After several minutes, I felt sensation returning. First, my heart and chest, then my neck and head. Soon my whole body felt bathed in a flush of life . . . I even noticed my left leg dropping some of its swelling.

I sat up more and looked around. Although I could not make out images with my eyes, I could *see* the room and beyond! Trusting this was not some other fluke or illusion, I forced myself to stand and hobble toward where I *saw* the entrance to the temple.

In pain and not used to walking, I fell several times. My vitality remained, however, and soon I cornered the entrance and headed down the dark, narrow corridor. Pain increased with each movement, and I found myself having to stop for long periods of time just to recover.

It was during one of these rest periods that I became aware of my throat . . . It was parched. I had no idea how long I had been in this cave. Not sure how long this renewed vitality would last, I chose to press on . . . push through the pain as much as possible.

An eternity later, I found the door; fortunately, it was unlocked. Relieved, I forced it open, only to be confronted with a bifurcation in the corridor - a fork in the road! Knowing that a

202

wrong decision would probably be my last, I chose to sit, meditate, and *see* the right way. Part of me wanted to surrender to the inevitable. Part of me wanted to lie down and . . .

"*Intent!*" Pachili's eyes stared into me as a knife into warm butter.

"Two decisions . . . It doesn't really matter."

I let go of the need to be right. Even the need to live. I forgave everyone I ever knew or met; I was in the hands of *intent* now. Focusing on the puzzle before me, I noticed a kind of flavor . . . a strand of bliss that hung in the ether. The familiar aura of *knowing* surrounding my body and mind.

A few seconds later I could *see* a large, vibrant silver chord leading down the right corridor, while the left one revealed a weaker, shriveled chord. Gathering my last bit of strength, I painfully dragged my useless body and leg to the right, maintaining a pace worthy of a paraplegic turtle. Steady pain ripped through my body. I kept going. Steady. Easy. Steady. Easy . . .

No end came. After a while, I labored to catch my breath. For what seemed like hours of tortuous drudgery, I strained to see some glimmer of the outside world . . . *any* glimmer that would give meaning again to my life . . . some fresh air . . . water . . .

Then I realized: I had been breathing the whole time! The air smelled a little fresher in this corridor. I kept a steady pace for about another twenty or so minutes until a glimmer of light hit the wall. I stopped, straining my eyes to check out whether or not it was real. More . . . Steady. Pain had turned into a throbbing torrent . . . my left leg took on a life of its own that threatened to separate from me at any moment. I talked to it with as much compassion as I dared. "There's light! Be patient with me, dammit! Just a little longer . . ."

I must have passed out again. When I awoke, I checked to see which reality I had stumbled on this time . . . the walls of the corridor were clearly discernible. Same cave. Same reality . . . and there was light . . . and plenty of air! Not a moment to soon: my mouth and throat were greatly swollen. I gathered as much energy as I could muster and dragged my ailing carcass to the entrance of the cave, and into the blinding morning light.

My vision was failing me, but I managed to see two human beings emerging from the wooded area below, one wearing an orange robe. I had just enough energy to raise my hand in the air and wave before collapsing into a small mat of grass. I heard the soft rustling sound, like feet crackling through some underbrush. I had the sensation of being gently hoisted . . .

Then passed out.

Chapter Thirty-Eight

Everything was flat: no taste, emotion, or fear . . . but much activity around me . . . I was still alive.

I awoke to find myself in a small ashram or temple, sitting on a mat in front of someone wearing a white robe. His head was turned and facing the window in back of him. Outside the window was a familiar-looking garden. Someone offered me water; I drank until my thirst was gone.

For a minute, I had no memory of anything, then slowly pulled myself into a space of clarity. Something about a window . . . *that window*, I thought as I glanced at the opening to my right whose satin curtains still flowed gently in the breeze. I had dreamed coming here . . . or was it a dream?

My body ached, but I could move without much pain. Actually, as I moves some more, it felt pretty good! My hosts had apparently bathed and dressed me in some local clothing.

Before I had a chance to check out my wounds, the man at the window turned to face me, shifting only his direction while remaining in lotus posture. My eyes and heart seized the memory like a sword and carved it into my waking consciousness. . . it was the old man! The *same* old man - the Veddha - I saw in Balangoda many months ago!

I suddenly harbored an intense desire to run . . . as I did during our first encounter. My body froze, however, while my turbulent mind sifted through options. This time there was no escape. No hedge to hide behind. No car to drive. Just him. And me.

The old man looked at me with eyes that glistened with such depth I had to take a breath. Intense feelings of love rose from deep within me, as I felt all anger and fear escaping from my back, around the middle of my spine. My body jerked a few times, and I closed my eyes and settled into an upright sitting posture without strain or effort. Suddenly there was no need to run. The aged fellow spoke in an unfamiliar sing-song accent:

"You awake now," he said, opening his palm in a gesture of friendliness. "You have come a long way. There is no need to leave so soon this time." He remembered my spying episode. I felt slightly embarrassed, and didn't know what to say. But, somehow it didn't matter. I felt explanations were not necessary.

As the old man spoke, I became aware of another presence that slipped out of the shadows. I glanced as the moving figure quietly set a cup of tea in front of the old man then moved to the corner of the room. Pachili! I had found him again.

I had so many questions, and could not turn away from the aged gentleman's eyes. They were so soothing and compassionate, I found myself releasing all concern. I devoured his striking features: high cheekbones and a long, white beard that flowed in the soft breeze around his creamy satin robe. He wore plain sandals. I saw the weathered cane in back of him, next to a mural painted on the wall.

As he stared at me softly, I took a deep breath and poured myself out to him as easily as if he were my best friend. He closed his eyes, and for a long time there was silence. I waited. Finally, the old man spoke to Pachili, but only in a foreign dialect. I waited for them to complete their discussion.

"Bija wants to know if you are prepared . . . if you have purged your killer?" I sat in silence, unsure of what to say. Did I? I didn't know. My head spun as I tried to think of the right answer. I didn't even know what they were preparing me for.

"I don't know," I said honestly. A lengthy dialogue ensued, as my Buddhist friend seemed to be arguing something with him. After a few more minutes of debate, the old man turned to me and said:

"You are not ready."

"Ready for *what?!*" I insisted looking over at Pachili.

"You must purge before fully *knowing*," explained my friend. As he spoke, I detected a hint of sadness, "otherwise your thread of *intent* is lost."

"And how do I do that?" I asked, trying to be practical. I wanted nuts and bolts instructions, but suspected I would be getting the Zen treatment instead. More conversation ensued, then the old man rose to his feet, grabbed his cane, and left the small temple.

"Bija says go home," said Pachili coldly. I felt utterly nonplussed.

"Go *home?!*" I sputtered, "Home where? To *what??*" I didn't know what to say to him. For some reason I felt my whole world collapsing. I pinched myself to see if this were another one of those Zone nightmares . . . like Dorothy must have felt before the wizard. How would I get that *stupid broom* and get back to Kansas?! This felt so . . . so real . . . and yet so surreal!

"Will you go with me?" I asked.

"If you wish," he responded softly. I felt slightly relieved.

"Go outside and wait. I will come soon."

In spite of my leg and back pain, and teetering between rage and numbness, I managed to rise to my feet and find the door . . . at the end of a long, purple hallway. The blue and white arched wooden doors squeaked as they opened, and I noticed the hinges were rusty. Somebody ought to replace them . . .

I aimlessly walked out the front of the small ashram into what appeared to be a large alley, highlighted by the hot, mid-morning sun. I felt a sudden intense wave of heat and almost passed out. A beggar approached. I quickly brushed him off, staggering toward an area I had never been before. I didn't know where I was, or where I was going. Pilgrims were everywhere, bearing offerings and burning incense. As I looked back, I caught a glance of these same worshippers pouring into a tall, white shrine with elaborate carvings on the door. The ashram had disappeared! I felt dizzy.

****

"*Am* I going to die?" I asked Pachili soon after he just appeared out of the crowd. We were winding our way through the thinning mass of pilgrims along the road leading away from town. The whole thing still smacked of acute unreality although my body still ached from the previous beatings.

"Eventually," quipped Pachili in a manner I had come to accept as his unique form of sarcasm.

"That's a relief," I interjected, adding to the sarcasm. I no longer feared death - I guess I'd faced it enough times - but suddenly I felt hungry for sanity again . . . some continuity. The last time that happened was during my run on the beach south of Mount Lavinia. After that? Strange things . . . but my memory of intervening events was cloudy at best.

"What town is this?" I queried.

"Kataragama," he said, "a very holy place in Sri Lanka; a place with much active *Chi.*"

"You brought me here?"

"No," said Pachili mysteriously, "You arrived on your own." Before I could ask for clarification he added, "You're very creative. Most local people are very frightened by the *Yaka Raume,* or 'devil circles.' With your complete innocence, however, you walked right into one."

"What's a 'devil circle'?" I queried my older companion, displaying my ignorance.

"You will see."

"Where are we going?"

"Back to the cave entrance."

"Cave?" I questioned, vaguely remembering something about stumbling out of one.

"You found the *Yaka Raume;*" he stated, "now you must know their purpose."

As we walked, the memories started coming back: The cave temple. The attackers. The cobra bites. The fire! My God! No wonder I forgot . . . I probably blocked it out because of my terror! Curious, I posed the question to Pachili, who seemed to understand what transpired.

"How . . . why . . . did I survive?" I asked, feeling a sudden urgency.

"Your *intent* guided you," he explained, "But it's a tricky thing. Until you made the choice to find me, I could only observe. You are still not out yet . . . but you came to me. I can help you as much as your *intent* will allow."

"I'm still in the Zone?" I exclaimed. "You mean, this is not real?!"

"Don't confuse reality with awareness," said my guide. "There are many realities. It all depends on your focus. The Zone is actually a state of acute awareness - a state far more 'real' than normal human waking state . . . just as waking is considered more 'real' than dreaming.

"The Zone is the playground of pure consciousness, or *Chi.*"

The afternoon was intense, bright and hot, creating a thousand shades of color in the passing greenery along our path. After walking some distance in silence, the monk spoke again: "You are in a critical phase now; your body is changing. Whenever you are thrust into a new state of consciousness, your body must adapt."

"Adapt?" I inquired, feeling rather concerned. "And what happens if it doesn't . . ?"

"You die. *Chi* leaves the body," he said abruptly, anticipating my question, "But that has already happened: you left your body. But you came back. Now the body must change quickly . . . purify. Others who enter the devil circles do not often adapt so well. Most die. It's too much for them." As he spoke, Pachili's description touched something deep within me; I didn't even know why.

"Your body is simply a vehicle for consciousness. Remember that," he continued, "without flexibility it will not be able to absorb the rush of pure awareness. To do so, awareness must move into the next phase. *Intent* is not yet solidified . . . still too weak and diluted."

As he spoke, I had a strange, sinking feeling in my gut. Before today, my tendency would have been to question everything he said. Not now. As we traveled along the country road, I became aware of a mixed emotions: mortal fear of the unknown, accompanied by a deep love for the man and a total awareness of the moment. Nothing external, just an abiding sense of admiration and bliss that went beyond my ability to describe.

This was new to me. I felt helpless, like a newborn baby. Having made the decision to trust, I now had no other choice. My very existence depended on his presence.

As we walked some more in silence, I reached into the small package of lunch I bought before leaving town: a leaf packet of rice and curry. By now it had lost much of its warmth. I also detected a change in my appetite and taste. Normally averse to spice, I found the food suddenly rather bland . . . very unusual. Despite this, I felt an urgent hunger and suggested to Pachili we stop and eat. He agreed; we soon parked under a tree off the road, surrounded by jungle and a large field.

It was early afternoon. I had asked Pachili what date it was, but he said it didn't matter. The sun disappeared behind some light cumulus clouds, a welcome relief to the scorching heat that permeated this land. There had been no rain for some time, and the forest seemed much quieter than usual. I opened the rice and curry leaf and offered half of it to my companion. He accepted and offered me water from his goat-hide flask. It, too, tasted different. We ate in silence.

A hazy light spread out in the east over a field of bushes, framed by forest to the north and south. I suddenly remembered my left leg . . . and the cobra bites! They had not been hurting recently. Curious, I started rolling up my pants leg to observe the stab wound. I kept rolling, but no wound. Finally, I stood up and took off my pants. I felt my legs on both sides. There were no wounds anywhere! Neither could I find any snake bites, sores, or cuts. The only things I found were a few bruises on my hips and arms, and some minor contusions on my face.

"I've been *healed,* Pachili! The stab wound is completely gone . . . the snake bites are gone. . . whatever happened back there also *cured* me!"

"Relax. There was no stab wound or snake bites," spoke the older man in a fashion so matter-of-fact, I assumed he had forgotten what I had gone through.

"I was *there,* Pachili!" I said, trying to avoid patronizing him. "I didn't dream this . . . did I? I was stabbed, bitten, beat up, and physically and psychically tortured! I was attacked by a gang of four or five young Tamils, or Veddhas, or whatever they were, and . . ." Pachili waved me to sit down. I put my pants back on to oblige him, though still protested his obvious ignorance in matters that concerned me.

"The second remedy. Higher awareness centers . . . activated, that's all. It all happened in the circle . . . nothing now."

"But my experiences . . . so *real* . . . as real as me sitting here talking to you!" I blurted out, suddenly doubting my own sanity. My body's lack of injury confirmed Pachili's words . . . That many cobra bites would surely have killed me in minutes. Was I going crazy?

Sensing my fear, the older man put down his curry and spoke softly, as if he were my big brother explaining how to act on a first date. "Remember," he said, "without flexibility you will not be able to absorb the rush of *Chi*. Take it easy!

"You think you experienced the Zone?" added the mysterious monk as he picked up his meal once again. Indeed, if you can call it 'your' experience, then you did. But Zone experiences are not even *your* experiences! You enter a state of no-mind. No-experience. All you become is a witness . . . a spectator . . . watching a movie. Sometimes, it's an old movie with 'you' as the only actor."

"We will be there soon," he added. "Patience is most important." I reluctantly agreed to wait, nervously fidgeting with my potatoes.

Chapter Thirty-Nine

We arrived to a forested plateau shortly before dark. Although my companion showed no signs of fatigue, I was sweaty, and quite exhausted.

"Your body is still not strong enough," said Pachili as he strode briskly through a dried meadow. I tried to follow, but kept falling behind. When I finally caught him again, he looked at me squarely in the eyes, saying: "Your *intent* is solidifying - but in death. Are you aware of that?"

"No," I puffed, "I just thought I was tired."

"Look again. Close your eyes. Go within."

I did as instructed . . .

****

I lay in a bed at some hospital. Tremendous pain seared through my body, mostly in my groin area! I didn't recognize my surroundings, but struggled to sit up. I couldn't. All I could do was raise my left hand . . . it looked withered. Deformed. I was hooked up to some intravenous feeding device.

As the room swirled around my head, the dizzy memories of Pachili began to fade. I was dying. The pain . . . I needed more morphine . . !

Suddenly the pain was gone. The silence, however, was deadening.

****

"Enough!" I cried as I opened my eyes. Apparently, I was now able to shift awareness at will! I understood, but still felt helpless to alter the course laid out for me. Pachili motioning me over to a clump of trees. Beyond them, I spied what appeared to be the overgrown side of a mountain.

213

"There is your cave," announced the Buddhist nonchalantly. I studied the location where he pointed, but couldn't make it out.

"What cave?" I asked, not recognizing anything except a few carved stone Buddha figures. Pachili walked closer and put his hand on the side of a smooth column of rock, maybe fifteen feet tall. Suddenly I saw it.

"That's it?!" I exclaimed. "That's the cave I came out of?!" I shrank from the view. It appeared covered with forest vines; almost impassable from where I stood. "How . . ??"

"This was one of the *Yaka Raume* - or devil circles " said Pachili. "focal points, or connections to the Zone. I felt I should tell you about them."

"Tell me *what*?" I queried while knocking my shoes on a stump, trying to loosen some impacted mud. Pachili stopped fumbling with the vines and came over to sit next to me. His eyes betrayed an unusual compassion.

"These places were discovered by the Veddhas thousands of years ago. Since then, all but a few lost the knowledge of awareness travel. Others built a temple here."

"A temple! That's what I saw!" I exclaimed, suddenly feeling validated. "But this cave looks nothing like the one I came out of!"

"What you came out of existed hundreds of years ago," stated my guide tersely. My mind went blank. Then I understood his meaning of "the rush of pure awareness."

"Since then, the *Chi* has shifted; moved on. These *Yaka Raume* are entrances to the Zone, but are not really needed to enter the Zone.

"This place used to be one of thousands . . . a connecting point . . . *ein Knoten* . . . or cross point to universal awareness. These are like acupuncture points for the earth; black holes of consciousness. Dangerous for those without strong *intent*.

"Your perception was not of this time," he continued as I sat dazed and enthralled. "Remember: the Zone is the playground for the *Chi*. Your *ku* will unleash space-time warps and other strange things . . . all of them real, yet unreal. None of them belong to the person identified as 'you'."

"But," I protested, "I saw you and another man approach me as I fell! You picked me up . . . took me to the ashram!" I sat on a log facing him while Pachili got up and wandered towards the old cave, seemingly ignoring my question while exploring the overgrowth. Finally, he spoke:

"More mind games," he said simply, "All you see is a projection of your mind. In the Zone, it is instant. You saw us, but only after you arrived at the ashram."

"How . . ?" I started to ask, then remembered what he just told me about universal connecting points. Apparently the ashram was another one. "What kind of temple was this?" I asked instead, remembering the bizarre drawings on the walls and ceilings.

"A Tibetan Buddhist temple," answered my guide.

"Tibetans?" I smirked, "In Sri Lanka?"

"Yes, more recently," he said. "The *Yaka Raume* are actually left over from much more ancient times . . . useless relics."

"How's that?" I asked.

"They can only be appreciated by those who *know* - those who will not perish in them. But," added Pachili, "those awakened beings who *know* have no desire to use them!"

"So why do they exist?"

"Somebody's idea of fun, I suppose. This is how the so-called 'gods' and 'spirits' appeared in Sri Lanka from India, Tibet and elsewhere. This is the original purpose of the temples - and of acupuncture for that matter - to take awareness into the Zone and beyond. I discovered its connection with certain homeopathic dilutions and made use of it. The whole thing is a farce. A game."

I absorbed Pachili's words like a dry sponge in water. Somehow, it all made sense.

"Millions of impressions have been made on the *Chi* for thousands and thousands of years. These impressions are compounded each second. You are just seeing a reel of three-dimensional film unrolling, in and around you. Millions of people dying in suffering . . . millions of *Chi* impressions . . . stirred up by their unenlightened *kus*. You think you can avoid feeling that? You cannot.

"The more aware you become, the more you see. Let it go. It's not your concern. You will see many things before it's over: thoughts and impressions of bodiless spirits . . . *geisten* . . . ghosts. These things exist around us all the time. Yet, most people are completely unaware of them. Because of ego, they think these feelings and impressions belong to them - their *own* feelings and experiences. They are totally asleep, as they must be. The surge of experience is too much for a single 'individual' to absorb."

I *knew* he was right. The things I saw were too strange, yet surprisingly familiar . . . Suddenly I understood how the idea of past lives came about. It made sense to me how one could live completely in the *now* and still have these so-called past-life experiences.

"But, what about the attack?" I persisted. "The people who kidnapped me? It was all so . . . so REAL! The old sailing ships. I saw a battle with muskets and soldiers. I thought they were filming a movie! The details in the Cave temple?! What about . . ?"

"Not important," he said, emphasizing a point. "Don't get trapped into that. You can die a thousand deaths, none of them truly yours. The only 'you' is pure *Chi* . . . the screen behind the movie . . . the watcher of the movie. The movie itself is not so important."

I started to say something else, but experienced another wave of deja-vu. Former excitation turned to bliss. His words catapulted me into a space where speech was unimportant. My mind fell away to reveal the silent blissful state I felt before. For a brief moment, I *knew* without thinking! The dots connected. My head, previously swirling with thoughts, opened like a morning day-lily.

"Be kind to yourself," he said softly, just as he had long ago. My body relaxed. "You are still part of the Zone, but have nothing to fear. Just *know*. All events in the Zone happen out of the body. Out of this world . . . a parallel place and time where thinking is useless. Where ego absorbs into *knowing*. Don't be captured by the immense beauty . . . or terror. Just watch. Follow the thread of *intent*. That is all that matters."

I sat there, swimming in the rarefied absence of continuity. I could no longer make the distinction: was I a patient sitting with his homeopathic doctor? A son sitting with his father? . . . Or a disciple sitting at the feet of his master? Somehow it all blurred together. This holographic, archetypal image expanded, became more pervasive.

In this elaborate tapestry, Pachili's words settled softly, hypnotically, into my consciousness. The encounter with him in the beautiful, small room with satin curtains. The flight to his cabin. I already *knew* . . . I could navigate through states of consciousness as easily as I could glide a canoe through a lake. It only took one realization: that I was not *doing* anything! I wasn't even who I imagined; this "I" was simply a part of some vast and eternal cosmic play . . .

"It's time now," spoke the master cryptically. I immediately stood up and followed him as he led me further into the forest. Soon we reached a dirt path bordered - for miles it seemed - by Asian cypress trees.

"Are we going back to the ashram?" I asked.

"No. To the jungle," was his simple reply. I accepted the answer as completely natural, although I had no inkling of the purpose of this excursion. As we walked along the road, my head and legs began to feel heavier, as if I were passing through thick syrup.

Chapter Forty

My travel companion, although appearing to be in his mid- fifties, was in excellent physical condition. I tired easily, and often asked to stop for rest. The road seemed endless and circuitous, and the grueling march almost too much for me. It was getting dark. We had no more food and little water. Strange environment. And my body . . . I felt sore, nauseous, and had strange sensations in my head, stomach, and down my legs.

I attempted to pass the time in conversation, but Pachili rarely obliged me. He remained absorbed in the simple act of walking. Left to my own resources, I plodded along wearily behind him. I also couldn't help noticing the feelings of self-pity that crept back into my thoughts. I felt the matted, slippery terrain beneath my feet, the heavy weight of my head, and the aches and pains in my stomach and legs increasing with each passing mile.

Finally exhausted, I demanded that we stop. I suddenly felt sick and could barely manage to stay conscious. The constant exercise was sending me into another space. I fought to hold on as we continued on. Pachili still gave no indication of our destination.

Feeling pale, I hurried over to the side of the path to throw up. Nothing came. I had already emptied the contents of my stomach earlier, but still felt the need to purge. Now, all I had were dry heaves, cramps, chills, and an overwhelming desire to curl up somewhere and die. I also had cold hands and feet and an oozing boil on my right leg that made its first appearance between here and the cypress avenue.

"I can't go on," I implored Pachili with a force of will seldom expressed to him. "You'd better get me to a doctor, quick." I no longer thought of him as a doctor. At this point I only saw him as my slave driver, tormentor, and assassin. He was killing me!

Pachili sat next to me, chewing on some grass or herb. He offered me some, but I declined. I turned my head and tried continued to dry heave until it my head was spinning.

"Take this; it will help," he explained. "Chew it slowly, then swallow." I did as instructed. The weed was bitter, but tolerable and the pain in my stomach immediately abated. Soon my head cleared and my whole body felt better.

"What was that stuff?" I queried, amazed at the sudden turnaround of my symptoms.

"Temporary relief," he said. "An ancient Ayurvedic remedy. You are purging something deep inside you. This will help for a while." I had little more than a passing acquaintance with Ayurvedic medicine, but now it intrigued me.

"Will this herb help me to complete the purge?" He did not answer; just continued his walk in silence. I decided not to press the matter since I was at least well enough to travel; he had given me a small cache of herb to use whenever I needed.

"There is much *Chi* in this place," declared my guide as we approached an old oak tree in the middle of a clearing in the woods. We had completed a march of several miles.

"Much of it is ancient *Chi*," he announced "many old impressions; old disciplines. This *Chi* used to be at the cave temple. Now it is here. And very potent. Keep awareness close. Memory will fail unless *intent* is strong. Concentrate on every detail. The illusion will fall away."

I suddenly stopped, sensing a flow of vague memories. Nothing particular, just a sense of nostalgia; I asked my leader about the significance.

"Let go," he replied, "Relax into it." We sat beneath the tree in silence. I observed Pachili almost immediately go into deep meditation. I was hesitant at first to close my eyes. The nostalgia was getting stronger. I started getting images of everything: my first pet, the day I lost my stamp collection, a bicycle injury, recess at school . . .

Remembering my guide's instructions, I let them go. I did, then felt a deepening of awareness as I spontaneously closed my eyes. The images came and went. I felt drawn to focus on my breath.

Time went by. I don't know how long we sat. Often, the temptation made me want to jump up, declare the whole thing a sad mistake, and run away. But to where? Totally lost, I sensed not the faintest clue on how I might recover the path to the last village. I also notice my aches and pains returning, occasionally dipping into the herb cache for relief. Each time I would return to my breath, diving deep, then surfacing again, diving deep, then surfacing.

Darkness approached. My mind stayed busy, pondering the wisdom of leaving, versus staying with Pachili in meditation. Each time, I chose to stay with my breath. Soon, darkness overcame us. I knew now it would be futile to attempt any separation.

Stuck for the duration, I lay down next to the indefatigable Buddhist and drifted off to sleep. Before falling asleep, however, I couldn't help noticing the lack of bugs and ground critters that usually torment me in wooded areas. A few insect and bird sounds were there, but less than I would expect. The twilight was calm. A deep relaxation settled in, but I noticed I was not sleeping. A pleasant void persisted, and I melted into it, aware I was again losing all sense of continuity.

****

Swirling . . . falling . . . a maze of alternating darkness and light. A type of slow-motion chaos was all around me, but I had no fear. I passed through it, emerging into an area that glowed with a soft, bright amber light. I could *see* the area surrounding the tree with eyes closed. A hushed quiet fell as the image of the tree, of Pachili, began to fade, then disappeared. I was alone. There was no movement. I noticed the air, however, hummed with a tangible eeriness.

Then it happened.

My body twitched and my face felt suddenly distorted. I gasped and gargled . . . like a wolf! I watched as my jaw drew back and swallowed my head! Out of the throat emerged more tunnels . . . a network of circles, spirals, and personal passageways. Each had their own flavor. I immediately ceased to be, as reason relaxed its grip on my consciousness.

Out of some misty awareness came a pair of wings at my side, fluttering . . . majestically guiding me into what appeared to be a large valley surrounded by mountains covered with tea plants. I felt a subtle lift. Almost discernible, then . . . Gone. Wings. Trees. Rivers. Ocean. An intense emerald streak melting into deep blue, then yellow.

Things happened so quickly: moon . . . stars . . . faster. Another circle. Approach . A tunnel of streaked light. No light. Emptiness. Darkness mixed with heaviness. Feel. No place. Heaviness in the heart. Heaviness. Relax . . . Mountains. Valleys. Circling. Looking. Moving towards the sea . . .

Moving into yet another circle . . . I felt encased in a heavy light. For a while I couldn't move. Chord attached. Left all bodies. I was afraid. Go back? No. Follow *intent* . . . On and on . . . Closer. Spiraling. I descended

Eyes closed now . . . now open. I saw humans as figures suspended in frozen light. Pure bliss swept over me, knocking me on the floor and bringing a flood of tears to my partially opened eyes The figures settled into their motions as if guided by a giant, invisible hand.

"Keep awareness close. Concentrate on every detail. The illusion will fall away."

I again saw the world of color and light, a place where fantastic things . . . Then I remembered my guide.
"Pachili! *Wait!"*
Forcing awareness back, I called out to the robed man who was far ahead of me, angrily waving me off, then disappearing into the crowd. I ran to catch up, but soon became aware I had lost him. Separated. My heart leapt into my throat. I was alone in a strange place . . . I quickly shook it off, then felt a chill rising on the back of my neck.

Someone was watching me! Hooking into my field of awareness by some force! Eyes open . . . This was no daydream.

Everything seemed normal except the colors: brilliant, enhanced tones and tints surrounded me.

I turned slowly as the crowd milled around me, like visitors in a dream. Nothing. I then stood face to face with something perched on a window ledge across a narrow street - a large crow whose glaring eyes were unmistakable. I had seen those eyes before! A chill that emanated from them into my spine.

The bird looked squarely at me, spread his wings, then flew off in a way that invited me to come. He rose to the roof, then glided across to my side of the street a block away. He looked back again, silently. Then flew away again.

I followed, soon finding myself outside the small town, on a shallow hill leading to a wooded area. The crow parked himself on a lower branch, as I found a comfortable spot across the road, next to a tree.

More time passed. The crow and I just sat . . . staring at each other . . . Those *eyes!* I instantly knew they were the eyes I had seen in the mirror . . . *my own!* We remained frozen, rooted to our respective spots. The crow appeared to respond to my thoughts, as in a meditation. When a thought came, he flapped his wings as if to take off. When I settled into a simple space, he did likewise. When my mind would ask a question, he seemed to respond with some unspoken look of concern, anger, sadness, or joy. I also discovered he spread his feathers, took on an attack posture, whenever I felt the least bit of fear or doubt. I continued this dance with the crow for what seemed like hours.

Suddenly a shot rang out. I felt a sharp pain in my stomach as the big bird fell out of the tree. I noticed a large dark native person in a loincloth and rifle walking toward him! The man had long hair and a stubbled beard. His eyes were intense, like fire.

I instantly disliked him, and ran towards the crow, reaching it before the hated visitor. Watching the now-helpless body writhing in the dirt, I suddenly felt anger and hatred toward this errant hunter . . . The loin-clothed beast just sneered as he approached his prey. He seemed aloof. Evil. Unconcerned about life.

"You bastard!" I yelled as I glared at the man. "You did this .. !!" He didn't even listen to me, which provoked me even more. I felt uncontrollable rage and lunged at him.

The moment froze . . . I passed right through him! Before I could react, he flipped out a knife and quickly severed the bird's leg, then walked off, leaving it to die. I felt seized by the same familiar chill in my left leg. Darkness spread over me . . .

"You have put yourself under my care. Ego must be destroyed . . . this is major surgery you have agreed to."

The floating seemed endless.

Chapter Forty-One

I had left the ashram as instructed, and waited across the street from a large white temple. For a moment I could have sworn I was somewhere else! I felt I had shifted into a different place - a different time. Yet, everything appeared normal. My mind was playing tricks on me again.

As I watched pilgrims pile in and out of the temple with alms and incense, I shook my head, suddenly trying to remember where the ashram had been. It was getting late and Pachili had not yet arrived as promised. Why was I even waiting for him?

"To hell with him!" I muttered, as I picked myself up and headed towards the outskirts of town . . . the east side of Kataragama, towards uncharted territory. I didn't care. The only feelings I had were numbness and rage. Then I remembered: the old man kicked me out of the ashram! I stomped over to a tree by the side of the road and kicked it, grabbing my toe in agony. "You damn son-of-a-bitch!!!" I yelled in complete frustration as I grabbed the nearest cool spot to sit down.

I was angry . . . totally disillusioned! "Not ready yet," he said?! I wanted to kick the false teeth out of that old man, but I knew kicking trees was not helping. Instead, I grabbed a few pieces of roadside grass and started chewing. I wanted to be alone. Fortunately, passersby probably sensed this and left me to my misery.

After a few minutes of grazing and silent nothingness, tears came to my eyes. I wanted to feel sorry for myself. This felt like the time I lost Paula . . . the loneliness was almost unbearable. I couldn't - no, I *wouldn't* - face *that* again!

But it wasn't Paula. I was losing my mind! I had already lost Cheryl, Ruth, Jon, and now even Pachili and the old man. I was far from home. I never even knew whether any of this was real anymore. Colombo was 175 miles away, I was sick, maybe had five rupees left, and I didn't know how to get back to Mt. Lavinia except by walking and hitching rides.

I asked a local merchant the date. He said December 17th, 1987. I laughed cynically, realizing I was now an illegal alien. A bum. Me, the famous doctor! I hadn't renewed my visa again, and Christmas was only a week away.

I had come to Sri Lanka yearning for pain relief and spiritual knowledge. Instead, all I got was more pain. I cursed the day I set foot in this horrible country! My body responded with more nausea. I leaned back and vomited behind the tree. Fortunately, the grass had given me some bulk and I temporarily avoided the dry heaves.

I had no idea what I was going to do. My leg was developing more oozing pus scars. I didn't want to stay here . . . but walk *back*? The prospect of home held nothing for me. Once gone, I knew I would never return. Would I even make it home alive? I didn't care anymore.

After the cursing and the sobbing came the fatigue. And the rain. By late afternoon, I hadn't moved from my spot. I hadn't eaten in more than a day and my body ached all over. The thought occurred to me to start begging, but I knew I wouldn't get very far with that one! With all the professional beggars around - the ones with no arms or legs - I would look pretty silly asking for handouts in my western casual outfit, even if it *was* a bit dirty.

I paid for a king coconut with a two-rupee piece and tried to force the normally tasty milk down my painful, rebellious body. I was only able to retain a small amount at a time by taking small sips. Afterwards I just sat in my same spot next to the tree and the road as the soft rain pelted the dusty street, turning it into mud.

I hated myself and wanted to die. For real. Maybe *then* I would find out what this was all about! I got up and walked further out of town, determined to get as far away from civilization as I dared. I headed east along the partially paved road leading towards the isolation of Ruhuna National Park, also called Yala Reserve. I had read about it in the guide books, but never thought I would venture this far from the familiar.

226

I figured maybe a cobra or charging water buffalo would quickly end my misery.

****

My first night out of Kataragama was cruel. Death wasn't supposed to be this complicated. I had options: get killed by a wild animal, die of starvation, infection, disease, or maybe a combination of all of them. The prospects were many; none of them appealing. Why did I do this? I had no food or water. I needed shelter, and might be eaten alive before I could secure any of these. If I had really wanted to commit suicide, there were better ways to go about it.

I had left Kataragama on foot, lucky enough to get a ride into Ruhuna National Park by one of the locals, a Sinhalese farmer who said he had business on the reserve. I didn't ask him what his business was, nor did he ask about mine. I gave him all the money I had left - four rupees - and mentioned I wanted privacy. He told me he knew just the place for it, dropping me at the edge of a thorny scrub forest and warning me of the snakes, leopards, wild boars and sloth bears.

It looked like the pictures I'd seen of the African bush. Sparse but beautiful, especially after the rain. I immediately saw a couple of elephants in the distance east, and spied some deer grazing on some grass in the north. As the individual drove off in his dilapidated truck, however, I remember having instant regrets.

This first night was forgettable. I lay curled up under a large scrub tree, shivering uncontrollably while fighting off bugs, mosquitoes, crawling things, and ghosts of my own fears. Although the short rain stopped hours ago, it was very dark, and the shrill sounds of the jungle were everywhere. I hardly slept at all . . . too busy scaring away the bugs, rodents, monkeys, and other denizens of this strange land.

The approach of dawn was painfully slow. My leg sore had opened to the point where pus was flowing from it constantly. Flies found it an attractive target. I bound the wound with some wet leaves; this stopped the oozing a little, but not much. My head was splitting, accompanied by back pain, body

227

sores, dry mouth, and an intolerable nausea. I had no appetite, which was good; I had no idea what I could eat in this alien environment. Prompted by misery and thirst, I decided to move on.

Walking was difficult. My right leg had swollen considerably, and my stomach pain kept me doubled over most of the time. Still, I managed to hobble into a clearing where I saw the dusty path leading off into another distance grove of trees. Hearing a sound, I turned and saw a huge elephant grazing on some nearby foliage with her calf.

"Didn't see you there, fellas!" I exclaimed, shocked that I didn't notice them before. They glanced in my direction, still chewing, and making no effort to acknowledge my presence. I worked my way towards the tree grove, guided only by my mysterious bodily needs.

Once at the opening of the forest canopy, I collapsed in pain. I had lost my leg bandage, and a clear fluid flowed from my wound. I also felt a stirring in my bowels as I crawled towards the nearest tree. I slid down my pants with difficulty to relieve myself, but couldn't. Nothing came. I waited, agonizing over the violence occurring in my midsection. Still nothing.

What, I wondered, had I eaten that was causing me so much trouble?? I knew that both cholera and dysentery were common in these parts, but figured I would also have diarrhea. I obviously didn't. Five minutes passed and I witnessed no bowel activity. I slowly pulled my pants back up, also noticing the internal pain had subsided a little.

Why was I here? Despite my continued agony, I now had mixed feelings. I realized it wasn't my *intent* to die, much as the signs were there. But, I didn't even want to think about *intent*. Pachili's stupid lies! I wanted to end this pitiful charade . . . either get the *real* truth . . . or *die,* dammit!

I started laughing and crying at the same time. What was *real* anymore? What did *I* feel? I didn't even know. My life had been spent living other people's dreams and fears . . . other people's. What was inside of *me*? I sat quietly, letting my thoughts rise into the fluttering branches above. Nothing was real anymore. *This* was all I knew. This place. This time. This feeling of lingering pain and death.

Did I really hate Pachili? Or did I hate myself? What would happen if I just . . . let go? Forgive. What would happen if I just watched the whole thing silently unfold in front of me? Keep centered? Die peacefully?

I closed my eyes, silent. Waiting. If death comes, let it come.

I waited a long time, moving into the pain - acknowledging the discomfort with all my heart and mind. After a while, a deep relaxation came over me. I felt the earth moved steadily beneath me toward the warmth of the eastern sun. Funny. I no longer saw or felt the sun "rising." The earth - my earth - was moving! Like a gigantic moving Ferris wheel, the ground beneath me pulsed with an awesome vitality.

Suddenly I *knew*: I would *not* die here. I was being tested. But why?? I hadn't a clue as to my suffering, but resolved to stay conscious to that being presented to me.

Chapter Forty-Two

Three days passed, by my estimate; almost Christmas. A shame . . . Christmas had never been this ugly. No signs of anything remotely merry. It was hot. Muggy. Every hour went by slowly and painfully. I managed to pass the time, however, looking for water and edible plants. Not knowing what to eat, I practically fasted the whole time, drinking what little water I could find from wet leaves and morning dew.

To keep down the hunger and thirst, I also chewed on fresh grasses, leaves, and other things I recognized from my boy scout training. I avoided, however, drinking from the puddles and small lakes in the area for fear of cholera and dysentery. My leg had stopped oozing, but my stomach pains and headaches continued. I made broad-leaf poultices and scrubbed myself with some plant that seemed to help keep the flies and mosquitoes away.

I also constructed a temporary treehouse shelter designed to keep away the rain, bugs, snakes and mosquitoes. This helped, but was no guarantee against danger. A large, female spotted leopard climbed through my tree two days earlier, but was either not hungry, or decided I was too much trouble to attack. Elephants were my constant companions, but thankfully dodged my wooded abode in search of less crowded fair. A few playful peacocks, spotted deer, gray monkeys, and giant squirrels provided me much needed entertainment.

At one point I almost headed back to Kataragama. The thought of begging Pachili and Bija occurred to me, but I quickly came to the realization my supplications would go unheeded. What would I get by doing that? More rejection? No; I was finished with gurus, guides, and teachers.

I made plans to find a park ranger station, knowing I would die if I allowed my condition to get much worse. My body kept a continuously elevated temperature, indicative of an internal infection or disease. My right leg by now had grown numb and I feared gangrene. I didn't, however, have diarrhea and spiking fever, indicative of malaria or cholera. Whatever was killing me remained a mystery.

It was getting late as I broke down my makeshift shelter and set off down the dirt road, hobbling on my good leg with all the strength I could muster. One agonizing mile later it hit me. I would never make it. Death was near. Nearer than I thought. My midsection suddenly coiled shut like a collapsing iron spring as my legs buckled underneath. I crawled torturously to the side of the road to rest, but the stabbing pain almost knocked me out.

"Keep it together, Matthew!" I implored myself. It was laborious. I slipped in and out of coma for what seemed like an eternity. Each conscious moment was torture. My abdomen was splitting with a pain I could only previously imagine. I wanted a shot of morphine . . . if only . . .

I heard a growl and managed to look up. It was my friend the spotted leopard. About my size, she glared at me with a predatory intensity I had never experienced before. The beast appeared hungry and I was the slowest thing around. This was it. Somehow, I had been wrong; I would never make it out alive. Not this time.

The female leopard came nearer, snarling. Aware that it was useless to fight, I embraced her . . . welcomed her presence. Death could be actually beautiful. A total relief. As I labored to breathe I stared at her almost lovingly. She returned the gaze with such raw energy that I almost felt love in return - eating me was her gift to my spirit.

She approached . . . closer . . . closer . . . looking to see if I would present any sort of tactical problem. I wouldn't. I could barely breathe from the pain, and had no thought of a struggle. I closed my eyes, falling on my hands in the dirt and waited for her teeth to sink into my now-useless body.

I waited, but could only hear a faint rumbling in the background. I looked up to see the leopard freeze, her eyes glued to the distance. She backed off, reluctantly disappearing into a nearby clump of bushes.

Barely conscious, I could hear a vehicle approaching. In the remaining light of day, I saw the image of a vehicle . . . a Land Rover. Saved again. This was getting to be a habit. Why the last minute stuff?? This time instead of joy, I felt anger. Why didn't life just let me *die*?!

The park rangers who stopped to pick me up were also angry. Their questions were unrelenting. Who was I? Was I a poacher? If not, why was I out here without a tracker? Or a passport? Or even food or a vehicle? If not, didn't I know there was danger here?? I barely responded, instead moaning and passing out. The pain was too much . . .

****

Fresh water touched my lips. As I swallowed the pain returned. Stomach. Legs. Head. Back. Hell, it *all* hurt! The park rangers attending me had ceased with the questions long enough to carry me into their first aid cabin on the edge of the park.

"Sir, if we cannot identify you," announced a tall, skinny ranger with a baton and safari hat, "we will have to take you to prison in Colombo as soon as you can walk."

"Oooh," I squealed weakly, "a promotion! Make sure I have room service, would you?" I railed sarcastically, no longer caring what happened to me. If they wouldn't let me die, at least I would help them out! The ranger obliged and slapped me across the face. I hardly felt it, focused as I was on the pus from my unrelenting leg wound . . . and the horrible cramps.

"It does no good to do that!" yelled his shorter, companion. "He is delirious. Leave him alone. We can deliver him to George . . ."

Delirious. That was it. I was almost giddy. My awareness had gone beyond the pain into something akin to angry serenity. I wallowed in it. Pure hate. Nothing else seemed real except pain and passing out.

The next time I awoke, I felt the searing pain of being jostled into another Rover, this time by a large lighter-skinned native person with a thick mustache and a gentle smile. He looked a little older than me, wore civilian clothes, and appeared much more benign than my former hosts.

233

"Come, we take you home now," spoke the gentleman as he climbed into the driver's seat. I was lying prone in the back and observed dust rising from the other rangers' vehicle as it headed out in the opposite direction. Apparently, they had given me over to an intermediary for the trip to Colombo.

"Am I going to jail?" I moaned faintly, remembering earlier threats.

"No, no, my friend," laughed the big man. "They just like to scare people, and want you out of their jurisdiction . . . We have so many poachers here. I'm taking you to my grandmother. She lives in the jungle, and you need help quickly. She will know what to do with you."

Grandmother? The individual himself looked to be about forty years of age. What could a feeble old woman do for me? I didn't know, nor did I care at this point. It was a no-brainer. There probably wasn't a hospital within a hundred miles. I didn't have a choice: I would die without some kind of help.

With that thought, I relaxed just a bit. The pain was remarkably less, although I noticed I had a prevailing numbness all over my body. Was I better? Or was this the first stage of dying? I had no energy to care, still drifting in and out of awareness.

Some time later, my new friend - he told me his name was George Vidiya - delivered me to the front of an old coconut-leaf thatched cabin at the end of a long drive into the forest. He stopped the Rover, jumped out and went the door, yelling something in Sinhala.

"*Kohomada,* Hanna!" I could no longer see, but I heard the door open and some feet shuffling. I strained to understand what was happening. Suddenly, I looked up and saw the face of what appeared to be an old Caucasian woman. Her light wrinkled skin portrayed an individual of ninety years or more, although her face was clear and her eyes sparkled. She surveyed the damaged body before her.

"Bring him inside," she said in English with a slight accent. I realized they must be Burghers. But what brought them way out here? I hadn't the strength to ask. George lifted me from the jeep with two arms that doubled as tree trunks and carried me inside the small shack.

234

Before I had a chance to look around, I slipped into another half-coma, awareness intact. I learned from their conversation that the old woman was a healer of some sort, and the driver was her grandson from Galle. Before I knew it, she was burning some herbs, and pouring strange tea down my throat. Some were so bitter, I immediately threw it back up.

"They found him in the jungle," explained George. "I'm surprised he's still alive . . ."

"Parasites!" exclaimed the old woman as she made me swallow another of her bitter herbs, this time in leaf form. "Some dead; others trying to come out. He might have a touch of cholera as well."

Hearing that, I lost consciousness.

SECTION IV: THE FINAL REMEDY

Chapter Forty-Three

I awoke to a writhing in my stomach. It felt like a convulsion. Horrible, bitter. I doubled up and screamed.

The old woman yelled something Sinhalese as the big man ran over to steady me on the edge of the bed. My sudden feeling of deja-vu appeared, but became quickly overshadowed by the pain. I felt a ripping in my bowels . . . an intense burning. I was guided over to a large bedpan and prepared. Normally modest, I had no thought of any shyness here as agony threatened to overcome me.

Two minutes later it happened. The stench of the massive stool made me vomit. Afterwards, I collapsed back on the bed, feeling more relieve than I had felt in weeks. More conversation in Sinhala followed, as George quickly disposed of my fetid remains. I was afraid to ask what was in it, figuring it was something fairly horrible.

I immediately felt less pain. My head cleared. My stomach, previously swollen and tortured, began to show signs of recovery. Even my leg stopped oozing. The old matron shook her head in relief.

"You will recover, child," she said warmly. "The creatures hiding in you are mostly gone." I nodded weakly as she wiped the sweat from my face and chest. I could only imagine what happened to me, but figured it could wait. Exhausted, I fell into a deep slumber.

****

"What day is this," I chirped hoarsely as I opened my eyes and looked around the room. I could barely get the words out. The old woman stopped mixing something, went over to what looked like a small kerosene stove, and poured out a cup of hot fluid from a boiling kettle. She then approached my makeshift bed set up in her living room and offered me a sip. The first taste was slightly sweet.

"I'm not sure, but I think it's December 22nd," she said in her low, gravely voice with a slight accent, "Tuesday."

"I slept a whole day . . ?" I asked. She nodded.

"Thank you," I said, "for saving my life."

"Drink some more of this," she insisted, again touching the cup to my lips. As I drank slowly, my silent thoughts drifted home . . . to my mother, sister, brother and their families. . . to Christmas trees, presents, nephews and Santa Claus. I wondered how they were doing. I hadn't contacted any of them in over a month.

"What are you making?" I asked the old woman, mixing something on the table next to her little wood stove. I was suddenly curious.

"Herbs for my grandson," said the slight but sturdy elder, not bothering to look up from her work, "He sells them in the city to doctors and pharmacies. I also take care of sick animals in the park. The rangers bring some here, maybe two or three times a week." She pointed out the small kitchen window to a shed and corral in a clearing next to the woods. "Then they are turned loose again after a few days."

"*Elephants* come here?" I asked incredulously.

"Goodness no, child," she said, reassuringly. "Small animals. I go to the bigger ones. Usually, I just look at them, then give the park ranger the right medicine, along with instructions on how to give it. Nature does the rest."

"How do you know what's wrong with them?" I queried.

"Nature is not that difficult," she explained softly. "Animals respond well. Very quickly. People . . ?" she sighed, pausing for a moment, "Most people are so . . . well, so *complicated*." The old woman went back to her chopping and mixing. "Their habits. Their diets. So unnatural. The way doctors treat them . . . its all so complicated. But most misery is not so difficult to understand. "

I asked her what was wrong with me. She paused for another minute, surveying me up and down. "Liver and lung flukes . . . also in small intestines . . ." she said, "Worms."

238

I remembered vaguely her mentioning it before, but somehow blocked it out of my mind. It was too hideous to contemplate, even now. I shuddered.

"Did I pick these up in Sri Lanka?" I asked, trying to ascertain the origin of these villains.

"At first, I thought you might have the cholera, but you didn't. How long have you been here?" she queried.

"Almost six months."

"Then," she stated frankly, "you had them before you came here . . . probably for many years. Often they will just seem to appear in the blood out of nowhere." I was speechless. Worms? For years??

"How . . . when??" I beseeched the woman. She offered only a momentary glance up from her work. I then decided to ask her at a more appropriate time, as I lay back on my bed and closed my eyes. Although I couldn't sleep, I spent some quiet time surveying my body, still quite groggy, but amazed at how differently I felt . . .

"What is your name, young man?" snapped the matriarch while pouring the ground-up herb mixture into a large bowl.

"Matt . . ." I said, "Dr. Matthew Cannon from America. Please. Call me Matt."

"Very good, Dr. Matt," she echoed while bringing over a small handful of herb mixture. "My name is Hanna Vidiya. Now I want you to hold this in your mouth." I took several pinches and stuffed the strong-tasting blend into my mouth while she added forcefully, *"And keep it in your mouth as long as you can!"*

The mixture burned . . . slowly at first, then more. The stuff was both hot and bitter. Immediately my eyes began to water and my nose emitted streams of phlegm and mucous. The sensation shot straight through my sinuses into my brain . . . I was on fire!!!

I blasted the hot stuff out of my mouth into a large pot she had conveniently placed on the floor for just such a purpose. I gasped for air, spitting and stuttering, mouth and head aflame with a burning so intense I wanted to dowse my head in cold water.

"WHA . . . WHA . . .!!" I screamed, as I hopped around the room. Uncontrollable body language and gibberish were soon followed by a very clear "WATER . . !!!" Hanna handed me another herb. I snatched it greedily.

"Chew it!" she said. I crammed the new substance into my ignited orifice and chewed for my life! After another minute I stood in the middle of the floor, astonished. The burning had subsided, although streams of mucous still poured out of my nose and eyes, mixed with blood. As I blew my nose into a small rag she had given me, I noticed tiny, thread-like creatures swimming in my bodily fluids.

"Gross!" I yelled, flinging the rag into the same pot. "More worms?? That's disgusting!" I continued blowing to clear my head off as much of the stuff as possible.

"You had headaches?" observed the old woman wisely, handing me some water in a tin cup. I blew my nose again, then downed the fluid before answering.

"Many years, yes," I answered, impressed with her insight. I was such a sucker for people with insight.

"Eggs. Parasites trying to multiply as fast as possible," added the old herbalist. "You had done something to disturb their home in the organs. They were moving around in your body trying to survive. To multiply. I gave you medicine to kill them."

Pachili! *His* remedies did this . . . stirred them up. He knew I was sitting on a time bomb. Was *this* my killer?!

"I've had these things for . . . *years?!*" I reiterated, trying to comprehend how such a fetid condition could persist in the western world . . . in *me* of all people!

"It would seem so," she said, in her soft but slightly hoarse voice. Hanna's manner was such that I immediately trusted her. Despite her age - or maybe because of it - she had a real gentleness that permeated everything she said. "Most people have them, but never find out."

"But how . . ?" I asked.

"How did *I* know?" she said, her eyes laughing. "I had them too, child. We all had them. They live in our organs from such an early age, they become a part of our lives. We get them eating meat, around animals, or just being in nature. Most of the

240

time they don't bother us. But sometimes . . ." Her words trailed off slightly.

"Sometimes . . ?" I asked, prompting her to continue. She stopped mixing herbs and ambled over to a small stool, sitting.

"Don't worry," she said gently, "I will tell you . . . I just have to sit down." I paused, forgetting she was so old. I wanted to ask her *how* old, but didn't want to divert her attention from my other question.

"Yes," she continued, wiping her brow with a small lace handkerchief, "Sometimes they begin to move, or reproduce larger numbers. Sometimes they magically change form; bacteria cells and viruses can change into tiny parasites, then become something else. This can obviously cause health problems." She paused for another minute.

"Many diseases, most of them long-term things . . ."

"Chronic?" I asked, wanting to clarify.

"Yes, chronic diseases, like joint pain and problems, organ problems, blood and body fluid disorders, such as your headaches, skin problems, and . . . strong feelings . . . emotions."

"Strong feelings? That's not a disease, is it?" I questioned.

"Oh, forgive me, young man," she sighed humbly, "I am not a doctor, just an old woman who mixes things . . ." I suddenly felt ashamed for trying to correct her.

"Hanna!" I said lovingly, "You are maybe the greatest healer I've met on this island . . . and I've met many!"

"Thank you," she said simply, "I know I have a talent, but I just don't know the words how to tell you what I mean." As she spoke, her eyes shone with the clarity of a newborn baby.

"Please try," I said.

"As you wish," she said, continuing, "These parasites who cause troubles - they take on a life - a spirit of their own. I don't know whether they contain that spirit, or the spirit contains them. All I know is . . ."

"Please continue."

"All I know is they urge you toward addictions . . . Alcohol. Food. Betel chewing. Sex. Worry. Anger. Fear."

"Anger? Fear?" I interrupted, surprised.

"Yes, emotions can be addictions," she explained. "Not all are caused by worms, but worms are always present when you are always afraid . . . or consistently angry. They seem to be attracted to it. . . cause weakness in the organs, the blood. More fear . . . more doubts come." As she spoke, I remembered my horrible visions and nightmares after taking Pachili's first remedy.

"Can worms cause hallucinations? Delusions? Near-madness?" I asked nervously, trying to define my state for the last few months.

"Sometimes," she said, "But usually it's because death is near. Either they are dying, or *you* are dying, so they multiply faster, especially during a full moon."

"Every time you pass fear, a kind of death happens . . . much to learn on nights of the Full Moon."

His words rang in my mind so clearly, I almost turned around to see if he were there. I felt a sudden clarity, as if my brain had just become a fine-tuned short-wave radio. "Do you ever hear things . . ?" I asked, almost embarrassed to admit my sudden dysfunction.

"Most of the time," she said laughing, "although my hearing is not what it used to be."

"No, I mean HEAR things . . . like, inside your head?"

"Oh, goodness yes," confessed the gentle matron, much to my relief. "I've been alone here for so many years, my voices keep me company . . . they tell me which remedies to use. But be aware, though, most of those voices come from 'worm talk.'" We both laughed at her little joke. "Once you are free of such problems, though, these sounds can come from other sources."

"Like what?" I asked, suddenly intrigued.

"Oh," she paused, cocking her head to one side and smiling, "I think it is different for everyone. You will probably understand that on your own. Then *you* can tell *me.*"

I had a special feeling about this gentle old woman. I fell in love with her. She was wise. Simple. I felt unconditional acceptance from her. *Me,* this strange, angry and sick person who appeared on her doorstep looking for help.

"Are they all gone? The worms, I mean?" I asked, hoping to be rid of this plague conclusively.

"Probably not," spoke my newest friend. "We will know within the next few days . . . then you will have to take herbs for a few months to kill any hatching eggs."

"That long?" I exclaimed, "Why so long?" The old woman expressed a faint chuckle and shook her head.

"Are all Americans in such a hurry?" she asked cogently. I sighed, realizing I had nothing urgent to do except call my family. I related this to Hanna.

"They will probably think I'm dead if I don't show up for Christmas," I added.

"I understand, child," spoke the matriarch gently. "I lost most of my family. It's hard . . ." She didn't elaborate, but turned back to her herb table. "But you will be home for Easter, yes?"

"I should hope so!" I affirmed with enthusiasm, then lay back down to rest. I looked around her quaint thatched-roof masonry hut as if it had been home for ages. Feeling a quiet acceptance, I soon drifted back to sleep.

Chapter Forty-Four

December 31, 1987: my tenth day with the kind, elderly Hanna. During the time of my stay, I progressed well; my body felt stronger. So strong, in fact, I couldn't remember a time when I felt better!

I enjoyed her food, but could only handle it in small portions. My host served mostly roots and herbs: sometimes lightly steamed, other times hot and spicy, with a flavor I found enchanting, and surprisingly tolerable. The teas were different: bitter and sour. She plied me with several cups a day, saying I needed them for several months. I reluctantly agreed to abide by her regimen.

The torment in my abdomen had ceased. My sores had healed, other than for a few slight scars, and my headaches were a thing of the past. I knew this because my eyesight - always an indicator of imminent head pain - had been completely restored! I was no longer nearsighted, and would spend hours gazing at the evening sky in astonishment. Each of the constellations spoke to me in a language I had forgotten since childhood. Even my gray hair was darkening and my skin was growing softer and healthier.

Hanna's grandson George would be arriving in two days for his semi-weekly visit from Galle. During his last call, he had promised to drive me back to Colombo. Grateful to the Vidiyas, I was nevertheless sad to be leaving the warmth of Hanna's home. It was my haven from the world . . . and I had *so much* to learn from her.

"So, how old *are* you? Where do you come from? . . . Why did you come *here?*" I finally asked her that night, a cool one by Sri Lanka standards. I had just learned she was not from the island. She giggled like a little girl with a secret, delighted someone wanted to know.

"Have patience, my young friend," she said, "I will tell you; but please . . . one question at a time for my feeble old mind!" I apologized, but still smiling with eagerness to know her. She leaned back in her rocking chair in front of the small fireplace and related her story.

"I came from Europe," she said, "Holland. Many years ago - when I was 22. The Big War had just started, and I just didn't want anything to do with it."

"You mean . . . World War I?" I deduced, quickly adding she must be about 96 years old!

"Yes," she said, "it was 1914 when I got on the boat. It was a long journey back then, but I wanted to get as far away as I could, so I came here. I met and married a local man in Colombo: a brilliant poet whose ancestors were part of the original tribe on this island. He wooed me with his words and letters." She looked away a moment, and I could tell she had tears in her eyes.

"What is it, Hanna?" I asked, concerned. "I didn't mean to . . ."

"Oh, there's nothing you did child," she said, clearing her throat and wiping her tears. "Its just memories, that's all." I had mixed feelings for making her dredge up all this old stuff. "My husband George was a Burgher, but dark-skinned. His father was a hunter from the mountainous region, and his mother a half-English, half-Sinhalese farm girl. Because his father had no surname, they gave him 'Vidiya' from his mother's side . . .

"Anyway, George himself was rather brilliant. He came to the city as a young boy, worked, finished school and got a good job as a ticket-taker in the ports; a good position at the time.

"Only a year after we married, he enlisted in the British army, went to Europe, and was killed by mortar fire in Belgium . . . on the border of the Netherlands. They never found his body."

"What did you do?"

"Me?" she laughed gently, fighting back the tears, "I stayed in Colombo, pregnant with our only child. After he was born, I named him Arthur. I almost called him George . . . he was the same spirit as his father. I thought he'd come back to me. Conscious. Alive. Daring. Wise. But, Arthur it was. His

246

father and I both liked that name. We used to share stories with each other . . . about Camelot and the round table . . ."

As she spoke, I stared into the small crackling fire of dry twigs, then added a few to keep it going. I wanted to listen to her gentle voice forever. She paused for a moment and looked at me.

"Arthur died too," she added, then paused again, eyes dropping to her folded hands on the table. I relished her silence as well as her words. She had reached another difficult point in the story, and I urged her to continue.

"What about Arthur? Would he have wanted you to tell me about his death?" I asked. She smiled gently and nodded.

"Yes, he would," she responded. "He would have liked you . . . you are different, child. Open." I felt a warmth inside, and tears rose to my eyes. The old woman's lilting voice and kind words helped me more than all her remedies.

"Arthur grew up and loved the outdoors, like his grandfather, the hunter-tribesman. He was always bringing home wild animals to me to heal. He called them 'his animals' . . . Anyway, that's how I learned to care for them. We had moved to this small farm community near Ruhuna, and both of us felt welcomed here. Those were happy times."

"In this house?" I asked.

"I moved here later," she said, clarifying. "This house is in the jungle. After Arthur died I moved here. Before that, we lived in another place nearer to Kataragama, just outside the jungle . . ."

Hanna excused herself to make tea. I was sorry to have broken the spell of her narrative, and agreed to help by bringing out the cups. A few minutes later, we again sat in front of the fire with hot beverages. The tea was bitter as usual . . . I had almost gotten used to such fare.

"Anyway," she continued after setting down her teacup, "Arthur was a great boy; had a natural talent for healing too. He also loved to travel, but was also very angry and stubborn . . . a fighter. Often in trouble with the authorities. I spent most of my time worrying about him when he went on his long trips to the jungle, bringing home sick animals. I tried to help by learning the ancient herbal medicine myself . . .

"Well, one day it happened . . . he was attacked by a spotted leopard. Ripped up fairly badly," she said nervously. I hung on her words, sure that this was the end of Arthur. I felt as if I knew this person.

"He survived that," she added, "but barely. I took care of his wounds for weeks. He had a fever for a time, and almost died from it." She took another sip of tea as I fed the fire with a few more twigs. The chemistry of the moment was magical. Loving. Warm. Completely safe. The old woman's story contained the stuff of legends, and I felt myself melting into her words.

"Like his father, he wanted to go fight. So when the second world war came, he begged for them to allow him to go to England as a soldier. I don't even know why. He said he just had to go. Restless, I suppose . . . had to get away from this small island. It was not easy for him or me. I didn't want him to go, and colored soldiers were urged to stay home and fight on the Asian front instead. He was denied a visa.

"But because he was so determined to fight, he enlisted with the Allied forces stationed in Colombo. When the Japanese bombed Ceylon ports in April of 1942, he was there. I started to go to him . . . couldn't bear the thought of losing him . . . again."

"Did you go?"

"Not right away. I stayed here, taking care of his beloved animals. Later, after the danger had passed, some soldiers came to get me. I found out Arthur survived the attack . . . wounded, but in one piece. They had put him in a hospital and said they needed more help treating the wounded. After he was better, Arthur and I stayed on to help . . . mostly because of our talents for healing."

"How was he wounded?"

"From a piece of metal," she said, "shrapnel from one of the bombs. Legs and stomach. These wounds bothered him, but he kept on working. Helping others. Studying the herbs and medicines until he changed . . ." Another pause. I said nothing, figuring she was working her way around to it.

"He just went crazy one day," she said plainly. "I was heartbroken, but determined to do all I could for him."

"When was this," I asked, trying to get some fix on the story.

"Oh," she said, leaning back in her chair, "about thirty-seven or so years ago . . . in 1950. He was only 33."

"What happened?"

"He fell off the edge of World's End," she said. I instantly felt a chill in my spine. "He had just lost his uncle, but I thought everything else was fine. He was married to a lovely Sinhalese woman outside of Galle. His son, little George was just three years old. One day, he went into the jungle to search for his father's people, and just . . . went crazy."

"Does this have anything to do with *'Yaka Raume'*?" I asked, suspicious.

"How do you know about *that*?" she responded curtly, as if the name itself were a curse.

"Apparently, I experienced one myself," I sighed. The old woman stopped rocking and leaned forward in her chair. She glared at me skeptically, then shook her head and relaxed back into the chair.

"No, son, you just *think* you did," she said assuredly.

"But Pachili said . . ."

"Pachili?!" she cried, then leaped out of her chair towards me. Getting closer to my face, I could tell she was noticeably paler. "A Buddhist monk?!"

"Yes, why . . ?"

"He's alive??! Where . . . what you doing with *him?!*"

Suddenly I felt like a pariah. The normally loving Hanna glared at me desperately, as if she had seen a ghost. The old woman grew still paler, her chest heaved, and she gasped for breath. I was speechless and feared for her life . . . heart attack! I jumped up, held her hand while squeezing her little finger to ease the stress - a little trick I'd learned from Alfred.

It worked. After a couple of minutes, she sighed some relief and settled back into her chair. Her color, however, had not yet returned; I still worried about her . . . Why would a normally sedate human being go into such shock? Her breathing again became labored and I was afraid I would lose her. I quickly made her some of her own prescription herb tea, following brief instructions. She drank two cups before finally sinking into the

249

safety of her rocker. I wanted her to lie down, but she insisted on sitting, waving me off.

"I'm better now," she panted, "thank you." For a few minutes, Hanna just stared off into space with eyes as wide as I'd ever seen. Finally, she looked and me and asked, "How do you know, child?"

"Know *what,* Hanna?" I puzzled innocently. I was starting to realize there was something about this mysterious monk that many people on this island found rather unsettling.

"This . . . Pachili . . ." Hanna sat curled up in her chair, softly weeping. I wanted to comfort her, to tell her I was sorry. But I didn't know why . . . or when this monster hurt her.

"I met him in Colombo," I said. "He gave me homeopathic remedies, that's all." Hanna started breathing a little easier, although I remained very concerned about her condition. I could only just sit and wait while she rested. Eventually her breathing became normal again.

"Pachili . . ." said the now-fragile old woman, finally uncoiling herself from her seat, "was . . . or *is* . . . my older brother."

Chapter Forty-Five

"Brother?!" I exclaimed in response to an item that defied all logic. It was my turn to be shocked. *"Older . . . brother?!"*

Hanna's words hung like suspended particles in the air. For a full minute, I couldn't bring myself to move . . . barely to breathe. The moment was supercharged. My mind rebelled. "Naaaaah!" I groaned skeptically, "That can't be! The Pachili I know is middle-aged. There must be some mistake!"

"He's slightly balding? . . . a Buddhist monk?" she queried, "Healer? Likes to walk everywhere? German accent? Missing part of a little finger on his right hand?"

"That's him . . . but how??" I implored. Suddenly, my mind ceased to operate . . . and the old woman was no help. After laying this bomb in my lap, she rose from her rocking chair and disappeared into the next room. I was left with my emptiness.

"Will is free in the Zone. No rules . . . Fantastic things ."

Hanna returned with a handkerchief in her hand. She ambled slowly to her rocker, paused, then sank into it once again. "If he's still alive, I wonder why he never bothered to visit me . . ." she continued, almost as if talking to herself. "Then again, you may have met his ghost." Mind spinning, I tried to pull myself out of shock, but my eyes and mouth couldn't seem to respond. Finally, I was able to mutter a few words.

"I'm sorry, Hanna," I said, begging indulgence from the aged matron while hyperventilating, "I . . . this . . . is almost too much for me to take. I . . . I need to walk." With that, I got up from my cushion on the floor and headed for the front door. I needed time to sort things out. Once outside, I began to hike, heading down the long, wooded driveway to the main road about two miles away. I had walked this path many times over the last few days, and felt safe in the waxing moonlight.

Logic had failed me. The mystery, the magic was so tangible I had trouble staying centered. I felt the urge to leave my body, to travel . . . to fly again into that imagined Zone. Nothing else made sense - that, and walking.

Was the old woman lying? I hardly think so; it's difficult to mimic a heart attack. Then *how . . ?!* A hundred year-old Buddhist who looked fifty and had the stamina of a twenty-year old? Pachili? Was he really a ghost? If so, how . . ?

"Death? . . . You get used to it."

World's End?? Veddhas? Crows? *Chi? Knowing?* Killer. Death and sex. Magic; it came at me from all directions. I stopped walking to calm my mind. I knew if I started rationalizing, I would go insane.

"Fantastic things . . .Trust even when there is no reason to trust. Ghosts . . . these things are around us all the time."

I let out a giant laugh, interrupting the screeching cacophony of the jungle. I then started spinning . . . spinning . . . like a whirling dervish, or a child in the middle of a field, drunk with bliss. Suddenly everything seemed so bizarre . . . funny . . . *hilarious!* I whirled out of control . . .

"WHOOOOO CAAAARES . . ?!"

I shouted it over and over again. I howled at the moon and the owls. I talked to the crickets. I ran. I jumped and crawled. I had no boundaries anymore . . . nothing. Finally - exhausted from whirling and screaming - I collapsed in the middle of the dirt road and wept.

Chapter Forty-Six

"What happened to Pachili?" I murmured hesitantly.

"He started traveling when I was still at home," related the old woman as she poured my morning tea. "Pachili never followed the rules. He made his own."

I listened, wide awake but still feeling the effects of my cathartic night. I didn't sleep the whole evening: wandering wild through the jungle . . . yelling at the moon. Climbing trees. Or whirling in total silence. Hanna told me today was New Years Day, 1988, but I had no sense of time at all. Purged of intense feelings, I just sat at the old woman's table, listening to the rest of her bizarre tale unfold:

"Child, I've learned to keep things simple," she continued, "I don't get too amazed or upset about things anymore, but what you said shocked me." I sat mute, just staring at her.

"My brother would be old . . . older than me, and I haven't seen him in over fifty years. Alive? How?? I thought surely he was dead. How is he?"

"He hasn't aged a day over fifty-five," I reported.

"Well," she shrugged, "he certainly hasn't aged as much as I have! He always seemed to be up to something."

"Like what?" I asked, prepared to hear anything.

"Oh . . . like yoga, meditation, ancient Tantric rituals. Mostly, though, he just studied his books; ones he got from our father . . ."

"But, even if we are talking about the same man, how could he be your *brother*?" I asked, "The man I know is German. *You* said you came from Holland!"

"I did, that's true," she acknowledged, "But our family is originally from Bavaria. Around Regensburg. Father's name was Franz Buchhauser, a homeopathic doctor who died in a

253

hunting accident when I was two. After a few years of trying to feed and clothe us, Mother finally sent my brothers and me to Holland to stay with relatives, then joined us later.

"Karl - or Pachili as he calls himself now - didn't like it and ran away . . . back to Germany," she added, shaking her head. "He was about 14 at the time, I was eight, and my younger brother six. Nobody knew where he went until years later when he wrote us from Istanbul. That was in 1905."

"So," I interrupting Hanna after doing some quick math calculations, "Pachili is over a hundred years old?!" I felt a lump in my throat as I said the words.

"It doesn't seem possible, does it?" She chuckled softly. "He was always fascinated by mysterious things. I guess he found a way to live forever . . . or come back as a ghost. I know not which. He scares me, that Karl. Used to return home with wild stories of his travels. His letters and postcards were filled with accounts of new discoveries, strange people, new lovers . . ."

"Pachili," I giggled, "had lovers??"

"Oh yes," she said emphatically, "He was quite a lady's man; wore the latest styles and lived in the best luxury. We always wondered where he got his money. He said he had wealthy patrons who loved his skills as a doctor and his zest for life. He knew some very influential people.

"Then he went to Russia." Hanna paused a moment, drank a sip of tea, then offered me some. I declined. "Russia changed him," she said solemnly.

"How so?"

"He wrote us that he met Rasputin." My eyes widened.

"Wasn't he the mad monk who cared for the Czar's wife and ailing son . . . and was murdered before the revolution?" I asked for clarification.

"The same," she said. "He mentioned Rasputin, but never wrote us much about him while in Russia. We thought Karl had gone crazy. His letters were filled with wild, prophetic things . . . many of which have come true."

"Like what?"

"Oh," she sighed, "like the Russian revolution. That wasn't so difficult to see coming . . . after all, he was *there*.

254

"But then there were other things," she added with a sigh while pausing to reflect as she leaned forward in her chair. "He said Germany would lose the war, then go through a terrible time: inflation, starvation. He also predicted someone would lead Germany into a second disastrous war . . . all within thirty years!"

"How did he know these things?" I queried, amazed at the man's abilities.

"He never said," she said, smiling. "All I knew is that I respected his wisdom, even if I didn't understand it. He always turned out to be right . . . Anyway, when he wrote, begging us to leave Europe, we did. He said the world was turning upside down and it was not safe. That's how I came here."

"What happened to your younger bother," I asked. The elderly Hanna's eyes misted over again.

"The first big war took him," she declared sadly. "Philip insisted on staying and enlisting with the Kaiser's army. He said he had a duty to perform."

"What happened?" I repeated hesitantly.

"Nerve gas," the elderly matriarch sighed as she fiddled with her teacup handle. "They took him to a field hospital where he died, apparently after lingering for hours . . .

"Anyway, after Philip's death, Karl visited me once in Sri Lanka and spent much time with Arthur. They walked all the time; went on these long trips . . .

"Then Karl just went away. To Tibet, then India. That's where he changed his name and went into silence. After a brief correspondence, we never heard from him again. Arthur was devastated, swearing he would go there and join him."

Suddenly, she gave me a funny look, as if she recognized someone. We remained in this pregnant silence for almost thirty seconds; the ancient figure just stared at me. For a moment, I thought she was going to climb inside my head.

"What is it, Hanna?" I queried, unable to cope with the sudden intensity.

"I'm not so sure," said Mrs. Vidya, shaking her head as if to wake up, "I just saw something familiar in your eyes."

"More worms?" I quipped. She giggled; apparently, this broke her spell.

"No, child," she said as she struggled to rise from her chair and hobble over to a shelf on the wall. She retrieved and small item and ambled over to me. "Arthur idolized Karl, er . . . Pachili. Wanted to be like him," she said softly, showing me a piece of blue tartan cloth as she unraveled it before me. "Anyway, this is Arthur's scarf. Its the last thing I made him before he died. I want you to have it." As I studied the texture of the gift, I felt confused.

"Wh-Why are you giving this to me?" I asked, hoping the light of reason would give me something to hold onto.

"Maybe I'm getting a little too sentimental in my old age," said Hanna. "I suppose I am . . . Anyway, for a moment, you reminded me of Arthur, and I wanted to give you this . . . so I can finally let him go. Crazy, eh?"

I suddenly felt overwhelmed with gratitude. A jolt of energy surged through me, forcing tears to well up.   I fought to maintain composure and to understand what was happening to me.   "Not at all," I said, wiping my eyes, "Please go on." Hanna reached over and patted my hands. Her look was so loving and warm, I almost forgot where I was.

"Well," she continued, "Karl and Arthur truly loved each other. That's why I was so surprised when my brother disappeared so suddenly. He wrote us from India saying he would be retiring to an ashram, and that we would not hear from him again."

"After that, Arthur got very sick . . . crazy . . . When he realized his uncle was not coming back, he started living in another world . . ." she lamented. "I guess the loss of his only father figure was too much.

"My boy then went to be with his father's people, the Veddhas . . . Well, something happened to him. He came back different. Talked about the *Yaka Raume* . . . those accursed 'devil circles' that I used to dismiss as so much superstition. Talked crazy . . . said he was cursed . . . killed his *guru*. I tried every herbal mixture I could think of to bring him out of it, but it didn't matter. Nothing worked.

256

"Did he . . ?" I asked intently.

"Kill someone? Hard to say," she responded, "He acted so crazy. Maybe he did . . ." Hanna paused, shaking her head. I thought for a minute she might stop talking. Instead, she continued: "One day, he just left us: me, his wife and child . . . drove towards the interior . . . to the mountains. I feared for him. Word came back he became a primitive man again, killing livestock then escaping into the wilderness."

"Then what happened?" I asked with trepidation.

"I never saw him alive again."

"But how do you know Arthur's dead?"

"I saw his crushed body before cremation," explained my host, hanging her head, "He jumped off the edge of World's End." I sighed and leaned back against a low table.

"Did the police check for any foul play?" I asked.

"They had no proof of any," she said, "No witnesses; they called it a suicide. His wife just collapsed . . . gave little George to me to raise, then went to England to be a house servant. She sent us money for a little while, but died there a few years later."

This strange conversation was again taking its toll on me. I dismissed myself to go to her sink and wash my face, wondering what to make of everything. The feelings I felt were stronger than mere empathy. I speculated that Arthur, too, fell into the Zone, and that we were sharing the same bizarre experience . . . lifetimes apart.

I was also feeling slightly insane . . . ready to cut loose any minute . . . go on a rampage. Was I channeling her long-lost son? If so, was I also being urged to kill?! I felt nauseous again. Sick. I washed my face, trying to wipe off Arthur's guilt . . . a foggy film that stuck to my brain. There was something here for me, but no story could explain it.

"Let all experience be a meditation."

I let it go and returned to the table to listen without further thought or comment. "You mentioned your mother . . . Whatever happened to her?" I asked.

257

"My mother? When we left, she contracted Typhoid fever, and died after the war. I missed her badly, and begged her to come live with us; that I would take care of her. She never did. Having disowned Karl, she spent all her time mourning Philip's death. She was also angry at me for listening to Karl . . . leaving and marrying 'that primitive colored man' as she called George."

"Even after George's death?"

"No. She forgave me, but she still didn't want to come to Sri Lanka. Never met her grandson." With that, Hanna chuckled softly, "Maybe she was afraid she might love him - and this country - too much."

We sat quietly as the morning sun burst over the eastern tree line, flooding her small kitchen with a spectacle of light. I heard a faint rumble in the distance. Hanna got up from her perch and headed for the door.

Chapter Forty-Seven

"You heard *that*?" I asked in amazement. I could barely hear the vehicle approaching myself. How did the sensory acumen of this 96-year old develop so sharply?!

"That's the park ranger with another sick animal. I'd better go meet him," explained the old woman. "Would you like to come?"

"I'd better not," I said tentatively, still feeling the sting of our last encounter, "He might want to drag me away again."

"Not if you're with me," said Hanna, "but if you feel better, just wait here." The old woman then excused herself and walked out into her front yard, closing the door behind her. Still sitting at the window, I observed a familiar land rover approaching. It was the same park ranger that hit me - the tall one with the safari hat. He was alone this time.

My host greeted the ranger as he lifted a small animal from the back of his rover. Hanna then ambled over to her outdoor building or barn to make a place for it as the official followed dutifully, carrying the creature in his arms. Five minutes later he left, and Hanna returned to the house.

"You want to see the deer?" she asked as she came inside.

"I sure do," I affirmed. It was a rare opportunity to see the master herbalist at work on somebody other than me. I rushed to follow the spry young 96-year-old as she sprinted to her barn. There, in a small corral, lying in a pile of hay, was a baby fawn. My heart instantly melted as I saw the creature lying so listless.

"It's a spotted deer . . . a baby doe," said Hanna. "It got separated from its mother and is dying."

"What will you do for her?" I asked.

"Herbs, of course," replied Hanna with a solemn twinkle in her eyes. "She's just depressed. That's all."

I followed the progress of the small doe throughout the day. By the following morning, she was up and running around the corral. Meanwhile, she had tended a few dozen other small sick or wounded animals, some of whom had been there for days or weeks.

I was dying to ask her about the crows on the island. I finally had a chance to pop the question that evening, on the way back to her small cabin.

"The crows?" she chirped, "They own the island!"

"Own . . ?" I asked, slightly puzzled.

"Yes," she continued as we once again entered her front door. "You see, crows are different . . . they take on a strange power all their own."

"I discovered that," I said, taking the next few minutes to relate my experiences with the creatures. "What do you make of it?" I waited for her answer while she prepared another herbal compound and heated some water on her kerosene stove. I figured it best to move slowly with such an old person. I was hesitant to tell her everything; still afraid she might die on me or something.

"I will tell you, child," she grinned while serving me some of her famous bitter tea, "I've seen a few things in my years on this earth . . . and I've had many visitors . . ."

"Like who?" I asked, almost hesitant to find out.

"You see," she explained, "I believe the moment someone dies, his spirit travels. Goes places . . . or comes up in some other form" She paused.

"Yes?" I urged.

"Oh, I might as well tell you," she shrugged, "You handled the worm problem easily enough . . . You see, upon death, many spirits go into the bodies of these crows." Her words didn't surprise me. I sat enthralled. "Sometimes, the dead take on other life forms . . . like certain monkeys or langurs."

"I had heard the island rumors."

"These are more than rumors," she stated emphatically. "They are true."

"How can you be so sure," I asked my host, "that these animals hold spirits of the dead?" I had just swallowed my bitter tea too quickly, and was trying to speak through a sudden coughing spell.

"You have seen their eyes . . . and still you doubt?" she marveled. I noticed I dropped back into my old habits again: always thinking, always looking for proof. I admitted I wasn't sure of much anymore.

"You have a right to your doubts," stated Hanna sadly, "but a mother can always recognize her son." She looked at me with such limpid eyes, and such a sincere quality, I let all logic go.

"One day," she continued, "a farmer brought me a wounded crow shortly after Arthur died. He had a gunshot wound and was missing a leg, but still alive.

"He had Arthur's eyes," she concluded.

"What did you make of this?"

"He just came to say good-bye," sighed the old woman, "but didn't survive the night . . . more tea?" I sighed with her, feeling another rush of weird nostalgia, then finished my last gulp.

"Please, no thank you," I answered, thankful to be through with the last cup. I felt better, but still had difficulty downing all this nasty herb.

"And sometimes I see old friends in the eyes of monkeys," said my elderly host, her tone shifting noticeably. "When you live as long as I have, you see many people come and go . . . then come again. One particular old friend visits me quite regularly. He is a big langur that meditates on the edge of the jungle every morning. I used to see him during one of my long walks. I don't walk that much any more."

I stayed enraptured by the old woman's stories of reincarnated souls well into the night. Although she professed to be from a Christian background, I could sense her delight in discovering the mysteries life had to offer.

Chapter Forty-Eight

"Saturday, January 2, 1988" was the first thought I had upon waking with an inner calmness I had not felt in years. I was glad to feel balanced again. Normal. My joy was bittersweet, however: I knew I'd be leaving in a few hours.

I spent the morning helping Hanna with the animals, taking a walk, and meditating. I asked many questions about Pachili and Bija, but Hanna confessed she didn't recognize the name 'Bija,' or the ashram I spoke of in Kataragama.

"After Arthur's death, I never heard from Karl," reported my elderly host. "It was almost as if he had fallen off the cliff himself. I occasionally heard rumors about him. I knew he survived the Chinese invasion of Tibet, but that's all. I've not heard about him in on the island since his last visit."

"So, George has never met his great-uncle," I interjected.

"Oh, he remembered Karl from when he was a little one," she said, "and even checked into his disappearance when he was older. He could find nobody who knew anything until he met a disciple from a remote Mahayana Buddhist sect. The fellow claimed Pachili died in northern India at the ashram . . . swept away in a flood!"

****

Saying good-bye proved more difficult than I imagined. Although I had known Hanna only a short while, I felt she was almost family to me. George Vidiya arrived mid-morning as promised. His grandmother had packed a "goody bag" (as she described it) with Arthur's woolen scarf and some of her nasty-tasting herbs. George also carried a sack of herbs to deliver to pharmacists in Galle and Colombo.

I hugged my gracious host tightly. She returned the embrace, holding me for such a long time I felt she would never let go. Finally, she released her solemn grip, planted a huge kiss on my cheek, and looked me in the eyes.

"You know where your home is . . ." she said, tears falling from her eyes. "I may not be here, but somehow . . . I know we will meet again." I looked into her soulful eyes, tempted to just drop my bags and stay. Maybe she thought of me as her lost son, but it didn't matter. I had not felt such a complete love from any one person before.

Reluctantly, I climbed into the passenger side of George's rover. "Dear, dear Hanna," I said as the elderly figure climbed back on her small porch, "I don't know how to thank you . . ."

"Don't worry about it, love," she said, waving. "You already have. You are such a joy to me."

I smiled through the tears and waved to my elderly friend as I held one of her charges, the spotted deer. I had agreed to travel with George back into the jungle to help return some animals. The deer lay calmly covered in my lap, while a small monkey squealed nervously in a cage in the back. He had just recovered from a broken leg. I considered myself among these fortunates, having been under Hanna's care. It's just that George was taking me to a different jungle.

"Thank you again, dear woman. And God bless you."

"*Ayubowan!* See you next go-round," shouted George Vidiya as he cranked up the rover and headed down the small driveway. The deer, now healthy, found the noise disturbing, and wriggled to escape.

"Hold her," shouted George above the wind, "We will let her go in about fifteen minutes; I know the perfect place up the road." We soon escaped the wooded area and headed for a grassy savanna.

George did find the perfect place. Spotted deer families were in the area, and the tall grasses swayed with a majesty I'd seen only in video clips. I turned the deer loose; she instantly ran for cover behind some scrub brushes. We set the gray monkey free in another area more suited to his tastes: an area of dense foliage and many trees. He seemed pleased, smiling at me before turning and heading into the thick brush.

"I wonder," I said as we barreled out of Yala Park, towards Kataragama, "can we stop someplace in the city? I'm curious about something."

"Certainly," boomed George, "I know every building in the city. Where do you want to go?" I described Bija's ashram in detail, then told him I wanted to stop in and tell them I was leaving. I figured, with a little luck, we might even run into Pachili. For a while, George looked puzzled and didn't say anything. Then he asked me to repeat my description. After I did so, he puzzled some more.

"I am not aware of such a building in Kataragama," he said.

"I was *in* the building, George," I answered with a familiar sense of foreboding rising in my belly. "I practically memorized every detail!" George shook his head in silence as we approached the Holy City.

"Don't know of any building like it," he repeated. I had that strange feeling come back to me . . .

"Ancient Chi . . . impressions; the Zone hides in common places. Keep awareness close."

"George?" I said, turning to my driver, "Is there an old temple - tall white, but simple - with many carvings on the front entrance facing east?"

"Oh yes," bubbled the big man, "That's the *Maha Devala,* a shrine dedicated to Skanda, the Hindu war-god. You want to go *there?*"

"Have you found anything strange about the place?" I inquired, trying to fit pieces of lost memory together. George thought for a moment while he stuck his hand out the window of the land rover, as if checking for rain.

"Sometimes," he said hesitantly. "Sometimes when I am there, I get the feeling I'm sinking inside myself. It is a wonderful place for meditation, but some - a few people - find the place frightening; won't go near it. Most of those who go are religious pilgrims. They take some simple offering to receive blessings.

"Why do you ask?" he added.

"Nothing," I said, "It's just that I thought maybe there was some connection . . ."

"Here is Kataragama, doctor," interrupted George, "The temple is straight ahead. Do you want me to drive there?" Curiously, I said yes, while my *ku* was screaming at me to stop. Not knowing what this was about, I nevertheless decided to heed the warning.

"Stop here!" I yelled to George suddenly without knowing why. "I can't explain it, George, but I'm also afraid to go near that temple . . !" The big guy pulled over to the side of the road next to a crowded fruit stall and turned off the engine.

"The remedies are a only a window to the Zone. You must then use intent to walk through the door."

I turned to him, casting out all pretenses of sanity: "Do you know about the Zone?" I asked intently.

"No," said George as he looked me over, concerned.

"Devil Circles?"

"Yes, but why . . ."

"If you take me there, will you keep me close to the jeep, no matter what I say or do . . . and no matter what happens?!"

"Yes," he said, "but . . ."

"Another thing, George," I added, "If you see me looking crazy or something, will you stay with me and keep me safe until I snap out of it?"

"Yes, but I . . ."

"Please, George," I implored, "Just do as I ask. Maybe *nothing* will happen, but . . ." I found myself grabbing his shoulder as if making a dying request. Something in me had already snapped, but I chose to just watch . . . and then fell into silence. The big driver sat dumbfounded, silently staring at me, not knowing what to make of the whole scene. As a crowd began to gather, he looked embarrassed, then finally acquiesced.

"I . . . I will do whatever you ask," he said, "I do not understand this fear, but I will help you . . . Now can we go?" I relaxed my grip on his shirt and pointed to the rode ahead. George cranked up the rover, then honked at the crowd.

266

Was I crazy? Maybe so, but I could no longer hide behind the polite mask of reason. The pull of the Zone was too strong; the pull of Pachili's words too intimate. I fell back in my seat, unable to talk as our vehicle maneuvered slowly through the thickening crowd towards the temple.

Chapter Forty-Nine

I opened my eyes and looked around. A dream . . . but a fully conscious one. Surreal figures danced in my awareness.

It was late afternoon in a dimly lit room - at the same ashram as before in my visions, but much cleaner. I was sitting on a satin pillow in the middle of the shiny dark marble floor. The ashram had about two dozen disciples - some of them westerners. They sat, connected in small circles. I didn't know where I fit in, so I chose simply to stand and observe.

A beautiful Indian woman sat on the floor in the middle of the room, staring at me. I thought this odd . . . and rather uncharacteristic of Asian female behavior. She had on a luxurious purple robe, and sat with her hands wrapped around one of her knees. At first I reacted by averted my eyes, but decided to take a deep breath, let go of the false modesty, and returned her gaze.

The look was strong, and very familiar. Unaccustomed to such pure acceptance, I melted into the gaze, simultaneously aware of the subtle movement rising through my body towards the top of my head. I had a strong sexual desire for her . . . knew we had been together. But then my feelings expanded - transformed themselves into an ocean of exhilaration flowing into my senses, then out again. Soft. Rhythmic.

A figure emerged from the shadows to my left. It was Bija, the old man. Although he did not speak, I felt a magnetism swirling about him. He was obviously the master of this small group, by virtue of his quiet dignity.

As the bearded one approached, my heart spontaneously unfolded. I knew that, although I was not one of his group of followers, it didn't matter. The love he showered upon me was intense, unconditional and unremitting. Compelled to obeisance, I fell to my knees. He stopped as I saw his sandals turn to face me, his white robe rustling softly. He paused, then got on *his* knees in front of me. I looked up and saw . . . remembered . . . those loving, fiery eyes . . . burning into my very being. I froze, transfixed. He leaned closer. Closer, until his forehead touched mine. I closed my eyes, thoughts spinning wildly.

"Your mother had trouble; your grandmother had trouble. Now you have trouble," Bija said softly as he rocked his forehead back and forth on mine. "Compassion and anger . . . unbalanced."

I didn't know what he meant, but somehow it didn't matter. Light appeared in the center of my forehead, as if I were witness to an atomic explosion on the horizon. The luminous specter spread horizontally, then expanded . . . Before I knew it, I burst into tears. I became a dance. I became the dream. My body felt dizzy and nauseous as I floated in a rarefied mist-world between experience and magic.

I floated a long time, entering a world of dizzy inner discovery. Then deathly silence. I didn't dare open my eyes . . . waiting . . . waiting for some cue . . . some sign for action.

"Speak," came a voice at last, softly lifting my amorphous senses out of their deep slumber. I felt sick.

"Is this real?" was all I could ask as I opened my eyes witness the explosion of beauty happening around me. In the midst of this cosmic halo sat Bija.

"Quite real, *Govinda*," he answered, his eyes sparkling with life and love. *Govinda* . . . echoed the sound. I felt the nausea lifting, like a fog in the bright sunshine. The sound of the name brought memory and tears to my eyes . . . I could hardly bring myself to speak.

I wanted to ask the meaning of the name; instead I sobbed, choking back the flood of joyous tears that threaten to overwhelm me. My mind surrendered to the moment as the patriarch came closer to my face and gazed into my eyes for what seemed like an eternity. He then put his hand on my brow, and I felt a familiar electric sensation, as if suspended in a magnetic field. I totally relaxed.

"Master of the senses," he whispered, "relax and enjoy. I will guide you."

All others in the room disappeared; soon the room itself disappeared. I remained suspended in time and space. My body was an afterthought. The sound of *Govinda* engulfed me as I drifted. No feeling. No sensation. No thought.

There was nothing.

I opened my eyes. There was no indication of time at all. It simply didn't matter. My joyful attention danced to the window . . . the one I remembered. White silk curtains floated lazily into the clear, marble room. Outside, I could see a garden. It was all so *familiar!*
It *was* familiar! It was . . .
I arose and ran to the window. There in the glorious morning were trees and flowers - tulips; hundreds of them - spread out in all directions. And butterflies . . !
I looked around and realized I was alone. Then the thought came: "You have always been alone."
I understood.

Silence reigned; thoughts fell like light on the morning dew. My old questions already contained the answers within them. I never knew I was this . . . this *vast sea* of knowledge, bliss, and light. I felt at once both newly born and ancient.

"As long as the 'I' is trapped by continuity . . . expectations . . . you are a prisoner to the past and the future."

I was drawn inward, starting below my navel and rising to my heart, then out. Everything appeared to be connected to this bliss . . . this life-line! I found myself focusing on all the details in the room. I studied the majestic gray-black marble floors and columns, and the intricate murals on the curved walls and domed ceiling. I felt the satin pillows placed neatly around the room, and marveled at the bright diffusion of light that seemed to permeate everything.
I also noticed my body's manner, thoughts, and speech: separate, but not gone. Scenes in time unfolded before on a multi-dimensional scroll. The scroll material itself was my

271

unfolding consciousness . . . going both backwards and forwards in time.

I saw the vague memories: the healer, living . . . then dying, the old woman in the jungle, Sri Lanka . . . and Ruth . . . those same eyes of the Indian woman. I saw the pain of letting go of her . . . the searing pain of separation, and burning desire for enlightenment. There was no place, I said, for our union . . . something went wrong. I was supposed to die . . . to transform, but didn't. I jumped . . . then great darkness.

The scroll closed, then disappeared except for a thread. Fear. Great fear. Desires not fulfilled. Promises previously not kept . . . I fell silent once more, following the thread:

"Intent was established ages ago . . . follow the flavor . . .
"Bija is . . . the master . . . the deathless one . . .
"I am . . .
"I am . . .
"I've come home.
"I never left . . ."

"Intent," announced Pachili simply, "all the scattered remnants of *Chi* come back to you. As you see, I never left you as your mind insists."

I never questioned his appearance. It seemed so natural. Eyes now fully opened, I gazed upon my beloved guide, mute. Nothing needed to be said. We floated in a vast shared communion that seemed to go on eternally. Then, as easily as he came, Pachili disappeared. I felt a sensation between my eyebrows - a feeling of something opening. I watched as my consciousness plummeted boldly into the black spot before me. Afraid, I watched and continued to let go . . .

"Melt the fear . . ."

I plunged headlong into a darkness so black I began to witness a growing . . . light. A LIGHT, unlike any I had ever seen . . . a pool of clarity that exploded from the center of the dark space and poured into me. I lost contact with my body, with time, with all continuity . . . I was dying!

272

"Melt the fear . . ."

Hours passed. Maybe days. Or seconds - they all appeared simultaneously - my continuous climax subsided. In its place, the clarity of the sky. A glorious openness.

I opened my eyes . . . eyes that appeared in *knowing* as part of the whole, like operating appendages on the tip of a branch of consciousness that spread over millions of miles and thousands of years.   My hands and fingers - if you could call them "mine" - moved around the space before me as if caressing a lover. My body undulated softly to a low hum that permeated everything. I tasted a subtle sweetness . . .

"*Govinda,*" someone whispered, "is ready."

"Good," came the sound of Bija's voice. He then reached for his cane, turned to me, and whacked the top of my head . . . !

Chapter Fifty

Reeling from the sudden blow, I gasped as the room spun like a Ferris wheel loose from its moorings . . .

"Let go," came a familiar voice, *"Relax into it . . . Watch. Observe. Accept. Transcend the killer.*

"The Zone will pull you in . . . blinded by appearances and never get out . . .

"Stay awake . . . afraid, angry, or sad . . . can take one second, or lifetimes."

Suddenly I was acutely aware of death and chaos all around me.

"Death. . . outward expression of the gap."

I dropped the fear, emerging into an area that glowed with a soft, bright amber light. A hushed quiet fell. Again I fell into a deep silence. Alone.

The amber light had come within me. There was no movement, no feeling but a hum . . . a tangible eeriness. My body twitched and my face felt suddenly distorted. I gasped and gargled . . . like a wolf! My jaw drew back and swallowed my head . . . out of the throat emerged a long, dark network of circles - and wings fluttering at my side, majestically guiding me. I felt a subtle lift. Almost discernible, then . . . gone. Wings. Trees. Ocean. An intense emerald streak melting into deep blue, then yellow.

Full moon. Poya Day. So quickly . . . Moon. Stars . . . all came inside of me . . . *a part of me!* Faster. Another circle.

Approach . A tunnel of streaked light. No light. Emptiness. Darkness mixed with heaviness. Feel. No place. Lightness of heart. Circling. Looking. Moving towards the sea . . .

Two people in the midst of a crowd, one of them George. The other, familiar figure was whirling about in circles . . . gyrating wildly. Crazy. Ran into the side of the wall of the large temple. I closed my eyes . . . dare I open them again? No. I knew the figure was Matthew Cannon. I had left. What remained was dying . . . being pulled apart by the forces of pure chaos! From above I watched without concern. Without fear. Cold. Distant. Almost uncaring . . .

Shifted again . . . this time another circle, encased in a heavy light. For a while I could not move. Chord no longer attached to the figure. Tried again. No use. I was dying. On and on . . . Closer. Spiraling. Descending . . . then stopped.

Suddenly I felt pulled back - back to the ashram as if by a giant, invisible hand. I could not escape! The images of Pachili and Bija sat in the middle of the marble room, meditating. I also sat before them, staring . . . They looked so alike! Then I saw *they were only one.* Identical . . . one body, one being . . . *one Master.* Love poured out of me towards HIM. The radiance engulfed us all as I began to realize I had grown to encompass the room . . . even the Master!

Suddenly I *knew* . . . the Master and I . . . One. The same ONE . . ! I yearned to merge completely . . . to bind forever that which had been separate . . . to drop these bodies and flow eternally into the ONE I beheld within me. I had no more use for the illusions . . . the eternal ritual. The dance.

"Your intent is to kill . . . whole world dances to your song."

Without hesitating, I went to the wall and retrieved a curved dagger. Although my hands and arms shook violently, I had no feeling. None, other than a cold-blooded chill running through my veins as I approached the redundant robed body before me. This body had become too small to hold the love that

276

yearned to flow from us . . . from me! I was unafraid. I could never *really* kill that which was eternal, that which never died . . . I could never *really* destroy that which lived forever. We could only merge . . .

As a test, I thrust the dagger into my left leg, then pulled it out. Blood poured from the wound, but there was no pain. Only bliss!

"Do away with me . . . You are a killer. Accept. The seed remains. Trust . . . even when there is no reason to trust."

I raised the dagger over the form below me. "Namaste!" I shouted in reverence, then heard a voice . . .

"Arthur . . . *Govinda* . . ."

I looked up and beheld *him* . . . strangely familiar . . . average height and weight, about 35, reddish-blond hair, glasses. High forehead and ears, thin arms, delicate, strong hands . . . and those eyes! *Cannon!!* . . . Pus was pouring from his left leg . . . the same leg. He looked very sad.

"Let it go," he said, "Death. Just let it go . . ."

As consciousness dawned, I dropped to my knees. More blood issued from the self-inflicted wound. *Pain!* Suddenly, intense pain!! . . . There was no escaping it! I calmly placed the dagger before me, intending to fall on it myself. This form - the only remaining impediment to the Bliss of Eternity - would now dissolve.

The Master looked up, placed his outstretched hand on mine, and smiled knowingly: *"Govinda! Let it go! . . ."* he said in a voice that melted my mind and opened my heart, *"Let go of the pain . . . even the desire for enlightenment!"*

I gasped as the dagger fell to the floor, followed by tears. The cold-blooded chill was gone, replaced by the overwhelming relief of sadness and pain . . . and a love so profound, I covered my face, bowed and wept . . . then let it go. My head and heart

277

cleared. The Master would live. Arthur could rest. Matthew could heal. *Intent* was complete. Different bodies. One spirit.

As shocked devotees rushed over and wrestled me to the ground, it started raining. Pouring. Thunder and lightning rocked the hall as the sudden tempest rocked the ceiling and the walls. Torrential rain swept into the ashram as it fell from its foundation. The devotees released me and ran for their lives. I watched a deluge of water pouring in through the windows as dozens helplessly tried to escape through the only door. Flash flood!

My eyes followed suit, pouring out more tears as I released all remaining ideas about how I *thought* things were. Suddenly . . . I *knew*. I saw . . . and felt . . . and heard . . . but not with any senses I had used before. The deadly rising flood water swirled around and through me; connecting me to all things at once. All places. Events. People. The heavens unleashed their contents. I heard every sound. Felt every feeling. Every sight glowed with an intensity I had not known before . . .

"Concentrate on every detail. Silent witness. Illusion will fall away."

Again I flew . . . This time, consciously.

Chapter Fifty-One

"I'm O.K., George!" The words fell out of my mouth . . . "I'm O.K. . . ."

"Thank god!" sighed the big man as he let go of my shoulders. "I thought you were going to hurt yourself!" I was leaning against the car door, standing in the road in front of the *Maha Devala*. George appeared relieved. The small crowd that had gathered began to break up.

"What happened to you?!" implored my friend, again grabbing my shoulders to assist me back into the jeep. "You were acting crazy . . . your eyes rolled up, and I was concerned you might leave us for good!"

"I'm not quite sure . . ." I admitted truthfully.

"Come," emphasized George, "We'll talk later. For now, let's get some lunch. I promised Hanna I would make you take your herbs!" I offered no resistance as he drove deeper into town.

****

"I" never fully returned to my body. Now, that body was *within* me . . . a Self so large as to defy description. My sojourn into the Zone made me realize how *small* the I had been. How *very small* . . .

I could see George, speak to him; share food; even carry on a normal conversation. But I wasn't there. The name of *Govinda* rang deep inside like an ancient tuning fork. Nowhere in my former memory or experience did I have anything to compare with what transpired.

"Keep awareness close. The illusion will fall away."

I was in the midst of a massive inner movement . . . silent and blissful. Those moments of insanity bestowed on me a delicious clarity that trickled its way through my senses and into my being, like leaks in a breaking dam. My so-called realities were coming together, like pieces in a huge cosmic puzzle. I felt an aloneness - as well as a strong link with everything - I had never known before. Even in the midst of friends, I held a silent awareness so intimate, so vast, that my futile words could only distort it. I simply observed . . . a tiny speck of thinking astride a huge mountain of *knowing*. I wanted to laugh.

"More *papadam*, doctor?"

"No, thank you," I said, responding to the simple words of a beautiful woman. I was in love with George's wife, Divapura, and not ashamed to admit it. Their children too: Nali and Lali, aged 8 and 5 respectively. George, observing my strange behavior since Kataragama, was no longer sure what to make of me. I wasn't sure either, feeling more like a newborn infant than a grown man.

I had little appetite, content merely to sit and stare at events unfolding around me, as if dropped in the middle of a cartoon. Although I responded when asked, I had no desire for anything. A deep-seated joy anchored what was left of my identity to the body wrapped around it.

As I witnessed my hostess serve dinner, I fell back into the ocean of silent bliss that overflowed with every thought, every gesture. This subtle feeling that began at the Devil's Staircase now threatened to engulf me completely.

"The sun and stars rise and set in your eyes, sweet Divapura," I said, almost in tears as I held Mrs. Vidiya's hand. It was my second day in their home, and I wanted so much to share my happiness. She, alas, responded with an embarrassed smile, then glared at her husband who had just returned from putting their two children to bed.

"What time is your flight tomorrow afternoon?" asked George curtly, attempting to rescue me from my own blissful folly. "Three-thirty," I said, now giving him my full attention. I remembered my call the previous day to schedule the flight.

"Then we will be there at two o'clock, just to be safe. I don't suppose you will have any trouble getting out," George reminded me. "Even though your visa expired over two weeks ago; I'll just tell them you've been ill. We will stop by and obtain a written excuse from your Dr. Alfred . . . I've placed a telephone call to him. He invited us to his place at 11:30 for lunch. Will you be ready to leave Galle in the morning at six?"

"Yes," I said simply, trying my best to stay centered. More tears and laughter welled up inside of me. I excused myself and went outside.

With each step, I found it difficult to contain myself. Energy flowed into me from all directions, through all my senses at once. I was in love: with the air, the grass, the pavement, the pounding surf coming into the bay . . . this body that I found constantly amusing . . . and the strange hum that perpetually enlivened my being.

I ran along the retaining wall that surrounded the old Dutch fort. The Vidiyas had a small home near the main entrance to Galle, a beautiful old city.

While running I thought of another great friend of mine in Galle - a Muslim gem dealer named Ifthikar Mahuroof. I had had the rare pleasure of meeting his father Siddick when I first arrived in Sri Lanka and before he died – a wonderfully happy old man who gathered rice and food for the poor people from his sickbed. Since his passing, I remained fast friends with "Ifthi" and had hoped to see him again before I left. This was not to be however since I suddenly remembered Ifthi was off in Europe on another sales trip.

George thought it best that I stay with them in Galle one more night - for observation no doubt - to make sure I wasn't crazy. He once threatened to take me back to Hanna . . . or to the authorities, depending on his mood at the moment.

My heart poured out to George. As many times as I promised to behave, occasional torrents of bliss would surge through my veins. I found myself singing to people on the streets and roaring in laughter at their responses, which ranged from amusement to looks of terror.

George, hardly amused, would always haul me in and apologize to the spectators. He had, after all, lost his father to insanity and seemed mortified of the prospect of losing me, although he tried to pretend otherwise. Most residents of the island, however, responded in kind. When I laughed, they laughed. When I danced, they did likewise. Sri Lanka overflowed with crazies! We danced together and I loved them all.

"Matt!" I heard a voice cutting through the darkness. "Matt Cannon!!" I almost forgot the name.

"Here," I said softly as the familiar figure approached me, running. George looked worried.

"You ran off so suddenly," he said, "I didn't know what to think. Are you sufficiently well?"

"George," I bubbled, "if I were any better, I would start floating away. In fact, you'd better hold . . ."

"Come on, my good fellow," said the big man, grabbing me by the arm, "let's go home. You don't need to be running around out here alone."

"Maybe you're right," I said, surrendering to the force of reason . . . and George. He had chased me to the other end of the city. I followed obediently, although I could barely detect my feet touching the ground. I still had not told him about my experiences in the ashram, figuring that would lock me up for sure!

"Where are these so-called Devil Circles, George?" I asked Mr. Vidiya as he led me by the arm, "and what do you know about them?" He relaxed his grip when he saw my demeanor change.

"Many places, Dr. Matt," he answered vaguely. "All I know is that some people experience nothing. Others a little bit, and some few go crazy . . . but you don't think about those things now!"

"Don't patronize me, George," I said, stopping to stare at him. He bolted in surprise as my eyes searched his. He didn't want to discuss it, already afraid I was trapped in one . . . afraid I would go back and get killed. I related these thoughts to him.

"Its true," sobbed George, sitting on the curb, "I . . . I can't think of those beastly places without . . ."

282

"Without thinking of the father you lost," I said calmly, finishing his sentence. "It's O.K., George, I know about it." The big man covered his eyes and wept softly as I placed my hand on his back. My love for him grew as his heart - and my memory - opened.

"I don't know," he sobbed, "the look on your face at the temple. I knew that look and it scared me . . ."

"Up there, George," I said, interrupting, "Look . . . the constellation Orion!" I pointed to the eastern sky. "As a kid, I loved to look through my telescope at a galaxy in the middle of Orion's belt . . . M32 as I recall . . . was a hellova thing to see. Over a million light years away, but I can almost see it now . . . and feel it . . . Can you? Isn't that absolutely amazing?"

"How can you be so happy?" boomed my large friend, "What did you really see back there?"

"I saw life . . . all around me, George. In me: the same life. That's all."

"Mmmm . . ." he sighed. "I don't know if I'm ready for what you have. I have so many duties . . . Besides, how can I be happy? I lost both my parents; I'm trying to give my children what I never had . . . a family."

"Your father never died," I interrupted boldly, then modified my statement. "I feel his presence very strongly . . . like its a part of me." George smiled, accepting the idea without question.

I helped him back to his feet and we walked the rest of the way in silence, sharing an unspoken bond. I no longer had the desire to find out about devil circles. Or Pachili's third remedy . . . the one I never got. For now, that chapter was complete. If I never saw one again, it would be O.K. with me. I had everything I came for . . . and more. My life in the present was unbounded. The past was over. Complete. Tomorrow would take care of itself. Everything was done; I was not the doer any more.

George and I quietly bid each other goodnight as I took my sheet and pillow to the guest room. I was asleep in minutes.

Chapter Fifty-Two

The return trip to Colombo was like a pilgrimage. An adventure. Everything seemed so new. My gratitude and joy, unabated, flowed from me like fragrant emanations from a rose.

Riding in the passenger's seat of George's rover, I realized my whole body, mind, and senses had changed. Every bump in the road, every sound of traffic was a different flavor: some sweet, others spicy. Some blue, others a tart yellow. I absorbed it all into my nostrils, through my skin.

Our destination led us north along the coast, towards the city. Rounding a curve on a hill, I spied the misty ocean landscape below, sprinkled by a splash of morning dawn. Coconut trees were everywhere. The morning sun revealed a color and freshness I had not seen before. I became intoxicated with the beauty . . . The orange light of morning mixed its splendor with the wide expanse of greenery and the deepening blue of the sky.

Colombo beckoned. Sri Lanka's largest city, a vague memory for over three weeks, was now my vehicle for a new transition: home. At 8 o'clock we reached Mount Lavinia, hungry and ready for breakfast. Although today was Full Moon day, a time when most businesses closed, we were able to find a small cafe and grab a bite.

"Dr. Alfred said he was inviting some people over to say good-bye to you," said George as he sipped his hot tea while I asked for some eggs and toast. "A good-bye party, I suppose." I smiled, remembering Alfred's penchant for festivity.

"You asked me in Kataragama if I knew about devil circles. Do you still want to know?"

"Yes," I said, "if you want to tell me." George put down his teacup, leaned back in his chair, and spoke, almost in a whisper.

"I met a member of my grandfather's tribe when I was nineteen . . . a long time ago. He took me to the little Veddha village of Rathugala, in the center of one of the eastern national parks, Gal Oya . . ."

"Veddha . . ?" I exclaimed, suddenly making the aboriginal connection to Hanna and George.

"Yes, they are my ancestors," continued George, "The Gal Oya Park was traditional Veddha territory for centuries . . . until they built that huge irrigation project after WW II.

"Anyway, Rathugala is nothing special . . . just a few bark huts and half-naked hunters with use old rifles and a few bows and arrows. The clan, however, is still active. Many of them have left and joined society. Out of the ones who stayed, there are only a handful who retain the old ways."

"Like what?"

"Oh, hunting. Storytelling. Magic lore. Anyway. . . years later I met another old Veddha hunter near the Horton Plains. On holiday. Very strange . . . those people hardly ever leave their village. Anyway, there were perhaps a dozen tourists at World's End on that Saturday . . . they come and go. Once you've seen it, there's not much else to do but leave.

"He said he remembered me from my visit and looked for me. He appeared safe enough, so I went with him and he showed me one of those so-called *Yaka Raume*. He told me strange stories about animals, creatures, and men appearing and disappearing in them. Traveling great distances; things like that. I sat in it. Nothing happened, so I left."

"Is that all?" I asked.

"No," said George, "He also said he knew my father. Said my father had a different experience . . . succeeded in resurrecting the tribal magic, but lost his mind and died there. 'Too much of the world' he said. That's why he jumped off the edge, I suppose."

"What do you make of all this?" I asked.

"Well," he grimaced, "I believe there is something to what the old man told me. One of these days I would like to learn about it . . . but not while I have a family!"

I smiled, genuinely happy for him.

286

****

I returned to Dr. Goonilike's guest house to retrieve my belongings. Although I had not paid any extra for January, he didn't complain. Instead, he graciously wished me a safe journey home. Everything was as I left it - scattered and untidy. I had not been back since December 5th, and the scent of purging was still in the air. With George's help, I quickly packed up while marveling at all the drama I went through.

After gathering a few belongings and arranging for the rest to be given away, I told George I needed to make a few phone calls. I had been away so long, my mail and messages had piled up, particularly from Cheryl and my mother. I needed to call and assure them I was O.K.

Before leaving the room, I sat on the bed and closed my eyes, wondering. Almost without notice, my state of bliss had melted away. Since breakfast I started feeling smaller again . . . like a so-called normal human being.

"Life is good. Life is bad. Existence gives you both. Just accept."

"Are you well?" asked my companion. I slowly opened my eyes, smiled at him and nodded. A slight nostalgia arose in my throat as I tasted a certain calmness. It was actually wonderful just to be normal again . . . just to be a simple player in this production called Life.

Chapter Fifty-Three

"Collect call to U.S.A., please . . ." I said to the operator. Although it was 9:50 A.M. in Sri Lanka, I figured it around 12:20 A.M. - the night before - in Atlanta. Knowing Cheryl, she would just be getting ready for bed.

"Hello," came the crackling voice at the other end of the line.

"Guess who this is?" I said rather awkwardly.

"Matthew?" she asked, almost mechanically. Something was amiss. I sensed another presence.

"I just got back to Colombo, honey. I've been lost, and gone a long time."

"Well," she continued flatly, "I'm glad you're alive. We almost called the American Embassy there . . . Are you O.K.?"

"I'm really fine . . ."

"Well," piped Cheryl superficially, "I suppose you'll tell me about it when you get back . . ." The energy in her voice was changed. I felt a resistance from her . . . a distancing.

"Something's going on. What is it?" I asked, addressing the emotional barrier.

"I'd rather not say until you get back . . ."

"Tell me, dammit!" I insisted.

"Well . . . I tried to call you . . . I was so lonely . . . needed you! Why didn't you come home?!"

"I don't know what to say, except . . ."

"There's someone else," she interrupted.

I held out the receiver for a moment, unsure how to react. Suddenly I realized: I didn't have to react at all!

"Pass fear. . . a kind of death happens. Then deep relaxation and happiness . . . Will is truly free . . . No rules."

289

"You . . . have someone else?!"

"I . . . well, we met at Donna's Christmas party about three weeks ago," she said meekly.

"Do you love him?"

"I think so . . ."

My heart fluttered briefly, then settled. A relaxation set in. I laughed quietly, amazed at the ease with which I was able to release anger, jealousy, and all those other emotions. The immense awareness simply swallowed them up!

"Your ku is connected . . existence takes care of the details."

"I'm happy for you, Cheryl!" I said, feeling a bubble of joy rising in my heart.

"Are you being sarcastic?" she questioned.

"No, actually - you may not believe this - but I found some real happiness in these jungles . . . something I can't describe. Something that shook my very being."

"Matt . . . can't we talk about this when you return?"

"What's there to talk about? Do you want a divorce?"

"I don't . . . well . . ."

"Actually, I met someone too," I added, sensing her fear of shocking me. "But, she's in England and I don't know if I'll ever see her again. Crazy huh? Life works out somehow. And, let's face it . . . we haven't been together for a long time. I know that now."

"I need more time," she said. I heard a few quiet sobs.

"I understand, Cheryl. I'll be home soon and we'll work things out . . . however it's supposed to be."

"Well," she added between sobs, "You know I love you, but maybe it's time to let go . . . It just hurts so much!"

"I know this pain too . . ."

For the first time in our relationship, I felt a *bond* with Cheryl . . . a connection in truth. We both shed a few tears, then ended our conversation on a lighter note: a few laughs, a few more tears. She said she would call my mother and pick me up at the airport. I thanked her for being honest with me, said I'd call when I got to the states, then hung up.

****

"Come in! Come in!" sounded the booming voice from upstairs, responding to our doorbell ring. *"Now all the important people are here!"*

I could hear a crowd of people milling around upstairs in Alfred's deluxe two-story Colombo apartment. It was 11:40 and the party had already begun. I looked forward to seeing the big doctor again; it was always party time at his house.

George and I climbed the winding staircase to the upper floor lounge. We passed rows of ostentatiously displayed diplomas, honors, and certificates that Alfred had accumulated from all over the world. As we stepped onto the landing, the big doctor voiced his welcome.

"Come in, please!" bellowed the big man. As we looked at all the faces, I wondered if Jayawardene hadn't brought the whole clinic home with him! I immediately spotted Jon, and made my way over to embrace him.

"Welcome home, Matthew!" gushed Jon warmly as we heartily embraced each other. "I worried when you didn't call . . ."

"*Here,* Ladies and Gentlemen," announced Alfred, the master host, "is the great American chiro-doctor who went searching for the mysteries of life in our jungles, and has come back to us still alive! Perhaps he will honor us by canceling his plane ticket and staying longer . . . Come! Come! Sit here!" he announced, pointing over to his sofa. A few helpers moved to make room for us as we obediently settled in.

". . . and the Sinhalese lunar astronauts just sat around on the moon doing nothing . . ." announced our master of ceremonies, applying the finish to another joke. Whenever Alfred called a party, it usually meant *he* was the entertainment. This time was no exception.

" *'No Sir!'* they said, 'You see it is our custom in Sri Lanka to take holiday on the full moon day, so we must *always* be on holiday here . . . It's *always* a full moon!!' And *that,* my friends is why we call it 'Poya Day'. . !" The crowd roared with laughter and approval.

Although I'd probably heard this joke a hundred times I, too, let out some genuine laughter. It still sounded as fresh as the first time.

"Where is she?" boomed Alfred. A hush came over the crowd. "Where is the lady from England . . . the one who will find our instruments?"

"Here!" shouted a familiar voice. The figure of Ruth emerged from the back of the room and walked towards Alfred. "Here I am!" My heart soared.

"Our friend here is remarkable," said Dr. Alfred as he put his big arms around her. "She has come back to Sri Lanka to help us import needed equipment for our clinic . . . at very good rates!" Alfred continued his speech, but I hardly cared. As she looked in my direction and our eyes met, time stopped. A wave of energy arose within me and painted the moment and our connection with such brilliance I lost all thought. We smiled together; in the silence, we *knew.* For the first time, I truly *saw* her.

"Knowing will reveal itself to you . . . all things will return through intent . . ."

"And now I wish to declare a toast," announced the vicar of Kalibuwila Hospital, "Pass out the drinks! Glasses! Quickly! The moment is at hand! Drinks, then lunch . . . ritual worthy of the holiest of saints! Come! Quickly!"

After a few instructions in Sinhala, Alfred's resident helpers scurried to the kitchen and back to bring a set of trays filled with enough scotch glasses for everyone. They also served five or six open bottles of *Arrack,* the local 100-proof whiskey. Not much of a drinker, I mused about how it might affect me *this* time.

But George and others seemed so delighted with the whole show, I caught myself surrendering to the moment . . . to the flow of spontaneous energy bursting forth on every face. I grabbed one of the shot glasses being passed around.

"And now, a toast to Doctor Matthew's safe passage to America," declared Alfred. "I have *no doubt* he will return very soon!" As he raised his glass skyward, all of us - his devoted disciples - did likewise. Dr. Alfred looked at me as he continued . .

"I would like to suggest that few have understood the true meaning of health . . . and those few are fortunate enough to know that needles and remedies alone will not heal the human heart . . .

"For those whose bodies are *acutely hurt* . . . we have *first aid:* medicine and surgery . . . for this is the only action for such traumas.

"For those who are *chronically ill,* we have a *second remedy:* acupuncture, homeopathy, and cleansing herbs and diet . . . for this is the only way for a weakened body to respond.

"And for those who are *spiritually sick,.* we have the *third remedy:* food, drink, love and laughter . . . for this is the only way *a soul can rise out of self-concern, relax into being, and unite with the greatest of humankind . . .*

Suddenly, a familiar face and orange color appeared out of the corner of my eye. When I turned to catch him, however, he was gone. I raised my glass with the others, let out a hearty "Cheers," and downed the fiery liquid.

Pachili had delivered as promised.

- DAS ENDE –

For other Books, Products & Courses
By Michael Craig, visit
www.LogicalSoul.com

www.ingramcontent.com/pod-product-compliance
Lightning Source LLC
Chambersburg PA
CBHW071449170626
46811CB00007B/2518